Fierce Voice

Fierce Voice

Susan Currie

Published by Common Deer Press Incorporated.

Published in 2025 by Common Deer Press
1745 Rockland Ave.
Victoria, BC
V8S 1W6

Library and Archives Canada Cataloguing in Publication

Title: Fierce voice / Susan Currie.
Names: Currie, Susan, 1967- author.
Description: Series statement: Métier | Sequel to: Iz the apocalypse.
Identifiers: Canadiana (print) 20250132907 |
Canadiana (ebook) 2025013294X | ISBN 9781998484065 (softcover) |
ISBN 9781998484072 (EPUB)
Subjects: LCGFT: Novels.
Classification: LCC PS8555.U743 F54 2025 | DDC jC813/.6—dc23

Cover Illustration: Bex Glendining
Book Design: David Moratto

Printed in Canada
www.commondeerpress.com

To John and Rachel
"I love you" scarcely seems strong enough.

"A part of all art is to make silence speak."

—Freya Stark

Chapter One

Don't be such a coward! Just walk in!

Fourteen-year-old Iz Beaufort clutched her guitar, staring up at the great brick expanse of The Métier School. Here she was on her official first day as a Métier student, with everything she'd ever wanted waiting inside those big wooden doors, but she was totally scared to walk up the steps.

A girl's voice pealed out. "Give it back or I'll beat you with my clarinet! I got that beret in *Paris* this summer!"

"That's why it looks so awesome on me." A resonant laugh filled the air.

Iz froze. She knew that second voice all too well. And he was the last human being she wanted to see at this moment.

She didn't mean to look but couldn't help herself.

A boy with floppy dark hair and a brilliant grin ran across the grass, pursued by a girl swinging an instrument case at him. He wore a bright red beret. He was laughing his head off. The girl was too.

Flashing his teeth like he was in a toothpaste commercial, he twirled to face her. "Oh wait, just a sec, let me see." He placed the beret on the girl's head. "Yeah, okay, it does actually look better on you."

Then—he lifted his eyes and looked directly at Iz.

Teo Russo.

Iz let out a panicked squeak. She couldn't talk to him. Not after what had happened during the summer.

Run!

In a total frenzy, she stumbled up the steps, through the wooden doors, and into the foyer. She wove blindly among Métier students, scarcely registering the laughing voices and spatters of music all around.

"Oof!" said the person she slammed into. He stumbled backward. Everything he was carrying tumbled to the ground.

"Oh, I'm so sorry!" Iz cried. "Here, let me help ..."

She dropped to her knees and grabbed at papers.

He began gathering them too. "Storming Métier again, I see. What a delight. How *are* you, Iz Beaufort?"

For the first time, Iz looked directly at the man. She gasped with horrified embarrassment. "Dr. Perlinger! I am so, so sorry."

He was only her favourite teacher in the world.

"Not at all. We have a new Neapolitan mastiff at our house, and I get knocked down daily." He beamed amiably. "And how about you? Settling in well to your new foster home? That was a wonderful newspaper article, by the way."

"Oh, uh, yeah ..."

She'd been so anxious when the reporter had contacted her after the concert she'd done last June. And she'd felt like a complete liar for leaving out a few key details during the interview. Not surprisingly, the published article had depicted a single-minded and confident girl she hardly recognized. *Foster Kid Makes It into Prestigious Métier School and Finds Her Forever Home.*

"And I mean, I love living at the Santoro's. They're awesome," she added.

"How's your writing?"

"Great!" She forced her voice to sound bright.

"Really? What are you working on?"

"Uh, you know ..."

Dr. Perlinger waited.

"Ha!" Iz said. "So much stuff."

Her insides felt like they were shrivelling up.

"I can't wait to hear about it," he said, his voice light. "You can share at the Manifesto rehearsal tonight."

"Uh, for sure, I will."

"And in the meantime, welcome, Iz! Welcome to your second term. What an exciting day!"

She was about to thank him when his words sank in. "Uh … *second* term? I think you mean *first* term."

"Oh, no, I think I mean second."

Iz stared. "But …"

"Yes?"

She hated to say the words. She lowered her voice, looking around to see who might be listening. "You guys … like … *kicked me out.* I'm starting all over again today. From the beginning."

"Yes. But the director has given you credit for your hard work before all of that happened. You don't want to argue with the director, do you?"

"Uh—well—"

"Of course you don't," Dr. Perlinger's voice was sunny. "What's more, if I'm not mistaken, you'll attack term two with your usual passion and creativity and come up with something outstanding and original, yes?"

Iz stammered, "Ha! Maybe!" Then she added, "Y-yes. Sure. Of course. Definitely."

Dr. Perlinger half bowed to her. "On that note, off you go to finish getting registered, and I'll see you at the Manifesto rehearsal after school. Iz, I absolutely *cannot wait* to hear what you've been working on all summer."

"Oh, yeah, I can't wait to show you."

As she walked toward the registration desk, her brain started screaming.

How was she supposed to find a project by four o'clock this afternoon?

And even if she found one, how could she handle walking into the rehearsal, with Teo Russo sitting right there?

Chapter Two

The day was jam-packed with all the classes Iz had been so looking forward to—Guitar with Dr. Nguyen, Voice with Dr. Henderson, Music History, Theory, Curriculum Studies, Choir.

Part of her brain was delighted to be talking again about classical guitar, theory and composition, producing her unique singing style in a healthy way, and studying regular high school subjects like math and English and science in a kind of mix that worked with the way that she thought. She was thrilled to be back in that heady Métier atmosphere of impromptu jamming, animated conversation, and helpless laughter. She was grateful to be a student in a place where everyone was passionate about the very things that made Iz feel like *herself.*

But the other part of her mind was churning over how to find something, anything, interesting enough to take to the Manifesto rehearsal. Everything she thought of was pointless, and her brain kept shouting unhelpfully that she couldn't let Dr. Perlinger down.

Furthermore, Teo Russo kept being everywhere Iz was. When she was trying to walk to class, he ran down the hallway with a group of hooligans, hurling a cake of rosin back and forth and yelling, "Go long!" When she was talking with Mrs. Harvey in the front office about a conflict in her schedule, he threw his arms around the shoulders of girls jamming in the foyer, singing along while they laughed. And later, when all Iz wanted to do was eat her lunch, he sprawled nearby and argued with his friends LaRoyce and Bijan about impressionist music while his eyes flashed. Distractingly, he kept throwing pretzels in the air and catching them in his mouth.

By the time of Iz's last class of the afternoon, Profiles of Composers, her agitation was turned up to about a million.

Dr. Warren strode down the aisle, clad in jeans and a T-shirt. The teacher vaulted onto the stage, then hurled herself on top of the desk. She settled there, legs swinging. The students burst into spontaneous applause.

Dr. Warren's husky voice boomed into the hall, amplified by the microphone.

"Welcome to Profiles of Composers. Nice to see so many of you here this afternoon! Are you ready to take a little trip through Romantic tragic opera this term?"

Someone hooted.

"Excellent!" Dr. Warren raised a fist. "Let's have big emotions, bigger deaths, and huge questions about humanity's place in the universe. Let's weep, let's rage, and let's *question*."

Dr. Warren's enthusiastic voice actually pierced through Iz's anxiety somehow. Weeping, raging, death . . . those things felt even mightier than Iz's worries.

"We're not going chronologically," Dr. Warren declared. "That's too easy. No, we're going thematically. And we're going to start with some difficult questions about birth and fortune and the different effects of societal conformity on men and women."

"Verdi!" someone shouted.

"Indeed. Giuseppe Verdi!" Dr. Warren's eyes flashed.

Vito's favourite, Iz thought. Her new foster father played Verdi recordings all the time.

"Before we examine any of his works, we need to start with the composer himself." Dr. Warren allowed a silence to fall, and you could hear a pin drop. "Sometimes maybe we think that composers are born fully developed, world famous, ready to step into their place in history. Blessed by the gods, perfect from the get-go. Yes?"

The students laughed.

"*No!*" Dr. Warren exclaimed. "In Verdi's case, his parents were poor. They bought him this battered little instrument called a spinet, which probably sounded awful. Still . . . he learned to play on it." She paused. "And he kept that spinet forever, even when he could afford whatever instrument he wanted."

Iz smiled at that. After all, she'd rescued her own first guitar from a dumpster and she was planning to keep it forever too—even though Teo Russo had actually given her a much better guitar last year.

She shoved Teo out of her head for the nine thousandth time.

"So," Dr. Warren murmured, "here's our question—how did Giuseppe Verdi go from poverty and a crummy spinet to being one of the greatest opera composers in the world?"

"Genius," someone called out.

She nodded. "Genius, absolutely. And something else."

"The ability to work hard, to focus, to learn," a girl yelled.

"Definitely." Dr. Warren smiled. "What else?"

From the back, a boy called, "Drive. Basically, hunger."

"All true. But there was something else." Her eyes narrowed as if what she was about to say was important. "He had a *helper*. A wealthy merchant who heard him play. That helper ended up giving the ten-year-old free room and board. He hired the best teacher around, the head of the philharmonic society. He opened that boy's whole world up."

Lucky kid, Iz thought.

Dr. Warren nodded as if she had heard Iz say the words out loud. "Imagine how much in Western music history depends on luck as much as talent. Being the right gender. Having a rich patron who hears you play at just the right minute and wants to help. How many other Giuseppe Verdi's out there never got heard? How many are still waiting to be heard?"

The teacher's expressive face matched her passionate voice as she asked them all to reflect on how fragile everything was. To consider how many children would never be given a helping hand out of the emotional poverty of their lives. To think about talented humans stuck in a monotonous *good-enough*, blocked from reaching higher.

Out of absolutely nowhere, a memory popped into Iz's head.

She was sitting on the floor in a circle with others, feeling furious.

Iz closed her eyes. Slowly she remembered the after-school program she'd attended for kids like herself who were at risk of exploding all the time. She recalled the insipid singing, useless crafts, and conversations that were supposed to be empowering.

Those activities hadn't done a thing to address the roiling, raging desire inside her. She'd wanted someone to say, *I notice how differently your mind works, how you can listen to a piece of music and see it drawn out like an architectural plan or something. I hear how you can make four melodies dart around each other when you play your guitar.* I see you. *And I will teach you everything you are desperate to learn.*

Iz sat there in Dr. Warren's lecture with tears in her eyes, unexpectedly grieving for that long-ago little girl. A helper! Yes, she could have used one.

A weird thought sprang into her mind. If only she could go back in time, she would reach out her hand to that young, desperate Iz. She would pull her from the darkness. She would show her *everything.*

Chapter Three

Iz became so utterly entranced by Dr. Warren that she forgot about the Manifesto rehearsal coming up right afterward. But when the hour ended, horror shot through her. She still had exactly nothing to show to Manifesto—and no idea how to face Teo Russo after everything that had happened.

Also, she was out of time.

Iz dragged herself to Seminar Room 3C where Manifesto held its rehearsals. For the second time that day, she stood in front of a door she was scared to open.

But Rina flew up behind her, pushed it wide and gestured for Iz to enter. "Welcome to Manifesto! Come in!"

"Uh . . . thanks." Iz's voice came out all wobbly.

When she stepped inside the seminar room, intelligent voices hit her ears right away.

"So, I want to somehow convey the grey-green of the light filtering through the forest canopy—creaky cello, laced through with streaks of flute . . ." That was Jasleen Singh.

"If we could actually code a series of notes and create different outcomes based on the order—" Becky, who was obsessed with Schoenberg and programming, was talking to Will.

Then Teo's voice oozed out like caramel. "But how do you actually musically establish a sense of *place* without stereotype?"

He was reclining against the wall, next to Kwame.

Seeing him there, Iz felt even more panic building.

Maybe she could leave before things got started.

But as she was turning to run, Dr. Perlinger breezed in. "Well, well, hello everyone! Welcome to the fall term! Gather round! What have we all been up to?"

"We all know what *Russo's* been doing." Ahmed spoke cheerfully, while everyone pulled up chairs.

Iz froze. She silently implored Teo, *Please don't tell them what happened.*

But his sunny voice betrayed nothing. "Yeah, I took off to Italy for the summer term. Little opera program. Whatever."

"I can imagine the reviews," Jasleen teased. "Young Teo Russo as Alfredo, blah blah blah, voice of the century."

He laughed, mouth impossibly wide. "No, the real supernova was Chloe Farrington, who was Violetta. Every time she sang, she totally broke my heart. She's going to, like, *dominate* stages. Plus, she was a nice girl. Fun to hang out with."

Teo's eyes flashed at Iz and away again.

"Anyone else?" Dr. Perlinger said.

One by one, everyone in Manifesto began to discuss the projects they were working on. Heavy metal Mahler. Syrian hip hop anti-war protest. Coding and atonality. The rest of the group analyzed, questioned, and extended the original ideas. People grabbed instruments and played out their thoughts, voices colliding with enthusiasm. They operated on two levels—as individuals and integral components of the whole.

Dr. Perlinger's keen eyes swung in Iz's direction at last. "And Iz Beaufort, welcome to you today! Your very first Manifesto rehearsal. How does it feel?"

Kind of like she was maybe going to throw up.

"Ha! Good. Great. It's great."

"Have you been writing any more apocalyptic song cycles?" Bijan's voice exuded gentle respect. "I loved that article about your scholarship concert, by the way."

"Uh ... yeah ... well ... not exactly."

"What *are* you working on?" Jasleen asked, eyes welcoming. "Something wonderful, I bet."

That was the thing about Manifesto—Dr. Perlinger had picked everyone for not only their talent but also the way they moved through the world. They were infinitely generous and supportive. They *built* each other.

Tears pushed at Iz's eyes. She glanced at Teo without meaning to, sure he was delighted at how she was failing. But his face was compassionate, which actually made everything worse.

"I, uh, I'm just, you know, like, in the beginning process of developing a project." She curled her hands into fists.

LaRoyce's voice pierced through her embarrassment. "Well, look at the summer you've had, though. Moving foster homes and everything. I bet you've hardly had a second to think about writing."

She looked up gratefully at his perceptive eyes and magnanimous smile. It was no accident that LaRoyce was Bijan's best friend—they were equally compassionate and tuned in. Though LaRoyce was a lot more forthcoming with ridiculous jokes.

"Yeah," Iz said, feeling braver. "I don't know, it's weird. Like ... everything is so much better now." She frowned, trying to sort her thoughts out. "But, somehow ... that's the problem, you know? I've always written angry stuff. B-but there's, like, less to be angry about."

She thought again about that little girl from her memory.

"I mean, I used to be stuck in these stupid little after-school programs that I hated, and I was just like *yearning* all the time for something more. That was what fuelled my writing. But now I've got what I wanted. So, what do I write about?" She rolled her eyes. "Okay, that sounds totally ridiculous."

"Tell me—imagine for a minute—if you could go back to that little girl and talk to her ... what would you say?" Dr. Perlinger's voice was curious.

"Huh! It's funny, I was thinking about that." She paused. "I-I guess ... I'd say, 'I know you're frustrated, but there's a whole world of music out there and you are actually going to get to be part of it one day. And ... it's going to be amazing.'" She laughed out loud. "'Until—one day, you're going to say, *I have nothing more to write about.*'"

They all laughed too.

"What was the name of this place?" Kwame asked. "Is it still there?"

She pulled the words out of her foggy memory. "The Eastbourne Centre."

Everyone wrestled their phone out. At almost the same time, they triumphantly called out its address.

Iz thought about Dr. Warren.

About Giuseppe Verdi.

The randomness of luck.

"Like," she said slowly, "I wonder what it would have been like to have had a helper when I was there ... a-a *teacher.*"

"Ahh." Dr. Perlinger placed his fingertips together. "Being a helper. Being helped. Sometimes that's a circular process—the one leads to the other and back again."

Teo's buttery voice rumbled out, "Let's suppose a helper did go in there. What would that look like?"

Iz peeked at him and away again. "Like ... maybe they could create classes that were actually challenging, exciting. Showing the kids what was possible. Opening up their minds, kind of."

"Reaching out to that long-ago girl." Dr. Perlinger nodded like Iz had said something profound. "Designing a program to ferret some other little person's talent in the here and now ... that sounds like a really *fascinating* project."

"We'd back you up," LaRoyce said brightly.

"Introduce them to instruments, teach them how to play," Bijan added.

"Help them develop their own voices and passions ..." Rina's voice was enthusiastic.

"Maybe a composition would come out of it, something that represents who they are ..." Jasleen's eyes flashed.

"Which could lead to a performance opportunity." Will grinned.

Iz gazed with gratitude at these supportive students, this nurturing group.

Being a helper.

Weirdly, if she could give back somehow, it would almost be like earning everything good in her life.

For the first time in ages, something creative stirred in her.

Chapter Four

Iz left the rehearsal in a whirl of surprised enthusiasm. She headed to her locker and began to wrestle materials into the new backpack her foster parents had bought for her.

Then Teo came striding out of nowhere.

Iz panicked. She crouched behind the locker door, watching him through the slats as he opened his locker, pulled out his Métier bomber jacket and did up the snaps. He swung his backpack over a shoulder, locked the door. Then he called to Bijan and LaRoyce and galloped down the main stairs like a colt.

Iz waited until she was sure he was gone. At last, shaking, she emerged.

Why did she feel all at once like there was a drain inside her and her spirits were pouring through it into a sewer or something?

Suddenly she wanted to run after him. But what would she say? Nothing he wanted to hear. He'd obviously had a wonderful time with Chloe Farrington the supernova during his summer opera program.

Still, something goaded her, urgent and demanding. *Don't think about it! Just go!*

Iz grabbed everything and ran along the hall, down the main staircase, across the foyer, through the doors into the late-afternoon sunshine.

Teo stood at the bus stop, hands in the pockets of his jacket.

Iz pounded up to him. "Okay. I-I just want to say something."

"Yeah?" His face was neutral.

"So ..." She gathered courage, shoved herself into the words. "I'm really sorry I didn't text you back this summer. Like, any of those times. Or take the phone calls. I don't know, I just—"

Teo raised a hand like she didn't need to go on. "Forget about it. I figured you had a good reason, like I'd done something stupid and offensive or whatever. Which I'm pretty good at."

"Yeah," Iz said without thinking. "I saw you this morning with the hat."

A weird expression shot across his face, like he wanted to fire some remark back at her but was stopping himself. "Well, don't worry about it. I got the message."

Staring down at the guitar he had given her, she spoke the intimidating truth. "I-I mean, I just, I got scared."

He frowned like she made no sense. "Beaufort, you don't have to be scared of *me*."

"Yeah, no, you don't get it. I'm pretty much scared of everyone."

His expression softened. "What did you think I was going to do?"

"I don't know. Be a human being. Those are the ones I'm most terrified of."

She knew how weird she sounded. But there was so much in her past that she couldn't tell him, couldn't tell anyone, about. All those foster homes. And the worst secret of all, That Place.

A ghost of a smile curled his lips. "Rigazza di cipolla."

"What's that mean? Loser chick?"

He threw his head back, laughing like a gregarious lion. "No. It means *onion girl*. Because you're made up of all these layers. And, Beaufort, I do not understand how you work at *all*."

Iz's heart started beating like a percussion instrument. "Fair. I don't either, if that helps." She gathered courage. "And ... I don't even know why I ghosted you, except that I just am horrible at, like, *knowing* people and I think I got freaked when, you know, that *thing* happened at Festa ..."

She waited for him to respond but he didn't. At last she muttered, "So, you could say something."

"Well, I didn't want to interrupt in case you weren't finished."

"I don't know if I'm finished."

And then—

"I'm finished."

He squinted at her. "Okay. So that *thing* you're talking about … let's remember that you kissed *me*. I was just sitting there minding my own business."

Iz opened her mouth to argue, but he kept going.

"And did I *once* pressure you about it afterward? No, because I figured you've, you know, been through lots of stuff and if you wanted to talk about it, you would." His voice grew strained. "But then, I went to Italy, and you stopped talking to me at all. It was like you vanished. At first, I thought, maybe she's busy with therapy and work and moving to the Santoro's and everything. But when I kept reaching out and asking how you were, and you still didn't answer … I realized you didn't want anything to do with me. And I'm going to admit, I was hurt. Because I thought we were at least friends. Like, *good* friends."

Iz nodded, wretched guilt seeping through her.

"So now what are *you* going to say?" He stared with those uncanny, light-brown eyes.

It took her a while to trust her voice to be steady. "You're right. I-I'm sorry. You didn't deserve that. We *were* good friends." She crossed her arms tightly, closed her eyes. "I wrecked everything."

"You didn't wreck *everything*. I mean, we're here talking. Which is an improvement over the summer." Teo's voice was kinder than she deserved.

Iz opened her eyes nervously.

He was gazing at her with lids half-closed.

"Stop doing the eye thing," she said in a tiny voice.

"Beaufort, Beaufort, Beaufort. For the thousandth time, there's no eye thing."

"Sure, keep telling yourself that."

A ghost of a smile played on his lips like she was some combination of exasperating and possibly not completely horrible. He said slowly, "So … like … I'm not exactly sure what you want now. Are we talking again? Are we acquaintances? Friends? Or … whatever?"

Iz shrugged and looked all around. "I guess friends, sort of."

His mouth wriggled slightly, and he shook his head. "Don't oversell it."

Iz gulped. "Yes. I-I want to be friends again. I just don't know if I'm ready to … to, you know, be *whatever*."

His smile grew, and he kicked at a pebble, sending it flying off the sidewalk. "So, we're allowed to acknowledge each other in the hallway."

"Yeeaah …"

"And maybe we can address each other occasionally."

"Sometimes."

"But texting is probably right out."

Iz flushed. "I-I mean, I guess texting is okay …"

Teo looked as though he was starting to enjoy this. "But, like, you would never want to go out and do something together …"

"Um," Iz said. "I don't know."

"Ahh. Right." He grimaced as if weighing something in his mind. "Like … you wouldn't want to go and see *La Traviata* or anything."

"That's very specific."

Teo's eyebrows arched in that way she'd sort of missed. "Well … I don't know if I should mention this or not …" He scuffed his foot through the dirt. "Before I went to Italy, I bought these tickets. I was going to surprise you with them, but you vanished off the earth. So, I meant to sell them or give them away or whatever, but I never did. And I wasn't going to tell you about them, obviously. Except … that now … we seem to be talking." He regarded her, daring and uneasy at the same time. "Yeah, they're kind of for this Saturday."

"Are you—what are you . . . ?" Something weird fluttered through her.

He gazed at the apparently fascinating sky. "You don't have to. And we would obviously go as *friends*. I mean . . . if you want."

"I'd . . . have to ask Vito and Gisele."

"It's Verdi," Teo said, "so Vito should be in love with the idea."

"Huh. Yeah. Right."

And then she was staring ridiculously at him and running out of words.

She mumbled, "So, I should probably get home . . ."

"Probably," Teo said.

"Bye, then. I-I'll let you know what they say."

Iz started walking backward along the sidewalk while he stared quizzically at her. She half saluted, turned, forced herself to take measured steps to the corner. Once around it, she took off running.

Her heart was lighter than it had been in ages.

She and Teo were talking again.

Finally, finally, she had a project.

Maybe everything was going to be okay.

Chapter Five

Iz pelted all the way to Festa, the restaurant that her foster parents Vito and Gisele Santoro owned. She threw open the door and barrelled right into Vito, who was polishing the brass on the lectern.

"Whoa, slow down! You being chased by elephants? You know this is a peaceful, nice place, right?"

"Oh," Iz said. "I thought it was the circus."

She could tease Vito like that. Before becoming his foster kid, she'd worked for months as a dinner musician in the restaurant. They'd been bantering back and forth for a while now.

Vito shook his head like she was the worst behaved kid he'd ever seen, but a glimmer of a smile played on his mouth. "So come in the kitchen. Tell us how it all went."

She followed him through the swinging doors. Fragrant aromas hit her nose immediately—garlic, butter, lemon.

Gisele, her foster mother, burst into a huge smile as Iz and Vito walked in. "Cara! Sit down. I'll get you something."

Iz settled at the long table where she had eaten so many meals when she was just their employee and not their foster kid.

Gisele placed a steaming bowl of minestrone and a plate of freshly baked rolls in front of her. "So, your first day! It went okay?"

Iz began devouring the delicious soup. "Huh! It was actually amazing."

She told them everything about her classes, about the loud and happy cafeteria where people burst into unexpected songs or jammed with impromptu instruments. She described how one kid did backflips down the hallway while everyone else clapped a rhythm that was some Métier in-joke.

"And then, I don't like even know *how*, but somehow during the Manifesto rehearsal I ended up deciding I want to do a music outreach program at the Eastbourne Centre. Manifesto is going to help me." She wrinkled her brow. "I don't actually know what I'll do yet, but I kind of think I'm excited about it. Well, also terrified."

As Iz spoke, Gisele patted her hand, face full of pride. Vito sipped coffee in a stony, supportive way.

"Oh. And you know, I was talking with … with … like, Teo." Iz made her voice casual as if she'd just thought of it.

Vito and Gisele exchanged glances.

She froze a little. "Uh … what?"

"Nothing." Vito's face was impassive.

"So you were talking," Gisele added.

The comfortable feeling began to seep away. What was wrong? It was totally not her imagination that the mood had shifted. "Yeah. A-and, well, he was asking … he just wanted to know if, like …"

They waited.

"Wanted to know what?" Gisele asked.

"If, you know, I just kind of wanted to go to this thing."

"What *thing*?" Vito's eyebrows crowded low.

Panic was building in Iz. "Um, an opera. *La Traviata*. Verdi! And you love Verdi, so I was thinking … like, maybe I could go?"

Vito frowned. "Who else is going?"

"Uh, just the two of us I think."

"How would you get there? How late would it go?"

Iz gulped. "W-we didn't talk about any of that yet."

"Where is it anyway?"

"I'm not sure …"

Vito's forbidding expression made her suddenly sure he was about to tell her to pack her bags.

"I'm sorry!" she gasped. "I-I'll find out!"

"Iz, of course it's fine." Gisele's voice was calm, like a caressing hand. "It's *Teo*. He's a good boy, Vito. We've had him here a hundred times. You know that."

"She didn't want to talk to him all summer long. I lost track of how many messages I took. And now, out of the blue ..." He stonily took another sip of coffee. "And she's fourteen, and he's fifteen. She's too young to be dating."

Iz stammered, "I-I'm fifteen in, like, a couple of months. And anyway, I said it's not a date. J-just two people going to an *opera*."

She didn't mention that Teo had had a birthday in early July and was in fact sixteen now.

"It's not like they're sneaking off to a rave or something," Gisele added.

Iz blinked, surprised that Gisele knew what a rave was.

Vito harrumphed, shaking his head.

Iz pushed up from the table, stomach hurting. "Th-thank you for the soup. And, I mean, for everything so far ... I'm sorry for asking about the opera."

"Cara," Gisele said gently. "You don't have to keep thanking us. This is *your* place now." She jabbed at Vito. "And ignore this one. Of course you can go."

"Oh! R-really? Okay. Uh—g-good."

Iz nodded rapidly, ran upstairs shaking.

In her hand was a roll that she'd slipped off the table. She stashed it under the bed, next to the toast from this morning. She felt totally ashamed to still be hiding food. She wasn't going to starve in a family that owned a restaurant, after all. But somehow she felt safer, less panicky, when she kept a few things in reserve.

Iz sat down in the little rocking chair and drew out the iPad that Métier had loaned her. She went to Messages, clicked on Teo's name after an anxious minute, and started typing.

I can go but Vito's going to do a stakeout in front of the opera house all night.

She hugged herself, walked around the room to calm her nerves before gathering the courage to see if he had written anything back.

If it helps, we could wear wires.

She laughed out loud, totally startling herself.

But the nervous feeling remained. She needed to be so careful to not put a foot wrong. Because if Vito was this upset at the idea of an outing with Teo, what would he say about the dark things she couldn't share with anyone?

What would he think about That Place, the nightmarish foster home from her past? He would be disgusted. He would kick her out in a heartbeat.

There were so many secrets she had to keep.

She needed to behave perfectly.

She had to earn this new life.

Chapter Six

On Saturday night, Iz stood outside the restaurant with Vito.

When Teo's father pulled up, she raced toward the car, planning to get in before Vito could go all nuclear dad figure. But as she reached for the car handle, the door opened of its own accord. Teo leaped out and held it open for her.

"Home by twelve." Vito eyed Teo with zero trust.

"Eleven fifty-nine!" Teo's voice was as exuberant as Vito's was not.

"We'll see to it!" Teo's dad added.

Iz climbed into the car, while Vito itemized all the things she and Teo were and were not allowed to do. She blushed with acute embarrassment.

As the car pulled away from the curb, she said, "I'm sorry about that."

"Ah, he's protective of his little girl!" Teo grinned.

"I'm not a little girl!"

"You're littler than me."

"That's because you're four thousand feet tall."

He chuckled and changed the subject. "So are you all ready for, like, big suffering and death?"

"Why are operas always *tragedies*?"

He laughed, throwing his head back. She was suddenly aware that he looked sort of good in his crisp shirt and jacket. And he smelled nice.

"They're not! Lots of them are comedies, like opera buffa, this kind of Italian comic opera from back in the eighteenth century. Basically, stupid plots. For me I'll take a tragedy any day. Rip my heart in half and stomp on it."

"I'll keep that in mind," Iz said.

When they arrived at the opera hall, Teo's father waved and drove away.

In the lobby, people milled around, all dressed up. Perfume hung in the air. Iz plucked anxiously at her dress, the one Gisele had bought her in the spring.

"Come on! Let's find our seats." Teo wove through the crowd, hand resting lightly on her upper back. Which was weird but not completely horrible—even sort of gallant. Iz wondered if Vito would approve or not. There were arguments for both sides.

They climbed a curving carpeted staircase to the second floor. Iz stared out at the panorama of Dennison Hall—chrome, glass, varnished light wood, grey carpets, and enormous windows opening out onto the city. The sun, still up in the sky, bathed everything in a natural light.

"Oh," she said, not intending to.

"Pretty, right?" Teo grinned down at her.

He showed their tickets to the lady at the door to the theatre.

"Down to AA," she said. "First row of the balcony."

When they'd found their seats, Teo pointed above the stage, apparently unable to stop talking. "That's where the surtitles will be in English. Because the original libretto is in Italian. And down there is the pit, where the orchestra will be playing. In a few minutes, the lights are going to dim and the conductor will come out. Then they'll play the prologue, which is super somber."

"Because this is a *tragedy*," she said, teasing him.

"Exactly. But, when the curtain comes up, the first scene is a big party, and you're going to hear the whole tone change—get bright, lit up, you know?"

Teo himself was lit up, she realized. His eyes sparkled.

She found herself smiling back. "How do you know so much about *La Traviata*, anyway?"

His eyes widened with disbelief. "Beaufort, I spent my *summer* with this opera. Every. Waking. Minute."

"Oh, is *this* the one you did in the fancy Italian program?"

"See what happens when you ignore people's texts? Yes, this is the one."

Iz flushed. "And you were Whoever."

"I was Alfredo, yeah."

"And some incredibly gorgeous superstar girl was the other lead."

"Chloe Farrington was Violetta." His eyes sparkled. "What, are you jealous?"

"No!"

He laughed. "Relax, Beaufort. Anyway, she has a boyfriend."

"That's nice." Iz crossed her arms.

"What, you don't want her to have a boyfriend? Poor Chloe Farrington."

"I'm delighted she has a boyfriend."

The lights began to dim, and clapping burst out.

Iz leaned over and saw a man walk through the pit to take his place on a little podium at the front. He raised his hands. Everyone lifted their instruments into position.

Through the darkness, she could see Teo smiling at her like he didn't want to miss a minute of her reaction.

The first aching strains of violins began. By the time the sound shivered to a close, she was frozen, unable to move, already caught in it.

Then, the music exploded into a bounding scale. The curtain rose onto a jewelled fairyland—an opulent room, all in velvets, with an overladen banquet table. Couples twirled in bright colours.

They burst into song, and—

A brilliant woman, practically shooting sparks, pirouetted with champagne in hand. Lots of men hovered around, but she laughed and deflected, utterly in control.

"That's Violetta," Teo whispered under his breath to Iz.

A man, all energy and humour, held up a glass to the dazzling woman.

"And that's Alfredo."

"He is totally into her," she whispered.

"Yeah, but she doesn't take him seriously. She doesn't think anyone would actually care about her."

"Why not?"

"She's like, a professional party girl, a courtesan. Completely brittle."

Someone said, "Shhh," behind them.

Iz turned her attention to the opera. Alfredo burst into a song about how much he loved her. His voice curled around Violetta like a blanket to keep her from freezing. She blew him off with a mocking melody that danced around his and kept him at bay.

But later Violetta sat alone and wondered what it would be like to be seen fully by someone who didn't care about her past. Maybe she loved Alfredo too. But she hardly dared to trust her own feelings.

Little by little, without knowing exactly when it happened, Iz stepped out of time. She walked beside Violetta. Her own heart swelled as Violetta accepted Alfredo's love at last and moved in with him—even though they had no money to speak of.

And she was as horrified and devastated as Violetta when Alfredo's father showed up and told her to get out.

Alfredo's dad didn't recognize Violetta as a human being. He saw the disreputable girl who operated on the outskirts of society. No matter how much Violetta tried to tell him she'd embraced a new life and loved Alfredo with all her heart, he didn't listen. He said she was harming the reputation of Alfredo's whole family by staying.

Violetta's arching, sobbing voice begged Alfredo's father not to make her go. But he argued back in a snakelike way—manipulating, infiltrating, twisting.

It made Iz sick to listen to. She knew exactly how that felt.

At last, Alfredo's father wore Violetta down. As she prepared to leave, she cried out to her love even though he wasn't there, begging that he might somehow still care for her.

"Love me, Alfredo—love me, my own, as I love you—"

Iz gasped. It was one of the most horrifying and transfixing moments she had ever experienced. Cold travelled up her spine and her neck into her scalp. Her arms prickled and the hairs actually stood up.

She glanced at Teo to see what he thought.

There he was, leaning forward, hands cupped over his nose, eyes full of tears.

Chapter Seven

At the end, Iz could scarcely shake off the spell.

"Look at the eyes on this one." Teo's voice was infinitely gentle.

"Are they red?"

"You look like a vampire." He smiled down at her.

"Great. Thanks."

"You're welcome."

There was a silence.

"So . . . have you ever had Giovanni's margarita pizza?" he asked.

"No."

"Beaufort, Beaufort, Beaufort." He sighed. "It's a three-hundred-year-old family recipe. Beautiful crust, flame browned, chewy. It's like *steaming* with tomato purée and garlic and the most flavourful, fresh basil you've ever experienced. It's dotted here and there with these creamy mounds of mozzarella di bufala, and then it's drizzled with this extra virgin olive oil. You take a bite, and it's like"—he waved his arms—"It's like heaven opened its gates. Seriously. It's like choirs are singing."

"Sounds intense."

He nodded. "Follow me."

Teo led her across the street to a restaurant called *Giovanni's*. A few moments later, they were sitting in a little booth next to each other.

Iz fanned herself, totally anxious. Someone had obviously broken the thermostat. Her brain started short-circuiting in the heat.

But Teo seemed completely comfortable. "Okay, so *Traviata*! Don't hold back. Honest review."

"I . . . loved it."

"Oh my God, that moment, right?" He beamed. "'Love me, Alfredo . . .'"

His rich voice rang out, and everyone in the restaurant turned to see who had just sung that beautiful thing.

Iz flushed. She said softly, "It's so cruel, how a woman in that time had no power except for, like, making sure nobody thought anything bad about her. The minute she did something wrong, she was *out*. And there was no way to fix it. It just . . . followed her, no matter how she tried to be better. No matter how much she wanted a fresh start."

Her mind was suddenly on all of those foster homes, all of those schools. The way her reputation would arrive at a new place before she did. The in-school committees waiting to manage her. The useless clubs designed to defuse her anger. And foster parents who had been thoroughly briefed about what to expect.

Teo's eyes glowed with compassion as if he could see her thoughts. "Too bad Violetta couldn't just push away all that judgment and not care."

"Ha!" Iz burst out. "But she would have to care. She'd be always worrying. I mean, *always*. About, you know, everything I've done—I mean, *she's* done . . ." She covered her face, overwhelmed with embarrassment. "Yeah, sorry, never mind. Way to bring down the tone."

"There's no tone."

Teo's phone buzzed. He took it out. "Hey! It's Dr. P!"

Iz leaned over so she could read her teacher's email.

> *Hello Manifesto and families!*
>
> *Sorry for interrupting your Saturday night. Just wanted to follow up on our last rehearsal. I've reached out to the Eastbourne Centre. They would like to meet with us to discuss our plans for an outreach program. The centre manager will join us at our rehearsal on Tuesday.*

Iz, why don't you and I hash out next steps in your tutorial on Monday?

Fun new adventure, yes?

Dr. P

Iz's eyes flew open, and her heart started beating even faster than it was already. "It's ... happening?"

"Of course, it is." Teo's eyes glowed. "It's going to be amazing."

"Ha! Right!" She took some deep breaths. Reminded herself about projects and giving back and helpers.

"What?" Teo said.

"What?"

"You look completely stressed."

She thought about telling him she was fine but other words came out. "Part of me is scared to go back. I wasn't very happy there." She noticed his worried face, shook her shoulders as if scattering her worries. "Yeah, never mind. It's good. It's going to be great."

"This group of kids is so lucky. You've got this." Teo leaned closer, candlelight reflecting in his eyes. "And ... I think you're relatively amazing."

At that moment, the pizza arrived. Teo filled Iz's plate and passed it over to her. "Okay, first bite at the same time. Then first impressions."

When Iz bit into the pizza, her eyes flew open, and she stopped thinking about anything except the rich flavours exploding in her mouth. The tomato purée, the creamy cheese, the fresh basil that cut through everything. And the olive oil!

"This is unbelievable!" she exclaimed.

"Right?" Teo beamed at her.

They ate in silence and nearly demolished the entire pizza.

Then Iz found herself actually sort of relaxing. "This whole evening," she said awkwardly. "Pizza and opera and—I don't know—like, us sitting here and talking ..." She waved her hand around, trying to figure out what she wanted to say. "It's actually been pretty amazing."

He grinned. "Should we do this again some time? I mean, as friends."

"Ha!" Iz thought about it. "Yeah. Okay. I guess. We should."

"Seriously, Beaufort, you have to stop over-enthusing. It's exhausting."

She burst out laughing. "No. Really. I want to."

"Good." His eyes crinkled at her.

The time passed quickly. Before Iz knew it, Teo's dad was pulling up.

When they arrived back at Festa, Teo hopped out, ran around the car, and opened Iz's door.

"Thanks for inviting me," Iz said shyly. "I had a really good time. Even though she died."

"Well, I did warn you she was going to kick it."

"How can you be so cruel?"

He laughed. "I'm immune to this opera."

"No, you're not. I saw you. You were a mess."

"Oh, really?" He smiled down at her. "You were supposed to be watching the stage, not me."

The door to the restaurant burst open.

"Hey!" Vito leaped out like some kind of vigilante.

Iz and Teo jumped apart guiltily, even though nothing had been going on.

"Eleven forty-two!" Teo exclaimed, holding out his wrist to show Vito the watch.

"Hmm," Vito said. But there was a glimmer of grudging amusement in his eyes. "Say goodnight, kids."

"See you on Monday," Iz said, slipping through the doorway.

"Yeah, see you, Beaufort."

She ran through the darkened restaurant before Vito could interrogate her. Because just for once, just for this minute, she wanted to feel like she didn't have to be careful of everything she said or did.

Chapter Eight

All weekend, Teo's encouraging words spurred Iz on.

That group of kids is so lucky.

I think you're relatively amazing.

By Monday, she had half filled a notebook with ideas for the outreach.

She burst into her Special Projects tutorial and thrust her notes at Dr. Perlinger.

As he read them, she couldn't help talking the whole time. "I feel like I want to challenge the way they see the world or something. I want this to be sort of *revolutionary* and totally unlike the stupid programs I had to sit through. It has to show the kids everything that's possible. It has to inspire them to reach out, to see people and ideas in a new light."

He smiled at her impassioned face. "Yes, most definitely. But bear in mind that you may not accomplish *all* of that on the first day."

"Right. No. True." She felt like a balloon losing air. "So ... is this completely unrealistic?"

"Not at all. I believe the main purpose of teaching is to encourage people to wrestle with big ideas. Anything else is scarcely of value at all." He paused. "But let's simplify this slightly for tomorrow's meeting. Focus on the basics—how a typical session will run, what materials you'll include, and so on."

"Okay." She felt like a fool. "I … I should have thought about the basics. I can do that."

"Of course you can." His voice was kind, like he could see her disappointment in herself. "But don't abandon those bigger ideas. They are at the heart of this outreach and of who you are. They'll emerge organically, taking us in unexpected directions. Then … *then* … you and I will have so much fun hashing out our next steps and talking music pedagogy together!"

His face shone. Iz's heart raced in response.

She'd really missed embarking on an adventure with Dr. Perlinger.

Iz stayed up most of the night making her notes simple and practical. The next afternoon, she entered the Manifesto rehearsal room with everything in order.

Dr. Perlinger was sitting there already with a woman who perched on the edge of a chair like she didn't quite want to commit to it. "Ah, Iz! Let me introduce you to Ms. Sole. She is the community centre manager. Ms. Sole, this is Iz Beaufort, the mastermind behind this outreach idea."

"Nice to meet you." Ms. Sole spoke like she had reservations about Iz, the outreach, and maybe the world.

"N-nice to meet you too."

Iz sat down, trying to control her nerves.

One by one, Manifesto tumbled in the door, while Ms. Sole eyed them warily. They seemed oblivious, laughing and chatting.

When everyone had arrived, Dr. Perlinger rose. "Let's welcome Ms. Sole to our rehearsal. She's here to listen to our ideas for an outreach and provide some feedback." He turned to Iz. "Would you like to say a few words about what might happen in these sessions?"

Iz gulped, cowed by Ms. Sole's forbidding expression. "Yes! I would!" She opened her notebook. "First, I-I have a kind of mission statement. W-we want to provide the basics of musical performance and songwriting. To nurture talent. To help kids work together to create music. And … to encourage them to see the world in a unique and special way."

She could hear how high and quickly she was talking.

Calm down.

In a more measured voice, she said, "Let me walk you through the first session. It'll probably be typical of how we'll run things." She forced herself to look right at Ms. Sole. "I'm thinking we'd all have nametags and maybe go round the circle telling something about ourselves."

She consulted her notes, eyes flying across the pages.

"Then, I think Manifesto could present something we're working on, tell its form and style and how we thought of it. We'd involve the students in performing it."

"How would you involve them?" Ms. Sole asked in a voice like thin gravy.

Iz gulped. "Ha! We have several ideas about that." Suddenly she couldn't think of any of them. "Uh ... anyone want to jump in?"

"There are lots of ways kids could be involved in a performance," Bijan said. "Like an ostinato, or a drum rhythm ..."

"Simple bass line." LaRoyce was nodding.

"Movement or singing ..." Rina added.

"Pitched bells," Jasleen said.

Listening to them all, Iz felt braver. Regardless of whatever Ms. Sole was thinking, Manifesto saw this proposal as entirely doable.

"And then," she said, "we'd encourage the kids to create their *own* music with our support. Like, we'd teach how to build a melody and how to add harmony ..."

Her voice trailed off, eyes on the centre manager.

She whispered, "So what do you think?"

Ms. Sole lifted a hand to her mouth and stared at some troubling thing in her mind. Finally she murmured, "It sounds ... like a very interesting program. I think the children would enjoy it."

"Really?" Relief burst all through Iz. "Oh! Good! I'm so glad!"

"*But.*" Ms. Sole's voice was saturated with caution. "These children are at risk. Some of them come to us from foster care, from refugee services, from shelters ..."

"Yes, yes, of course." Iz flushed.

"So you can see that we are very careful about what programs we run with them." Ms. Sole's pale eyes locked, one by one, with everyone in the circle. "Do any of you have experience in working with at-risk children? With vulnerable populations? With young people who have been through trauma?"

There was a silence.

Iz wanted to say, *I am one of those young people.* But she wasn't sure if that would help anyone's cause.

Ms. Sole cocked her head on one side. "You'd need to complete training before you could go in. And then there's the issue of a police check."

Iz sucked in a huge breath. "Oh! Yeah! A police check!" She tried to sound utterly confident.

But her brain started freaking out.

She would not pass a police check, not after everything that had happened.

"I have one, of course," Dr. Perlinger said quickly, "and would supervise every session. Will that be sufficient?" He glanced at Iz and away again. "Or do each of these young people need to get a police check as well?"

Iz held her breath.

Ms. Sole said at last, "No, I think not, as long as you are supervising."

Iz exhaled loudly. To cover it up, she blurted, "So can you tell us a little more about the training? And, like, about the kids?"

Ms. Sole nodded. "The group I have in mind is seven- to nine-year-olds. The training will be six hours in total. It covers a variety of topics to do with at-risk children and families. I propose we do it in two-hour increments. I can come here to facilitate."

"Excellent!" Dr. Perlinger rubbed his hands together. "When can we start?"

"We could begin tomorrow." Ms. Sole stared unblinkingly at them like a suspicious fish. "Bring something to take notes."

Chapter Nine

For the next three afternoons, Manifesto gathered in the little rehearsal room and Ms. Sole showed them slides about recognizing signs of trauma, abuse, and addiction. She talked about how to defuse anger, build trust, and diminish defensiveness.

The whole time, Iz could not help thinking about how the long-ago adults who had worked with *her* at Eastbourne must have had similar training so they could manage her unhappiness and desperation. She ached for that young girl who had been distilled down to a series of expected behaviours. She fought not to fall back into the anger she'd felt in those days. Over and over, she reminded herself that she was not that child now. She was, in fact, standing up for the younger Iz and all the other children in the Eastbourne Centre. This training was simply a trial to be endured and mastered, no matter how painful it might be in the moment.

The end of the third day came at last.

"I hope I haven't scared you all off!" Ms. Sole said with a watery smile.

Everyone spoke at the same time, assuring her that they were definitely not scared, quite the opposite.

Iz said in the clearest, strongest voice she could, "Let's set the date for the first session, Ms. Sole. I propose we start as soon as possible. Next week. What do you have available?"

The woman blinked at Iz's bold tone. She consulted her phone. "Wednesdays will work. At four o'clock."

"Perfect. We will be there."

At the door, Dr. Perlinger said softly to Iz, "Now that this training is out of the way, we can embark on those *revolutionary* ideas of yours, to show the world in a different way, to empower young people through music."

He smiled warmly as if he guessed how hard the training had been, how much she had fought to remain herself throughout. Her heart shimmered with gratitude for this teacher, and this school, where she was seen.

"Yes!" The word burst out of her with all the purpose in the world.

The days passed quickly, filled with epiphanies she scribbled down before she could forget them, exhilarating sessions with Dr. Perlinger, and passionate discussions in Manifesto rehearsals.

Before Iz knew it, Wednesday had come.

After school, she helped cram instruments into Dr. Perlinger's van—acoustic and electric guitars, amps, a keyboard, a drum set, Jasleen's cello, Becky's violin and oboe.

Dr. Perlinger cheerfully turned on the ignition. "See you there!"

Manifesto began walking toward the Eastbourne Centre, only a few blocks away.

As they strolled along through the warm autumn afternoon, Iz wasn't sure if she was excited, terrified, or a bit of both.

"You good, Beaufort?" Teo gazed down at her.

"Ha! Uh, yeah, maybe. If I don't have a heart attack."

"Probably you just need a distraction." He tackled Kwame, who chased after him and jumped on his shoulders. Bijan climbed on LaRoyce's shoulders and Will hoisted himself up on Ahmed's shoulders. They started bashing into each other, laughing like fools.

"We need energy!" Rina said. "Come with us. Becky, you too."

The next thing Iz knew, Rina and Jasleen had pulled her into a shop. They all ran to the counter, where the chocolate was.

"We'll need this . . . and this . . ." Rina picked out candy.

Jasleen added, "And the caramel one, LaRoyce likes that . . ."

"Also two of the chewy things . . ." Rina turned to Iz. "What do you want, Iz?"

"I-I don't know." She fumbled out her wallet.

"No, no, this is on us!" Jasleen said firmly.

Embarrassment rushed all through Iz. "I can pay for it! I-I have a job!"

"Doesn't matter. This is our treat for *everyone*."

"Oh. Uh . . . thanks." She picked up a bar at random.

Rina squeezed Iz's shoulders. "You're welcome."

"Love you," Jasleen added.

"Ha! Good! Okay!" And then a minute later, awkwardly—"That's like . . . really nice of you."

"Wait till you get to know us better! Our magnificence will overwhelm you." Rina turned cheerfully to Becky. "And now, what do *you* want?"

"This one." Becky held out a solid bar of chocolate.

"Why am I not surprised?" Rina grinned.

They reemerged from the shop a few minutes later and started passing out candy to everyone. The guys all dismounted and took something.

LaRoyce stuffed almost the whole bar in his mouth at once, and said, "What?" to everyone's laughing face.

When they arrived at the orange-brick building, Dr. Perlinger was unloading equipment onto the sidewalk. Everyone rushed to carry everything up the stairs and into the centre.

In the lobby, a woman darted forward, propelled by nervous energy. "Hello! Welcome! Thank you so much for coming! Oh, this all looks so interesting!"

Miss Cathy, Iz suddenly thought.

For a second, she felt like that scared kid who had attended here. But then she pictured Teo sitting in the candlelight at the restaurant. She listened to his rich and warm voice. *You've got this.*

The woman stepped in front of her, looking quizzical. "Iz Beaufort, is that you?"

"Huh, yeah," Iz said guardedly. "Hey, Miss Cathy."

"Do you go to The Métier School?" Miss Cathy's voice was frankly astonished.

"I do! Sorry, got to set up." Iz fled with everything she was carrying into the main room, where a bunch of kids had stopped what they were doing to stare at everyone.

A thrill ran through her when she saw them.

This was it. These were the actual kids.

Iz smiled and waved at them. A couple of hands waved back.

"Iz, where should we set up?" Teo carried the keyboard under one arm and the stand under the other like they were feathers.

"Uh." She scanned the room. "How about over here, and then we can sit in a circle in front?"

"Okay, captain." Cheerfully he put them down and began to assemble the stand. To the little girls watching him, he added, "Get back. This thing could blow at any minute. Also, which one of you hid all the plugs in this place?"

Iz sat on the floor to unclip her guitar case. That was when she saw a small body under a table, knees gripped beneath its chin.

She gazed at the figure for a minute.

Then she clambered to her feet, drifted toward the table. She sat on the floor so she was on the same level as the little person.

"Hey!" She tried to sound approachable. "I'm Iz. I used to go here. I'd hide under this table sometimes, but mostly I liked to go behind the coats."

The girl looked over Iz's left ear like Iz didn't exist. She sighed loudly as if all her time kept being taken up in annoying conversation.

Iz swallowed, pushed on. "So, yeah, we're here to do music with you today. We're called Manifesto. Everyone writes their own stuff, and it kind of comes out of research we do. They—we—tour around and perform in concerts. We're all from The Métier School. It's, like, a high school for music."

In the sour silence that followed, she began to wonder if she just sounded like a braggart. "But . . . I mean, I'm just new in Manifesto. I don't know much yet. Basically, I auditioned at the beginning of the winter term last year. And, like, I'm a foster kid with Dominion Children's Care, and my foster mother at the time didn't exactly know about me auditioning till later. I wouldn't recommend doing it that way, actually."

She stopped, shocked she had just blurted everything out loud. That was the *last* thing she'd planned.

"Skye, you should come on out and meet Iz! I think you'd have a lot in common." Miss Cathy materialized, all bubbly.

"Why, because we're both foster kids with DCC? She already told me."

"Oh, no!" Miss Cathy looked stricken. "I didn't mean that at all! Excuse me, I just have to . . ." Flustered, she took off.

There was an awkward silence.

"Ha!" Iz said at last in a light voice. "Looks like Miss Cathy is as smooth as ever."

She hoped they might bond over how tiresome Miss Cathy was. But the little girl sat silently like she'd been frozen into a statue of a kid.

Finally Iz stood up. "Well . . . bye, then. Hope you'll come and join us."

She walked away quickly. When she reached the far wall, she closed her eyes and imagined she was in a helicopter maybe, or a ski lift, or an elevator carrying her high into the air. From up there, she could see everything. She could remember she was at the Eastbourne Centre to give these kids the same view of the world.

"Hey, Beaufort." Teo's voice was confident and encouraging. "You ready?"

She opened her eyes. His smile gave her courage. "Yep."

Chapter Ten

Iz walked to the centre of the room. "Hey, does everyone want to come and sit in like a circle?"

She expected them to run over, but instead the kids kept careening around the room, paying no attention. Finally, LaRoyce clapped his hands and shouted, "People! Circle!"

At his words, they tumbled toward her like acrobats.

The minute Teo sat down, two little girls grabbed him in a headlock.

"Everything okay?" Bijan asked him.

"Great," Teo said in a muffled voice. He shook the girls off, but they flung themselves at him again. He put an arm around each and lowered them onto the ground. "Hey, whoever you are, sit down. We're getting started."

"Kid tamer," Rina said.

"I've got four thousand cousins. Tame 'em or they eat you alive."

"Hi!" Iz beamed around the circle. She took in each face, thinking of how well they would soon know each other. "How's everyone today?"

They all chorused, "Good."

"I'm so glad!" She took a deep breath. "We're here from The Métier School. We thought we'd come each Wednesday to do some music together—if that's okay."

She was just opening her mouth to say they should go around the circle and introduce themselves. But she was interrupted by a boy whose name tag read *Ezekiel*. "What kind of music?"

"Well, a lot of kinds." She waved around at the members of Manifesto. "I mean, each one of these people is writing something cool. We're all studying different music forms and stuff . . ."

"Like what?"

"Um . . . fugues and operas and sonata-allegro form and, I mean, symphonies, and song cycles . . ."

"I have no idea," a girl named Daniella said flatly, "what any of that means."

"No, right." Iz flushed. "But, like, we can teach you. And a-about instruments and how to play them . . ."

"Are you going to play us something today?" Ezekiel asked.

Iz blinked. If only they'd stop firing questions at her, she could think. "Uh, yeah, we definitely could. But first, though, I thought we should go around—"

"What are you going to play us?" This was Chanti.

"Let's hear it *now*," Daniella bellowed.

Iz's heart started racing. The kids looked chaotic and defiant.

She thought back to the rehearsal yesterday, when everyone had talked about works they could potentially perform for the kids. "D-does anyone want to go ahead and play something?"

She tried to ignore how ungainly her words were, how unlike what she'd planned.

"I do!" Jasleen said immediately.

With infinite gratitude, Iz said, "Jasleen writes this amazing stuff that's, like, science meets music. I know I'm probably not saying that right, Jasleen."

Jasleen twinkled at her. "You said it wonderfully." She gazed around the circle, eyes lingering on each kid. "Anyone here ever played with a basketball?"

A bunch of them put up their hands.

"Ahh, good. Lately I've been wondering what would happen if you were playing basketball but the basketball didn't want to stop bouncing." She opened her eyes wide, encouraging them to consider how remarkable that would be. "It's something called the law of inertia, which means, things like to keep doing what they're doing. They don't want to stop. Can you even imagine?"

They all laughed at that. A bunch of them made exploding noises, as if the basketball was destroying everything it smashed into.

Everyone in Manifesto went to pick up an instrument while Jasleen passed out the music. Iz perched on a chair with her guitar.

A voice echoed from under the table. "Boooooring."

Skye was glaring like Iz was the worst thing she'd ever seen. Like this was personal.

"Are we ready?" Jasleen said brightly.

"Wait!" Daniella jumped up. "Be right back!"

She ran out of the room, reappearing a minute later with a ball.

"What are you going to do with that?" Devanch's voice was scornful.

"Duh. Her song's about a basketball. So, I got a basketball."

"Yeah, but her song doesn't have a basketball *in* it."

"You don't actually know anything," Daniella told him. "Maybe I'm going to put a basketball in it. Maybe I'm going to throw a basketball at your head. I can do whatever I want."

Miss Cathy murmured by the back wall, "Let's use kind words."

Iz's gaze ricocheted between everyone talking, her hands in fists. *This was on the verge of being a disaster.*

But Jasleen's eyes sparkled. "I have an idea," she said to Manifesto. "What if every time the basketball goes to a new kid, we jump to the next key change or time signature change? Sort of like hyperlinks. We'll just keep circling the piece."

Manifesto laughed out loud with delight. Meanwhile, Iz's stomach felt like it was doing a thousand nauseating crunches.

Jasleen gave the cue. Together, Iz's classmates burst into a joyful, tumultuous sound that leaped ahead several bars every time someone caught or threw the ball. Before long, the kids were laughing and running around making spectacular catches and throws. And everyone in Manifesto was concentrating feverishly so they didn't miss a change.

Skye crept out from under the table, did some kind of interpretive dance to the music. But when Iz caught her eye and smiled, Skye's face closed right down. She stuck out her tongue and retreated underneath the table.

At last, everyone tumbled back onto the ground, out of breath.

Iz was just about to suggest that this would be a great time for each person to introduce themselves. But then the little girls flung themselves on Teo again.

"Hey, what's with you two?" Teo said. He read their name tags. "Poppy and K'Nesha. Nah, those aren't your real names. You're Matches and Dynamite, right?"

Poppy giggled while lying somehow on top of his head. "When are you going to do *your* music?"

"*My* music? You want to hear *my* music?" He deposited Poppy and K'Nesha on the floor, looked to Iz. "Should I?"

"Sure. Yeah." She cast aside her plan for what felt like the thousandth time.

"Okay, does anyone here know what an opera is?" He ratcheted his charisma up to the highest level.

A quiet boy raised his hand. His nametag said, *Shemar.* "Is it a song?"

"It's a story with a *bunch* of songs in it," Teo said. "Operas have been around for hundreds of years, and they have this style of singing that's really, really *big* sounding, because the singers had to fill whole huge concert halls without microphones."

"The singers *were* the microphones," Ezekiel said.

"Yes! Exactly." He grinned. "And I have a long way to go to grow into a voice that's *that* big. But I'm learning how to do it."

"Show us!" K'nesha said.

"You sure?" Teo looked around at them all, smiling and egging them on. "Aren't you worried I'll break the windows with my big, big sound? Aren't you scared I'll send you all flying?"

Their voices rose again in delighted cacophony, until Miss Cathy stepped in again. "Settle down, everybody."

Teo's mouth quivered with amusement. He inhaled, chest expanding. And then—

The kids' mouths fell open at the resonant sound of his voice.

At the end, Teo grinned and did an elaborate bow.

"You didn't break the windows," K'Nesha accused.

"I held back this time. Didn't want to wreck the place. Besides, this song is an aria." He glided a hand back and forth slowly. "Arias are, like, gentle. The action stops, and the person just sings about their feelings—their biggest fears, their most important dreams, what they want out of life, their goals for the future . . ."

"Like praying," Shemar said, out of nowhere.

Teo's eyes glimmered with wonder at the little boy's words. "Yes, like praying. Like opening yourself up to the universe." His voice got quicker. "What I just sang was a love song this guy Alfredo sings about a girl he likes named Violetta. And it's also sort of an apology, because he's wrecked *everything*, and she's dying, and it's at least partly his fault."

"How did you learn how to sing that song?" Ezekiel asked.

"I played Alfredo in a student opera this summer. Also . . ." He glanced sideways at Iz. "Iz and I went to see it on Saturday."

Iz flushed, as Chanti said loudly, "Oooh, was it a *date*? Are you two *dating?*"

"It was an *outing,*" Teo said, raising his eyebrows at Iz.

Under the table, Skye made puking noises. Because Iz was so disgusting and horrible nobody would ever want to go on a date with her.

Iz felt like she herself was going to puke for real in a minute. This was totally out of control.

"What did she die of?" Shemar asked. "The girl. Violetta."

"C*onsumption*." Teo spoke in a diabolical voice.

"What's consumption?" K'Nesha said.

"It's this thing," Teo said, "that gets in your lungs so you can't breathe."

"I had consumption last winter," Devanch told him.

"I had bronchitis," Chanti said. "I coughed so hard I barfed."

Skye shouted right at Iz, "I wish *you* would get consumption!"

Iz inhaled sharply.

Miss Cathy scrambled to her feet. "Skye, that's enough." She hurried to the table and spoke in a quiet voice.

Iz forced herself to regroup. "Ha! So! Anyone want to try one of these instruments today?"

The kids started yelling over each other about Jasleen's cello, the drum set, Becky's oboe and violin, the electric guitar.

But Iz could barely hear them because Skye's hateful words rang in her ears.

She saw herself through the little girl's eyes. She was a complete fraud, just as insipid and irrelevant as those annoying adults who had once pestered her into singalongs and crafting sessions.

This whole thing was a chaotic and profound failure.

Chapter Eleven

Iz lay awake most of the night, glaring at the ceiling and berating herself.

Stupid! Disorganized! Irrelevant! Arrogant!

Who was she to have imagined she could make some magnificent difference in these kids' lives? She was everything she'd always hated.

Fear prickled through her too. This bargain she'd made with the universe—to earn her lucky fortune through doing good and giving back—it only worked if she accomplished something worthwhile. Otherwise, safety could easily slip away. That Place was always only an arm's length away, like some goblin king galloping up behind.

In the morning, she huddled at the breakfast table, hood pulled over her eyes. She couldn't face anyone, including herself.

"I could get you more toast," Gisele said.

"*No.*"

"Bad sleep?" Vito rumbled.

Iz shot upright, realizing how rude she was being.

"Uh … yeah." She flushed. "Sorry. I'm sorry. I-I guess I'm in a bad mood. I shouldn't take it out on you."

Gisele looked concerned. "Cara, if you ever want to talk about anything … or we could set something up with Meredith …"

"Uh, no, I'm okay for now," Iz stammered. She and her therapist had agreed to a break while Iz settled into her new life.

She pushed her chair back, stood up. "Thank you for everything. I, like, have to get ready for school."

Iz practically ran down the hallway. She shoved the rest of her toast under the bed. Then she locked herself in the bathroom, found the cleaning stuff and spent the next twenty minutes scrubbing everything until it shone.

Afterward, she grabbed her backpack and guitar and strolled back to the kitchen like she was exactly the kind of easy-to-deal-with kid she should be.

"So," she said brightly. "See you tonight!"

"See you tonight." Gisele looked a bit worried.

Iz scrambled down the stairs and out into the street.

When she got to Métier, she fled upstairs to the cafeteria. Her plan was to get some hot chocolate and nurse it alone in the farthest corner possible until classes started. But to her chagrin, most of Manifesto was sitting at pushed-together tables, cackling and bellowing over each other.

Iz gulped, froze. She didn't want to talk to them about yesterday's disaster, wasn't sure she could handle the compassion in their eyes as they tried to soften the failure the outreach had been.

But Bijan saw her and waved. "Iz! Over here!"

She couldn't pretend she hadn't heard him. She forced her jerky limbs to walk over and collapsed into a chair. "H-hey!"

Bijan's eyes danced with enthusiasm. "We were just talking about that *moment* when Shemar said an aria is like praying."

LaRoyce added, "And when Daniella went and got the ball—"

"And we ended up improvising around Jasleen's piece—"

Kwame blurted, "And Ezekiel said opera singers *are* the microphones!"

Teo slammed into the chair beside Iz, all high good humour and unlimited energy. "Beaufort! Where did you go yesterday after the outreach? I turned around and you'd taken off."

"Yeah ... I had to work."

She wasn't about to tell him she'd run so her tears wouldn't fall in front of them all.

Jasleen called down the table, "So . . . Teo . . . Iz . . . I understand that you two went on an *outing*?"

"Beaufort's planning the next one." Teo tilted back in his chair, grinning at Iz.

"Oooh!" Rina said to Iz. "What are you going to do?"

All at once, Iz felt like she couldn't breathe. "I-I don't know."

As they stared, she rasped, "I, um, I have some history stuff to finish. Just remembered. Sorry—I'll see you later!"

For the second time that day, she shoved her chair back and stumbled to her feet. Grabbing her guitar and backpack, she raced out of the cafeteria.

Had they even been at Eastbourne?

Didn't they hear Skye yelling those horrible things?

Iz stumbled through the halls, unsure exactly where she was going, until she found herself outside Dr. Perlinger's office. She meant to walk straight by but instead stopped, closed her eyes, and knocked.

When Dr. Perlinger opened the door, Iz burst out, "I totally failed."

He looked astonished. "What do you mean?"

"Yesterday was a disaster. *I* was a disaster." She waved her hands around. "The kids were shouting and jumping on each other, and that girl Skye yelled at me, and nothing I planned actually worked."

"Ah. You'd better come in."

Iz perched on her usual armchair. Dr. Perlinger sat down in his. He clasped his hands behind his head, stretched out.

He said, "You wanted to introduce them to different instruments. You wanted Manifesto to perform some of their work. You were hoping it would be interactive. Yes? And didn't that all happen?"

Iz frowned. "But it was totally out of control."

"Ahh. Because it didn't follow your script. Because the kids changed the plan."

"They weren't changing the plan. They were yelling and screaming and jumping on people."

"Hmm." He smiled. "Have I ever told you my tennis theory of teaching?"

"No."

"You send a volley over the net—something new you want to challenge them with. They volley it back, completely repackaged in their own way of seeing things, quite different than you might have expected. It often throws you off balance."

She nodded, miserably ashamed. "Yeah, that definitely happened."

"But the next part is when it gets interesting. In real time, thinking on your feet, you have to figure out how to make sense of it—how to *build* it—and send a new version their way … only to have them shoot it back at you again."

"Huh." She considered it. "So you think they were volleying."

"They were." He smiled. "With tremendous enthusiasm, I thought."

"But … not everyone."

He narrowed his kind eyes. "Are you talking about Skye?"

Iz shot a glance at him. "She didn't even want to join us."

"Yet."

"No, not ever. She hates me."

There was a silence.

"I'm recalling a certain churned-up young person who sat on the bench outside of my door last term," Dr. Perlinger said. "And I asked myself, *how do I make a connection?* And she started telling me that we should study *Winterreise* together."

"I never said that."

"Not in so many words. But I sent out a little Schubert volley to see what would happen. And you whipped that ball back across the net, nearly taking my head off."

He laughed so heartily that Iz found herself half-smiling in response.

"Don't be too hard on yourself for not having a tidy first session with them." He passed her a tin of cookies and she took one. "Teaching is a terrifying and unpredictable and profoundly improvisatory business. It's not about *what* you are teaching, but rather *who* you are teaching and what they need at that moment. Anyone who tells you otherwise isn't doing it right."

"… Okay."

"And consider letting the children see who *you* are. They don't know yet, do they? They haven't met that rebellious voice who tore down the very fabric of the universe because it didn't fit her. They haven't been introduced to your passion, your drive for justice."

Iz found herself nodding slowly.

Dr. Perlinger added, "If you volley your own unique and human and questioning and vulnerable and powerful self over the net, they might just take their cue from you and volley back who *they* are. That's where the magic starts, you know."

Iz regarded this teacher who, against all odds, saw the raw potential inside her. For the thousandth time, she was profoundly grateful that she had fought for the chance to be his student.

"Okay," she said. "Okay. I can do that."

Chapter Twelve

Iz felt so much better after talking to Dr. Perlinger.

She spent the rest of the morning plotting how she was going to turn everything around. She would show the kids exactly who she was. She'd inspire them to show who *they* were. The outreach would explode into the stratosphere.

But her brain kept puncturing holes in her plans. *And who exactly is this amazing person you're going to tell them about? I assume you're planning to leave out all the bad stuff?*

"Shut up," Iz hissed back.

Her brain was right, though. She couldn't tell the kids about all those times she'd lashed out at teachers, about visits to principals' offices that had resulted in suspensions. She couldn't share about being arrested and appearing in court. And she definitely couldn't reveal anything about That Place.

How were you supposed to separate your bad behaviour from what was in your heart?

She was still wrestling with this question when she got to her Profiles of Composers class.

But Dr. Warren immediately commanded all of her attention. "'A third coffin goes out from my house. I was alone, alone!'"

Everyone fell silent.

"Such a random, horrible thing." Her teacher paced across the stage. "First Verdi's daughter, then his son, and finally his wife

Margherita. We'll never know what childhood disease took the children. But Margherita—his beloved 'Ghita'—died of encephalitis. His whole family, gone in a matter of months."

She paused.

"They got married the month after he'd landed a job that would allow him to support her. The babies came quickly afterward. And then ..." She brought her hands together like she was acknowledging a tragedy almost holy in its awfulness. "Everything destroyed. A reversal of everything good. No, a savage shredding of the universe. All meaning lost."

Dr. Warren jumped onto the main floor of the lecture hall and began to walk up the aisle. "The pain destroyed everything creative in him. When he tried to write, he couldn't. His comic opera was a disaster, not surprisingly. He threw his pen down and said he would never write again."

She held hands to her face, lowered her head.

The hall waited.

"So. How did he go from utter despair ... to *Traviata*, to *Trovatore*, to *Rigoletto, Otello, Aida,* and all the rest of the operatic masterpieces?"

Iz was leaning forward now.

"More helpers," Dr. Warren said softly. "A man named Temistocle Solera wrote the words for an opera. Then the director of the great La Scala opera house put it into Verdi's hands. The right libretto at the right time, an offer of a way back through the darkness." She paused. "He resisted it! He hurled it onto the table in his empty house. Only later did he read the words. Like atoms falling in the right places, they spoke to exactly the pain in his soul."

> *Oh, my homeland, so lovely and so lost! Oh memory, so dear and so dead!*
> *Golden harp of the prophets of old, why do you now hang silent upon the willow?*
> *Rekindle the memories in our hearts, and speak of times gone by!*

Dr. Warren looked around the hall, meeting everyone's eyes. "Those words were the ones he needed to see. They pointed out the agony of his losses but also rekindled the memory of when there had been hope and warmth."

She raised her hand, punctuating her words.

"Here's what he later said about beginning to write again. 'This verse today, tomorrow that, here a note, there a whole phrase . . .' He must surely have faltered, stumbled, questioned. But fundamentally, he looked despair in the eye and defied it with whatever strength he could bring to the task. A new opera emerged, born from pain but looking forward. *Nabucco*."

She clicked buttons on the remote in her hand, and an image came up on the screen behind her.

"Let's watch a clip of *Nabucco* now, thinking of how this work is his hard-won *way back*."

As the video came to life, Iz saw many people sitting on what looked like cliffs. When they began to sing, their hushed voices throbbed with pain almost too awful to speak aloud. But as they persevered, their voices grew. They became noble in their desolation.

Iz's eyes blurred.

She heard Dr. Warren's words again in her head. *Fundamentally, he looked despair in the eye.*

Empathy flared in her for this composer who had lived hundreds of years before. He'd had horrible experiences but faced them down. He'd gotten to know the demons that had decimated his life and taken his creativity. Somehow, he had sidestepped them, struggled on, even amid his great grief.

How had he done that?

"His music," Dr. Warren said, as if answering Iz's question. "His music was the roadmap we can follow to trace his path back to himself, to see his brave—no, *heroic*—determination to hammer out who he was going to be. And through his art, he was known."

At her teacher's words, Iz inhaled involuntarily.

Through his art, he was known.

After school, she ran home to Festa, flew upstairs, threw herself down on the floor, and pulled out the notebook of songs she had written over the years. In that little spiral-bound book, she had crafted all her messiness and doubt and faltering into lyrics that pierced through to her heart. That was what art did, after all—it shaped life's raw materials into something rare and meaningful. It said, *look at existence this way. Look at ME this way.*

She flipped through the pages.

"Paper Kid" was about how she was more bureaucratic paperwork than child, a kind of 2D representation of a human. But because she was so flimsy, so virtually nonexistent, she was able to slide under a locked door and escape without anyone noticing.

"Catapult" was about being slung from home to home, until she commandeered the slingshot, shooting herself into a place so high and far from where she was living that she could change the very rules of the universe.

Then, of course, there was "Refugee," Iz's original protest song, about how she refused to follow the route prescribed for her. She would rather be homeless, throw herself on the compassion and mercy of the world, than remain where she was. This song was like the heartbeat of her soul. It had been the soundtrack of her fight to get into The Métier School.

Yes, yes, her songs were a roadmap of her life, just like Verdi's had been of his. She would show the Eastbourne children who she was by singing to them.

Hope swelled in her, as if she was actually that confident girl in the newspaper article who knew exactly who she was and what she wanted to do.

But just then Vito's heavy feet thumped along the hallway to the home office, and back downstairs to the restaurant.

Iz froze.

His disapproving words from this morning burst into her head.

Bad sleep?

Without warning, her brain started doing the thing she hated. It started whirling like an out-of-control carousel, circling around worst-case scenarios. She was powerless to stop the horrible thoughts.

He was going to say, *We can't have a rude, ungrateful girl here. Go pack your stuff. You can wait for your social worker on the sidewalk outside.*

She tried to tell herself that none of it had happened. But her brain wasn't listening. It acted like she was already standing on the curb, like she had lost everything through her bad behaviour.

Iz scrambled to her feet, leaving the notebook and its songs on the floor. She stamped around the room, forcing herself to notice the steady floor beneath her feet. She touched the soft quilt, ran her hand along the desk, telling herself that those things were real. The other wasn't.

Not yet, anyway.

After a long time, the panic attack started to subside. Then Iz picked up her guitar. She forced herself to walk calmly down the stairs, through the kitchen, and into the restaurant.

Vito was going over receipts at the bar while Gisele hung clean wine glasses on the racks.

Iz pasted a huge smile on her face. She ran around the back of the bar and threw her arms around them both.

"What's all this?" Vito growled, but with a slight smile that felt immensely reassuring.

"Just happy to see you," Iz said brightly. "Just missed you. And now, I'm going to get my guitar and play in the restaurant. Gotta keep up my end of this bargain!"

"What bargain?" Gisele said.

Iz looked disbelievingly at her. "Uh, I still have a *job* with you. Three hours a week. Unless you fired me when I came to live here."

"Nobody fired you," Vito said. "But . . . you got homework?"

"I finished it at school." She summoned as much wheedling charm as possible. "You know I bring in customers whenever I play. Don't you want customers? I thought this was a business. I thought you, like, wanted to make money. But, I mean, it's your choice. Go bankrupt if you want."

She willed him to see how dependable and positive and responsible and low maintenance she was. Finally, his face transformed into a rare grin despite himself.

A few minutes later, Iz climbed onto the stool, tuned her guitar. Slowly, gently, she began to pluck a little melody woven through with folk songs the diners liked. She added hints of arias that Vito loved. Puccini, Rossini, Verdi. When she glanced at him, he was smiling and nodding his head in time to the music.

Her iPad pinged.

Iz brought the melody to a close. The early diners all clapped, and Vito raised a hand, paying homage to her.

She leaned over the screen. It was a message from Teo.

Hey B how are you?

Iz flushed. She needed to fix things with him too, needed to be bright and light. She wrote, *Güd! How are you??*

She watched the three dots for ages as she waited for his answer to come through.

Sorry I put you on the spot this morning saying you were going to plan the next outing. I'm an idiot.

Iz shook her head violently, even though he couldn't see her.

She wrote, *No I'm the idiot . . . I've just been worrying about a lot of stuff lately . . . But I totally have it out of my system.*

She watched impatiently as the dots appeared again.

I don't want to stress you out

. . .

I was just joking

. . .

You don't have to plan anything

Iz wrote, *I am so not stressed! I am awesome.*

Wow I wish I was awesome, Teo typed.

Iz debated various replies for a while.

At last, she wrote, *You are not not awesome.*

You are not not an onion girl, he shot back.

She could imagine his expressive mouth wriggling with amusement. She could picture his light-brown eyes, ringed in a kind of green, dancing with laughter—kind of like on the night of *La Traviata,* in the restaurant, with the flickering candlelight.

The dots played out again for a few long minutes.

. . .

You know I'm here for stuff though

"How are things?" Vito materialized at her elbow. He glanced down at the screen, saw who she was talking to.

"Uh, great! I was just saying this was not a good time to talk because I'm, like, working."

Hurriedly she wrote, *Gotta get back to work. TTYL.*

Ciao, Teo wrote back.

Iz picked up her guitar and tumbled into a tune. Only after a minute did she figure out that she had begun to play an aria from *La Traviata.*

It was the moment when Violetta was dying but trying to convince herself she wasn't.

> *The spasms of pain have ceased!*
> *I feel reborn in me the strength*
> *That once was mine!*
> *I feel I'm coming back to life!*
> *Oh, joy!*

It was a desperate, anxious, fevered cry, fighting back against the darkness. When Iz glanced at her foster parents, Gisele's hand gripped her mouth and Vito was swiping his eyes.

Good!

Relief fluttered through her.

She wouldn't step wrong again. Wouldn't lose their good opinion. From now on, she'd be dazzling and endearing and just the right amount of funny. She'd work hard at school, help out more around the apartment, play them beautiful music they could not do without.

She'd be everything they needed.

She'd be everything that everyone needed.

Chapter Thirteen

Iz blazed into the Eastbourne Centre on the following Wednesday.

Her line up of songs was ready. Her self-portrait was rehearsed, polished. After she finished showing who she was, the kids would be inspired to think deeply about who *they* were. The stage would be set for big thoughts and songwriting.

In her mind, this was going to proceed logically and inevitably along the path she'd worked out. So she didn't expect the arms that grabbed her as she walked in and the voices that yelled "You're late!"

"Hands to ourselves!" Miss Cathy was saying. But the kids paid no attention.

K'Nesha yelled, "Are we doing the basketball song again?"

"Did you go on another daaaate?" Daniella's voice was loaded with meaning, and the rest of them giggled.

Poppy asked, "Can I play the keyboard now?"

"When are we going to like learn how to be microphones?"

Iz said with confidence, "We are going to do *all* that stuff."

"We're going on a *date*?" Daniella said, smirking.

"Uh, well, no, I mean . . ." Iz extricated herself from their arms, annoyed with herself for blushing. "Let's get started. Come sit in a circle!"

This time, LaRoyce didn't need to back up Iz's request. The kids all slammed into position, some sliding across the floor.

"What are we doing today?" Ezekiel said.

Iz took a deep, powerful breath. "I'm going to introduce you to my guitar."

"Are you going to play it?" Chanti asked.

"In a second. First, I want to *tell* you about it." Iz ran a hand along the guitar's curved side. She willed the words to come out just right. "I found it in a dumpster when I was little—"

Their voices interrupted immediately.

"We have a dumpster."

"Same! In the alley behind our house."

"I never saw a guitar in it, but there was a raccoon."

"We had raccoons under the porch."

"There are lots of things in dumpsters," Iz said in an even voice. "Today we're going to talk about *this* thing. Okay?"

"Okay," Daniella said.

Everyone echoed her.

Iz waited until it was silent. Then she spoke softly, while they all leaned forward. "My guitar, this guitar ... it didn't even have strings on it. So, I got some from a kid. And then I put them on all wrong and I tuned them to these random notes I thought sounded good. But they were totally not the real notes a guitar is supposed to have. So, my guitar is different than any other guitar in the world."

"What does it sound like?" Shemar asked.

Iz thought. "It sounds like *me*, I guess."

"You sound like a guitar?" Ezekiel said.

The kids all laughed.

"Yeah, no, not exactly." She racked her brain for how to explain. "I have a lot in common with this guitar. For one thing, we're both sort of battered up."

"You don't look battered up," Daniella said. "You actually look pretty."

"Ha!" Iz said, totally thrown.

"What? You do!"

Then everyone was shouting out their agreement.

"What I mean is," Iz said loudly, "I sometimes *feel* battered up. I've been, like, through a lot of foster homes. I'm in home number twenty-seven right now. And The Métier School is my fifteenth school."

"Wow," K'Nesha said.

"Right. Wow." Iz paused. "And another way I'm like my guitar is, we both sort of look normal on the outside, but we're different in a way you can't see at first."

"Because of all the foster homes," Daniella said.

"Yes." Iz thought hard. "And also, because ... my brain kind of works in a weird way."

She was about to explain how she could see music in her mind, as if it were a structure getting built out of ropes of sound. She was going to tell them how she could have a melody in her mind when she was going to sleep and wake to discover she'd orchestrated it.

But Shemar's voice broke in. "My brain's weird too. That's why I'm so bad at school."

"Me too."

"Same."

"Oh!" Iz said.

This was where she'd planned to segue into songwriting. But somehow, she couldn't let their comments go unacknowledged.

"I-I'm sorry," she said in a low voice. "School was always hard for me too, until I got into Métier. And even then, I had to work like crazy because there was so much for me to catch up on. There still is, really. But ... it's the first place that I felt *got* me."

Will said slowly, "I bet a lot of people in Métier would say something similar. We fit in there, but not so much outside."

Becky added, "I had my own special bully in middle school. She used to call me *Freak* because I'm autistic and I'm really into patterns. But then when I got to Métier, Dr. Perlinger introduced me to twelve tone theory, and suddenly everything that girl had said was wrong with me, turned out to be actually really *right*." She grinned at Dr. Perlinger, who was beaming back.

Iz was struck then by how each member of Manifesto had a personal relationship with him.

She said softly, "Dr. P, how does *your* brain work?"

He slouched in his chair, placing his hands behind his head as usual. "Like yours. And like Shemar's and Will's and Becky's and Teo's and everyone else's here. That is to say ... it works *uniquely*. Everyone's brain does. Everyone's heart does, yes? And how we express ourselves is unique too." He smiled at Iz. "You, for example, write powerful songs about identity."

Chanti asked, "What's *identity*?"

"Who you are." Teo's voice rolled smoothly into the air. He grinned at Iz.

"You need to remind yourself about who you are?" Daniella said.

"Because you're sad about all of those homes?" Shemar asked.

Iz looked down at her guitar, slightly at a loss. "Sad ... yeah. Angry. Scared. I just ..."

They waited.

"I just wanted to escape. I wanted to be anywhere other than where I was. I ..." She paused. "I wanted to be anyone other than who I was."

This was not exactly going as she'd planned. Not nearly as inspirational and upbeat. A little too personal.

There was a silence. Then Daniella asked, "When are you going to sing one of your songs for us?"

Everyone erupted with enthusiasm, voices smashing up against each other.

"Okay. Okay then." Iz lifted her guitar into position and her fingers found their homes. She closed her eyes.

She'd intended to start with "Catapult" because it was strong and determined and had a literally uplifting ending. But instead, the words and notes of her song "Refugee" came out.

I will not walk the road you made for me
You say no road is there at all
But I think that it is all I see
And I'm running from you
A joyful refugee

Afterward, she sat there anxiously, unable to look at anyone.

She felt utterly exposed.

Chapter Fourteen

There was a short silence.

"What's a refugee?" Daniella asked.

"Who are you running away from?" Ezekiel said at the same time.

"A refugee has to leave their country because it isn't safe," Iz said softly. "But they don't have anywhere to go to. So, they need to, like, trust in the kindness of other countries to take them in."

"Did you run away from a *country*?"

Iz struggled to think how to answer Chanti's question. "Not a country, exactly. I wanted to run away from my whole *life*, I think. From Dominion Children's Care. From foster homes. All the craziness of it. You know, I used to think that if you made a map of my life, it would just be a random scribbled line going all over the place." She took a deep breath. "I wanted to be free of it. Even if that meant I didn't have a home anymore."

There was a silence.

"We didn't have a home," Chanti said then. "Me and my mom and my brother. We went to a shelter. I mean, we do *now,* but we just didn't then."

Iz blinked at this revelation. Her heart swelled painfully.

She remembered how, when she'd attended Eastbourne, everyone had always seemed like they were in a kind of way station, always in transit. Moms who had left dads, foster kids, refugees being sponsored by community organizations, families new to the country scrabbling to pay rent.

She said faintly, "I'm glad you do now."

"Same. It was 'cause my dad put his fist through the TV."

Iz drew in breath sharply.

That Place fluttered through her mind.

Lamely she said, "I'm so sorry about that."

"It's okay. We're not with him anymore."

Iz nodded.

She could not think of a single thing to volley back to Chanti that was worthy of what the girl had just revealed.

But then Bijan's soft voice broke into the awkward silence. "Refugees." His eyes seemed to be looking at something only he could see. "So, LaRoyce and I were up in the attic at my place, and we found these instruments."

"What were you doing up in the attic?" Daniella said.

"Long story." He glanced at LaRoyce, who laughed. "Anyway, it turns out that they belonged to my grandfather, my jidu. He was a musician and also a teacher in a school. When my aunt and my uncle and my cousins had to get out of Syria, they actually carried his oud, and his ney, darbuka—"

"Qanun," LaRoyce interrupted. "And what's the other one? It looks like it has a bulb on it, and you play it with a bow?"

"Kamancheh."

"What does that mean, they 'had to get out of Syria'?" Devanch said loudly.

"Well . . . there was a war there." Bijan spoke with care. "It's just like Iz said. They basically had to leave their home because it wasn't safe, but they also didn't have a place to go to."

His words were like a blanket protecting the kids from much darker realities.

"I-I'm so sorry," Iz whispered. In the face of Bijan's family's history, her own refugee song seemed like a pale, whining complaint. She flushed with shame. Had he been sitting there judging her for elevating her own story to his?

But Bijan flashed her the most generous of looks. "So many ways to be a refugee, right? From unsafe countries but also unsafe homes . . . Lots of different wars to escape."

"That's like *her*. A war." Poppy pointed at a girl whose name tag read *Kateryna*.

"She doesn't know much English yet," Ezekiel said.

"But she's getting better," K'Nesha added.

Miss Cathy put an arm around the girl, who smiled up at her. "Kateryna comes to us from Ukraine."

"Where's your jidu now?" Shemar asked Bijan.

Bijan didn't answer for a while. When he did speak, his voice was very quiet. "Remember, I said he was also a schoolteacher? Well, something happened to his school." He paused. "It got bombed. And . . . he passed away."

There was a horrified silence.

"So he didn't even *get* to be a refugee," Shemar whispered.

"No . . . He didn't get to."

Shemar frowned, clearly thinking hard. "But . . . but his *instruments* are refugees!"

"His instruments are refugees," Bijan repeated. "I love how you put that."

"My keyboard was a refugee too," Chanti looked straight at Iz.

Iz caught her breath at this newest volley. Finally, she murmured, "How did that happen?"

"Like, remember, I said we were in this shelter place. And my mom brought my keyboard with us. All the kids would come over to our room and fool around on it. And this one lady played songs, and we did these like singing games. They were sort of stupid."

Iz was just opening her mouth to say something about how precious a keyboard could be when things in your world didn't feel quite safe or right.

"When are *we* going to get to write a song anyway?" Devanch's words burst in.

Everyone started talking at once, and the sound rose sharply.

"Whenever you want!" Iz's heart leaped up at how Devanch had just put everyone on the path she'd hoped they might find. "What kind of song do you want to write?"

"About the instruments," Ezekiel said.

"Yeah, how they escaped and everything," Daniella shouted.

"How they were lonely," Shemar added.

Iz nodded, brain whirring as she tried to think about the best way to start. How did *she* write a song? With fragments and grabbed-at ideas at first, messy and raw and not the least bit polished. The precision came later.

Hoping she was on the right track, she grabbed a marker and wrote on the chart paper, *SONG.* "Give me your thoughts," she said.

There was silence while the kids thought hard.

"The instruments came from a school in Syria?" K'Nesha said.

"Yes!" Iz wrote the line on the chart paper.

Chanti added, "Where his grandpa used to teach the kids how to play them."

"And then Bijan and LaRoyce found them in the attic," Poppy said.

Iz kept scribbling, while the kids and Manifesto kept blurting suggestions. Soon the paper was full.

"You like it as is? Anything you think we should change?" Iz stood back, gazing at everything.

They studied the words.

"It's too bumpy in that part. His grandpa teaching the kids. It has too many bumps." Daniella pointed.

"Ah, right. I see what you mean."

"Bumps are, like, *beats.*" Teo's voice reverberated throughout the room. "You're right, that line has extra beats. How should we change it?"

Everyone started shouting out ideas.

"Oh, so, like *this*?" He clapped out the line.

Gratitude spread through Iz as she watched him interacting with the kids.

Over the next hour, Manifesto smoothly homed in on specific sections and asked the kids for their thoughts. Iz scribbled down each idea, crossing words out, adding others.

Meanwhile, the children bickered. They sighed gustily. They rolled around. They said they couldn't do it. They said they had a new idea. They said shut up, no, wait, what about *this?*

In the end, with Manifesto's help, they had actually built the lyrics for a new song.

The instruments were refugees
They came from a school in Syria
Where the grandpa taught the kids to play
The qanun, oud, darbuka, and ney
Till the school was knocked to the ground

The boy found them in his attic
He's learning to play them with his friend
He's going to write songs about wars and schools
And kids looking for somewhere to go
Like those instruments lost and found

When they'd finished, there was a silence.

"What do you think? Do you like it?" Iz could scarcely contain her smile.

"It's awesome," K'Nesha said.

"No, it's *incredible,*" Ezekiel added.

Poppy shouted, "We are so talented!"

They all started roaring over each other.

"Please," Miss Cathy said. "We can't learn if we don't listen."

Something daring reared up in Iz, emboldened by how everyone had come together to write the song. "But, you know, Miss Cathy, a certain amount of *chaos*, of *passion,* is part of the artistic process."

Miss Cathy stared, as if a whole new head was sprouting from Iz's shoulders.

"So," Chanti said to Bijan, "when do we get to play your jidu's instruments?"

"Yeah," K'Nesha said. "The oud and everything."

Daniella added, "The one that has the round thing on the end."

Bijan looked at Iz. "I can bring them next week. If you want."

"Yes," Iz said immediately. "Yes!"

She could hardly contain the joy shooting through her.

Dr. Perlinger had been exactly right. She'd shown them who she was, and they had followed suit with enthusiasm she couldn't have imagined possible.

This was going to work after all.

Chapter Fifteen

At the end of the session, Miss Cathy said, "Everyone! What can we say to Iz and Manifesto and Dr. Perlinger?"

They all bellowed, "Thank you!"

"You're welcome," Iz said, heart full.

She started to help put instruments in cases, while Miss Cathy herded the kids toward the kitchen for a snack.

Dr. Perlinger strode up to Iz, beaming. "Well, Iz Beaufort. Didn't *that* take us somewhere interesting?"

"Ah!" Iz's face burst into a smile. "I mean, it didn't really follow what I expected again, but ... it's like I knew where I *hoped* it would go, and we did sort of get there ..."

"We did indeed sort of get there, via social justice and some powerful lyrics. And let's see what they bring in next week!"

"You think they're going to bring something?"

"Of course!" he said cheerfully. "This is how the volleying goes. The fun part is waiting to see what it will be. Now, excuse me as I put these music stands in the van."

As he ambled off, Iz stood there marvelling at what a success it had been.

Would her younger self have been inspired by that conversation about refugees and instruments and songwriting? Would she have added her thoughts? Or would she have hung back, not yet quite trusting?

As she was thinking about this, something moved in the hallway.

A pair of legs extended from under the coats.

Iz exhaled slowly and softly. *Found you.*

She walked over, stood in front of the coat hooks, spoke loudly. "So, now I realize I should have piled up the shoes so nobody could see my legs."

There was silence.

"It used to get so hot in there, though. And sort of stinky. But, I mean, it was better than being in yet another self-esteem-building class or whatever."

She waited to see what Skye would volley back.

"Did you go on another dumb date?" Skye's voice was like a knife, precisely searching for the thing that would throw Iz off balance.

"It was an outing, not a date." She tried to sound lofty and unbothered.

"Whatever," Skye said. Then she added, in a pretend high-class voice, "The op-errrrr-a."

Skye's words made Iz sound privileged and obnoxious. By extension, maybe Skye saw this whole outreach as condescending—a bunch of rich kids strolling in and giving a glimpse into a lofty world that had no bearing on everyday life.

Iz wanted to walk away. But she imagined Dr. Perlinger encouraging her to keep going. Telling her to try to connect with however Skye saw the world.

Well, how *did* Skye see the world?

She was angry, for sure.

She didn't like anyone.

She was maybe scared of almost everything.

Mind racing, she said, "Yeah, I mean, I'd never been to an opera till the other weekend." She paused. "Actually, most of my music training has been me just writing, like, a bunch of angry songs like that one I played today."

There was a silence.

Iz said at last, "I don't know about you, but I pretty much hate Dominion Children's Care. Most of my songs are about feeling like

I was stuck in some kind of prison, wanting to just bust out and start over and be alone. And I was afraid all the time."

She let that hang there.

Then she swallowed and asked, "You ever . . . feel that way too?"

Skye rolled her eyes. "You like to talk about yourself, don't you?"

Iz forced herself not to take it personally. "Uh, no. Sort of the opposite. I think that's why I spend most of my time in my room with my guitar."

"Because nobody likes you."

"Ha! Actually some people do now."

"Like *Teo*."

"Uh, okay, sure, yeah." She paused. "And, I mean, my foster parents. Foster-to-adopt. They're kind of awesome actually."

"So why do you still spend most of your time in your room with your guitar if they're so awesome?"

This stopped Iz cold. "Maybe it's like Dr. Perlinger said. It's my identity . . ."

"Your identity is hiding in your room writing a dumb song."

"Well, you're hiding behind the coats." Iz spoke sharply, without thinking.

There was a silence.

She continued, "Also, I've written a lot of dumb songs, not just one. Y-you might even like some of them. You might connect with the feelings in them. Because—" Iz went out on a limb—"I sort of think . . . you and me, we're a bit the same."

"Nope." The little girl's voice was derisive.

"Okay, well, let me show you." Although Iz was pretty sure that whatever she said was going to be pointless, she took out her notebook. She started turning pages, saying the titles loudly.

After a bit, Skye interrupted. "What's that one?"

"Which one?"

"That one you just said. The shadow one."

"Oh." Iz stared down at the song. "Uh, 'Shadow Hands'?"

"Yeah."

"Ha," Iz said, something fluttering.

It had been about being trapped in a miserable middle space between life and death, at the mercy of wraiths you could not push away.

Skye was silent.

At last, Iz said in a small voice, "Want to hear it?"

"I don't care," Skye said dismissively.

Iz sat down cross-legged on the ground. She pulled her guitar into her lap.

She played to Skye's legs.

***

After Iz had performed several songs, the little girl said abruptly, "Well, I'm out of here." She slid along the coat rack till she was at the end closest to the main room. She wrapped a coat around herself like she was closing a door.

Iz sat there, trying to figure out what to do. She wanted to talk to Skye further but couldn't avoid the obvious message that the little girl wished to be left alone now. Finally, she got to her feet and walked back into the main room.

Manifesto was gone but Teo was still there, perched precariously on five stacked chairs, his long legs swinging. "Want me to walk home with you, Onion Girl?" he said smiling.

"Uh ... sure!" Her heart started fluttering way more than it had a minute ago.

Teo slipped off the chairs and held out a hand.

"What?" she said.

"Give me your guitar."

Face beating, Iz passed it to him. He slung it across his back.

When they left the building, the wind knocked them around like punching bags. They fought their way along the sidewalk toward Festa.

Iz's brain was on overdrive. She kept stealing glances at Teo, marvelling that he was carrying her stuff and walking with her. Also, she was totally on a high from the outreach, and even from that last conversation with Skye.

But she was also rapidly problem solving.

Because if Vito saw Teo walking her home, there was every chance her foster father would come out and interrogate Teo about his intentions or his financial situation or something. She didn't trust Vito-the-suspicious-dad as far as she could throw him, which wasn't far, because he was built like a mountain.

When they arrived at the restaurant, Iz said quickly, "Yeah, I should probably go in. Lots of, like, homework."

"Why's there a ladder on the ground?" Teo said.

"Hey," a voice called.

They looked up. Vito was crouched on the small ledge that separated the first and second storey, just above the awning.

"Can you put it back up?" Vito spoke like nothing was out of the ordinary.

Teo dropped Iz's things. He lifted the ladder like it weighed nothing, leaned it against the wall, then held it while Vito climbed down as if he was made of dignity.

"What happened?" Iz said.

"Ladder blew over. I was trying to fix the awning." Vito waved his hand like it was nothing.

Teo squinted upward. "What's wrong with the awning?"

"Wind bent it or something. Now it won't retract." Vito ran a hand through his grey hair. "Going to call the manufacturer."

"I could check it out," Teo said. "I've installed a bunch of awnings."

Iz and Vito both stared at him.

"What? My dad has a roofing company. I've helped him lots of times."

Vito grimaced, then waved at the ladder as if to tell Teo to be his guest.

While Vito held it steady, Teo climbed up and started fiddling with things. He called down, "It jumped the tracks, that's why it won't retract. I can probably get it in again. Also, it's full of gunk. If you could get like a cloth or some paper towels or something, I'll clean it out."

"Just a second."

Vito disappeared into the restaurant, and Iz took over holding the ladder in place while the wind buffeted her.

A minute later, he reappeared with a handful of cloths that he held up to Teo. Then Iz and Vito stood there and listened to metallic clinks and clangs.

"There, I think that's got it." Teo's head appeared at last. "Try retracting it."

Vito turned the handle, and the awning flattened against the wall. "Hey," he said with satisfaction.

Teo climbed down, while Iz held the ladder on one side and Vito held it on the other.

Vito clapped him on the back. "Thanks, son."

Teo burst into a huge grin. "No problem, Mr. Santoro. If there's anything else you need help with, I'm here."

"I'm not dead yet," Vito said.

Teo's face changed immediately. "Oh, hey, no, I mean, I didn't—"

Vito burst into a bark that could have been a laugh. "Relax. It's all good. And you might as well call me Vito."

He opened the door to go back inside, but the wind blew the door against the wall with a smash.

"Careful," Teo said. "I don't have any training in fixing glass."

Vito raised a threatening hand at him but smiled gruffly. "Funny man," he said, and went inside.

Then Iz and Teo stood there looking at each other, while Iz marvelled that Vito had actually left them alone.

Maybe he was cool with ... whatever this was, then.

Their heads moved closer.

The door flew open again. "You got homework?" Vito said to Iz.

"Ah! Ha! Yeah!"

She broke free of Teo's ridiculously compelling eyes. She waved, stumbled backward, whirled around, ran inside.

Chapter Sixteen

***Let's see what** they bring in next week.*

Iz absolutely couldn't wait.

On the day of the next outreach, she actually slipped out of her last class ten minutes early so she could head over to the Eastbourne Centre before the rest of Manifesto.

When she walked in, the kids all shouted and ran over.

"Where's everyone else?" Ezekiel said.

"Oh! They're on their way. I was just, like, so excited to see you I couldn't wait to come." Iz found herself beaming back at him.

"I couldn't sleep last night," Daniella told her. "I just kept saying the words of our instruments song."

"Me neither," Iz said. "And same."

She looked around surreptitiously for Skye. The little girl wasn't under the table or behind the coats. So she'd found a new hiding place. Never mind. Iz would find it later.

After a while, Manifesto staggered in the door with equipment. Iz jumped up to help. The kids scattered and buzzed around until everything was ready.

Then Iz called, "Hey! Let's get this started!"

Everyone ran over. Poppy and K'Nesha leaped on Teo as usual. Iz couldn't help grinning to see how he tried to deposit the girls on the ground while they clung to him and giggled.

"You're going to break my back!" he said.

"Goody!" Poppy shouted.

"So!" Iz said. "Has anyone noticed the instruments?"

"Duh!" Daniella exclaimed.

They were laid out on a blanket in front of Bijan and LaRoyce.

"Let's play 'em," Chanti said, reaching out for one.

Bijan laughed. "Let me show you how they work first!" He picked up a stringed instrument that had a body shaped like a pear. "This is an oud. It has five twinned strings. Sometimes six."

"It looks like a guitar," Poppy said.

"Well, it's sort of like one. But its tuning is totally different."

"Just like Iz's guitar," Shemar said in his soft voice.

"True," Bijan said.

"So the oud and Iz's guitar are like siblings," Shemar said.

Everyone in Manifesto grinned at each other. Shemar's observations were always so thoughtful.

"But they don't fight," Ezekiel added.

"I once shoved my sister's mattress out the front door." Daniella looked satisfied at the memory. "I told her to never come back."

"Listening," Miss Cathy said.

Bijan demonstrated how to play the oud, fingers fluttering over the strings. He showed some simple fingerings. One by one, the Eastbourne kids came up and tried them out. Then he introduced them to the rest of the instruments.

When everyone had had a chance to try everything, Shemar said, "Can we do our song from last week but with instruments now?"

Bijan strummed the oud softly. "Our song doesn't have a tune yet. What do we want it to sound like?"

"Taylor Swift!"

"Bruno Mars!"

"Beyoncé!"

Iz thought quickly. "What about a mashup? Something like this?" She picked through some notes on her guitar, sang the first lines of their song in a pop style.

They shouted and clapped.

"That's so good!" Ezekiel told her. "How did you do that?"

She thought about it. "Well, some of it is just coming from inside my head. But, I'm also learning about things called chord progressions and intervals and structure and phrasing. And I kind of took some of the phrases I knew from those artists' songs . . . and I sort of mixed them up . . ."

"Talk normal," Devanch said flatly.

"Huh! Right!" She wracked her brain for how to simplify her words. "Okay . . . see, I just took a little bit of Taylor here, and I put a little rhythm from Bruno in there, and can you hear Beyoncé in this part?" She demonstrated, singing those parts and exaggerating the rhythmic accompaniment.

The kids yelled, recognizing everything.

"But . . . I'm just wondering . . . does that tune really fit the *words* of our song?" Iz hoped her meaning would come across right. "I mean, we wrote about a war happening. About kids losing their school."

"The Grandpa dying," Shemar added.

"Wait a minute." Daniella sat up. She closed her eyes. She began to sing in a slow, throbbing voice, "The in . . . struments . . . were . . . ref . . . ugees . . ."

"Yes!" Rina said under her breath.

"They came from a school in Syr . . . ia . . . where the grand . . . pa taught the kids to play."

The other kids were swaying with her words.

Iz's fingers flew over her guitar, following Daniella's melody so quickly she was almost playing the notes before Daniella sang them.

"Beautiful," Bijan said softly at the end. "Teach it to us."

"Me?" Daniella said. "I don't know how to teach stuff. I was just singing."

"Yes, you do. Start again a line at a time and we'll sing it back."

"Fiiine." Daniella shrugged like Bijan didn't know what he was talking about.

She crooned the first keening phrase again. Raggedly, the kids joined to echo it. Iz scarcely dared to breathe—she didn't want to break this spell of the kids actually working together to create something new.

When Daniella had taught the whole melody, Bijan and LaRoyce lifted up the oud and the ney, looked to each other in that almost-telepathic way they had, and spooled out the opening line. Then Dr. Perlinger surprised everyone by picking up the darbuka and saying, "May I?" He shook his head as Manifesto cheered at him. "I am a complete beginner, believe me."

The first few times through the song were a mess. The kids sang at their own speeds and didn't really listen to the instruments at all. But when Iz pointed out places where they needed to be in sync with the accompaniment, they tried again and again, getting a bit better each time. Eventually, they began to sound like a real little group.

As everyone packed up at the end, Iz forced herself to not run around and scream with giddy excitement. They had written their first complete song! Not only that, but the kids had worked together without fighting.

A tight, little voice spoke behind her. "I wrote something."

Iz twisted around. Skye stood there, looking closed and slightly feral.

"Uh … you did?" Iz tried to sound calm, but her heart was suddenly racing.

Let's see what they bring in next week.

"It's about being mad." Skye pulled a crumpled paper out of her pocket. She shoved it at Iz.

"You want me to … read this?" Iz said.

"Duh."

Iz smoothed out the paper. It was covered with tiny, cramped printing. Her eyes flew back and forth along the lines.

Her astonishment grew.

And her excitement.

Skye said gruffly, "So?"

"It's … it's …"

"What?"

"It's really good …" She wished she could think of better words. "It's—it's powerful."

"I know."

"Like ... is it ... is there someone it's about ...?"

"None of your business."

"Okay." She decided to change the subject. "Do you, like, have any music in mind for it yet?"

Skye shook her head. "I just yell it. Like this."

Then, without warning, in front of everyone who was packing up, she launched into the angry lyrics.

Say my name but you don't know me
Now I'm gonna say something too
It's about time you knew
What's inside my head
And when I'm done telling you
You're gonna hate yourself
For trying to control me
For making me feel bad
With your mean mouth
And your snake mind

"Skye!" Ezekiel shouted like Skye had just solved the meaning of life or something.

Skye flushed and glared. But some small thing in her eyes looked proud.

Iz's brain scrambled to find the perfect volley back to Skye. It had to show that she *saw* Skye, and it needed to honour her ferocious writing without sending Skye running to hide.

She said slowly, "It's like someone's been telling you that you have to be a certain way or you're no good. But something snaps. And you finally shout at them to say how angry, how tired and frustrated and unhappy it makes you. And you get up the courage to say you're not going to take it anymore."

"Yeah," Skye said.

"Someone who's fighting back at last. Who refuses to be victimized." Teo's eyes were locked on Iz. "Like Violetta, if she had stood up to Alfredo's dad."

Iz flushed, again thinking of that night at the opera, with Teo smelling so nice and the two of them sitting next to each other with their legs touching.

Skye snapped, "It's not about Violetta. It's about *me*."

"No, I know," Teo said quickly. "I didn't mean it was. It just, like, reminded me about this part when Violetta gets kicked out of her home and it's totally unfair. I was imagining, what if Violetta had told off Alfredo's dad instead of running away? If she'd, like, shared what was inside her, made him see who she was."

"Yeah, okay, whatever," Skye said, her voice dismissive.

Shemar was clearly thinking about Teo's idea. He said carefully, "Because, nobody knows anything about anyone else unless someone tells them." He waved at Iz. "Just like we didn't know Iz was a foster kid till she *told us*. We didn't know these instruments were rescued till Bijan *told us*. And"—he twisted to look at Skye—"we didn't know Skye could write amazing songs till she *showed us*."

"Moral of the story," Daniella said loudly, "is tell people! Then they'll know!"

Something in Daniella's words hit Iz hard. She said slowly, "In our homes, in our lives, there are so many stories waiting to be told. Maybe they're in a person. Or maybe they're hiding in a shirt or some other object. And we'd never know unless we paid attention. Unless we listened and let them speak."

She hesitated, then decided to send the volley out.

"Maybe," she said, "something in your own home, your own life, is like that ... Why don't you see what you can you find this week? Bring it in next time."

Chapter Seventeen

"Why are you Onion Girl?" Skye stared up at Iz, all intensity.

Iz put down the music stands she was about to take out to the van. "When did you hear that?" she said at last.

"He called you Onion Girl last week when he was going to walk you home." Skye pointed at Teo, who was just walking out the door with an amp and a keyboard.

Iz tried to think of an explanation that would be appropriate for a kid of Skye's age. "Uh ... it's just a name Teo gave me. Because of, you know, layers on an onion. And he said I have, like, these layers."

"Bad layers," Skye said.

"Ha! What?"

Skye crossed her arms tightly across her chest. She squished up her face. Her next words sent a chill through Iz. "Where I live ... *they're* the bullies in the song."

"Ahh," Iz said.

She looked at Skye's quivering mouth, and her angry eyes. She saw the tense way the little girl held herself ...

That Place began seeping around the edges of Iz's thoughts, like a swamp alive with wraiths' fingers reaching and grabbing.

"Were you ever in a place like that?" Skye asked in a tiny voice.

Iz held her breath for a long time before letting it out. "... Yeah, sort of ..."

"What did you do?"

She swallowed, sat down cross-legged on the floor. Skye sat down too.

"I ... I asked to be moved," she said softly. "Like, twice. And nobody did anything. And I remember how hard that was. I felt ... *desperate*."

Skye waited.

"And, I don't know, when it got really horrible ... I did something sort of, like, bad. I shouldn't have done it, but I felt like I had no choice." She grimaced. "I kind of lost it. I ended up breaking her nose. And they kicked me out."

Skye considered this. "I don't think I'm big enough to break somebody's nose."

"I don't recommend going that route!" Iz cast her mind over what she knew about supports in the system. "Did you tell anyone you don't want to live there?"

"I told my caseworker to move me, but she didn't do anything. She probably thought I was making it up, or else ... maybe she figured they were being *mean* because I was being *bad*."

Iz's heart ached for the little girl. "But ... since she didn't listen, you have to try again. Or try something else. Till someone listens. You have rights. I found that out ..."

Skye nodded.

Iz stumbled on, "Because nobody ... should have to stay in a place where ... where they're scared, where it feels, you know, *bad*."

"Skye, your chili's getting cold!" Miss Cathy called from the doorway.

Skye jumped up guiltily. Iz knew that feeling all too well. Like you had to hide things and protect yourself. Like you were always sure you were in trouble.

"If I can help," Iz said, with far more confidence than she felt, "let me know. Anything."

"Really?" Skye said.

Iz nodded emphatically.

Skye regarded her. "Okay," she said. "Okay."

Then she turned and followed Miss Cathy.

Iz sat on her own in the empty room. She looked around at the piled-up chairs and the empty space where Manifesto had been a few minutes ago.

Right now, this minute, she felt exactly like the little kid who'd attended Eastbourne years ago. Trapped, traumatized.

"No," she whispered, pushing back against the suffocating feelings.

She was a different person now. She was looking forward, not backward.

Nonetheless, she leaped to her feet, tore out of the Eastbourne Centre like shadows were pursuing her. Outside, she gulped in fresh air and concentrated on the pure autumn sunshine.

"Beaufort!"

Teo leaned against the railing, grinning at her.

"Hey!" Iz said, ferociously tamping down on the darkness roiling inside her.

Cheerful, fun to banter with, balanced—that was who she was.

He fell in beside her as she walked. "So … I'm wondering if we actually *should* plan a new outing pretty soon?"

Iz forced her voice to be carefree. "Yeah! Definitely! Like, maybe a world cruise or something!"

He laughed. "I might have to save up for that."

She barked out a guffaw. "Me too."

She was trying to think of what to say next, when Teo's phone burst into a familiar tune. After a couple of seconds, she realized it was that moment from *La Traviata* when Violetta had sung "Love me, Alfredo." The moment when Teo had had tears in his eyes.

He pulled it out of his pocket and up to his ear, face bursting into a stellar smile. "Hey! Farrington!"

Iz stopped where she was.

Chloe Farrington.

The girl he'd spent the summer with. The one who was totally fun. Whose voice could make your heart break. The supernova.

"How are you? How's school?" Teo's voice was suddenly animated.

He listened, while various delighted expressions shot across his expressive face. "Yeah, I'm not surprised. You're such a star. You're going to ace all your classes."

Chloe was obviously saying more.

He burst into laughter. "No, sorry, I'm nowhere near the Met at the moment. I'm actually on the way to the best Italian restaurant in town." He glanced at Iz and grinned. Awkwardly, she grimaced back.

"What? No, I'm just walking my friend over there."

My friend. He said it so casually.

Iz felt a little pang then.

Which was ridiculous.

She was the one who had said she wasn't ready for anything else.

But there was something weird about him calling her a friend to Chloe Farrington the supernova.

"Iz," Teo said.

"What?" Iz said.

But then she realized he wasn't talking to her. He was answering Chloe.

"Yes, yes, it's fine. Everything's fine. Chill. I'm good."

Teo rolled his eyes then, half-grinning and listening to whatever was coming next. He said to Iz, "Chloe says she's heard so much about you, she wants to say hi."

She stared at him. "Like, what, right now?"

"No, after she hangs up." His laughter died when he saw Iz wasn't smiling. "I mean, nah. Forget it. I'll just tell her—"

Iz held out her hand. "Whatever." She held the phone up to her ear. "Uh ... hey. Chloe."

"So, *this* is the famous Iz!" Chloe's light voice sounded like music.

"Yep, that's me," Iz made her own voice breezy.

"I feel like I know you, after all the talks I had with Teo this summer."

"Um … oh, yeah?"

Iz felt some little thing twitching inside.

Chloe added, "Okay, I should explain that. A bunch of us would go out in the evening. There was this one place in the piazza. We'd hang out half the night. And Teo kept talking about this amazing girl."

"Uh, he did?"

"All the time. And he kept trying to get hold of you."

Iz glanced over at Teo. "Yeah?"

"You must have had a busy summer, though, right? I'm glad you're able to, you know, come up for air now."

"Uh …" Iz said.

"You must be absolutely amazing," Chloe added. "Because everyone was hitting on him all summer, and he just kept trying to get hold of you. We all wondered why this girl would ignore him. He was really depressed about it."

Iz's brain was already overloaded by her conversation with Skye. Now she felt claustrophobic.

"Uh," she stammered, "yeah, sorry, I've got to go …"

"Well, it was cool to finally hear your voice. And I'm so glad you're talking to Teo again. Hopefully we can meet sometime. I'm only a few hours away."

"Yeah. Bye," Iz said through gritted teeth.

She passed the phone back to Teo. As he continued to chatter at Chloe, she could feel a dark thing inside her getting bigger and bigger. It was made of guilt and futility and uselessness.

At last, Teo said, "Ciao, talk to you soon," and hung up.

They had arrived at Festa.

"Should we go in? We could sing." He said brightly.

"Uh. No … not today."

She didn't trust herself to say more. She needed to get somewhere quiet so she could recalibrate.

Teo frowned at her. Then he said in a casual tone, "Everything okay?"

"It's great."

She tried to get her feet under her. Tried to get back the Iz who made balanced choices that met the needs of everyone around her. But anger and panic fought for control.

Awful words spilled out, unbidden. "I'm so glad you had her to talk to this summer when I didn't, like, answer your texts. When everyone was hitting on you, and you were so depressed."

Teo blinked. "Is ... that what she said?"

"When you were hanging out in the piazza half the night."

A nasty little silence fell.

Teo winced. "Ahh. I'm really sorry, Beaufort." He crossed his arms, looked down at his feet. "Okay. I mean ... she was sort of, you know, protective this summer. Of me. That's all. And she just ... she doesn't know you yet." His eyebrows crowded over anxious eyes. "But Beaufort, it's nothing. I mean, she just happened to be there one day when I was checking for texts. And then it just turned into ... a stupid thing."

"I'm so glad she was there for you." Iz felt more unhinged by the moment.

Teo raked his hands through his hair. "There were just a bunch of us who would go out. Plus, the chaperone. They—ha—they called themselves my romantic consultants. But it was a joke."

Iz was feeling worse and worse. Fury was consuming her, mingled with intense shame. She saw herself through the eyes of these unknown people who had rallied around Teo during the summer. Everything was all mixed together with That Place too, with being at the mercy of too-personal gazes.

Tears pressed at her eyelids. If she wasn't so completely messed up, she could have reacted like a normal human being after that moment last spring in Festa. She could have spent the summer texting with Teo, and he could have been spared a whole lot of pain.

As if he sensed what she was thinking, Teo said gently, "Chloe doesn't know the whole story. None of them do. About you, Dominion Children's Care, how you got into Métier. I didn't think it was my story to tell." He shook his head, shrugged helplessly. "Maybe I *should* have told her. I don't know."

"Tell her whatever you want," Iz said coldly. "Really break it down for her, twenty-seven homes, fifteen schools. And don't forget my résumé of criminal activities."

He rubbed his head like he was trying to massage this argument away. "Oh, come on, Beaufort. Forget Chloe Farrington. She doesn't know what she's talking about. And you and me, we're back on track, we're friends again. Everything's cool . . ." His voice was light, but his eyes were blinking a whole lot.

"Oh good," Iz snapped, rage building. "If you say everything's cool, then it has to be."

"You're seriously overreacting. How do I fix this?"

Somehow, his reasonable words made her fury and shame grow, like bellows building flames.

"You can't fix it," she said. "You can't fix all the stupid onion layers. In fact, it's a waste of your time to try. You don't even know anything about me."

"Beaufort . . . Iz—"

"Forget it." She stumbled backward, out of control and hating herself for it. "I have to go."

Teo's face was tight. "This is a total misunderstanding—I'll call her back and sort everything out—"

"I don't want you to do anything! I just want you to leave me alone!"

At her words, his face changed.

A horrible pause went on and on.

"I will if you want," he said.

Inside, Iz screamed at herself, *what are you doing?*

Outside, she said, "Yeah. Good. I don't want you here."

"Cool."

He turned around and started to walk away.

He didn't look back.

Iz stood there staring after him, heart numb.

She wrenched open the door and pelted inside. She ran through the restaurant and up the stairs to the apartment.

In the little kitchen, she started prowling, searching for food.

A loaf of bread on the counter.

Tins of tomatoes, beans, artichokes.

Dried pasta.

Deli meat, sliced cheese, apples.

Anything to keep the terrible pain at bay. Anything to control the uncontrollable. Insurance against the darkness.

Iz carried the food to her room and shoved it under the bed. She stumbled back to the kitchen over and over, until the voice screaming in her head calmed down.

At last, she closed the door and crouched down, hugging her knees.

The tears erupted.

What had she just done?

It had happened so fast, the rage out of nowhere—just like the panic that had overwhelmed her when Skye's words dredged up those horrible memories.

A few minutes later, there was a knock on the door. "Iz? Are you okay, cara?" Gisele's voice sounded worried.

Iz quickly swiped at her eyes. "Fine! I'm fine!"

"You sure?"

"Yeah! Just practising a scene for my Profiles of Composers class. It's the part where Verdi's family all dies."

She realized how stupid she sounded, how implausible her story.

But she absolutely could not tell Gisele any part of this. One thread pulled would lead to other threads, and before long everything would unravel until that disgusting secret at the heart of it all was laid horribly bare.

There was nobody she could talk to without fouling the relationship.

"Can I come in?" Gisele asked.

"Uh . . . okay."

Gisele opened the door slightly and gazed at Iz with one of the warmest expressions Iz had ever seen. "Cara, I want you to know, you can tell me anything." She sat on the floor beside Iz. She put her hand on Iz's head and smoothed her hair back.

It actually felt really good.

Iz muttered at last, "I just did something horrible. I wrecked everything."

"Tesora. What did you wreck?"

Slowly it all came out, how she had gone ballistic. The end was half-muffled by tears. All the while, Gisele kept stroking her hair.

"Do you—think I'm bad?" Iz gasped at last.

"Iz, Iz, no, of course not." Gisele's face was a compassionate medley of light and shadow. "You have big feelings. You're human. And believe me, so is Teo. You can fix this. You'll talk to him. Cara, nothing, nothing is wrecked."

Chapter Eighteen

Iz did not at all want to go to school the next day. She dragged and dawdled around the apartment, packed and repacked her backpack, sat on her bed strumming her old guitar.

Finally, she trudged to Métier.

The lawn in front of the school was empty. The bell had probably just rung. Iz started climbing the steps as slowly as possible.

"Iz!"

Puzzled, she stopped, stared around. Nobody was nearby.

She started creeping up the stairs once more.

"Iz!"

Frowning, she halted again. "Uh … hello?"

"Down here!"

The voice was definitely coming from the bushes on the left-hand side of the steps.

Feeling like she was in some weird dream, Iz walked back down the stairs, then around to the bushes. Tentatively she called, "Who is it?"

"Me." The fronds moved slightly, revealing part of a face.

"*Skye?*" Iz's mouth dropped open.

"Shhhh," Skye snapped. "Just act natural."

Iz glanced around to see if anyone had noticed what was going on. She hissed, "What are you *doing* here?"

"I left," Skye said. "I'm done with that place. I'm not going back. I brought all my stuff."

Iz caught her breath. "Uh ... I mean, you can't just ..."

"You said you'd help me. So I'm going to live with *you*. In your foster family."

"What? No, that's not ... I mean ..."

There was a tense silence.

"You said you'd help me," Skye repeated stubbornly.

Iz's brain struggled to make sense of what was happening. One thing she knew for sure was that she had to find a way to control this. "Yeah, but ... my foster parents would totally, like, not be okay with me just bringing home a new kid and saying, like, *She's going to live with us from now on. Is that cool?*"

"You told me they were nice."

"They *are* nice," Iz said. "But ..."

She paced around for a while in front of the bush.

After a while she muttered, "We should let DCC know where you are."

"If you tell DCC, they'll just make me go back. That's the *opposite* of helping." Skye's voice exploded with bitterness.

Iz grabbed handfuls of her hair, trying to think. In her experience with the for-profit Dominion Children's Care, she had rarely felt particularly listened to, so she couldn't argue with what Skye was saying. But she also couldn't possibly allow the little girl to simply run away. That would be aiding and abetting or something, she was sure. "They ... they might not ..."

Skye said belligerently, "If you won't help, I'm just going to take off. I looked after myself before. I can do it again. Anything's better than going back there." The bushes rustled as she fought her way out, carrying a garbage bag. "I've got everything I need right here. So, see ya."

Skye took off along the sidewalk.

Iz waited for the little girl to turn around. But Skye kept going. Finally Iz ran after her. "Okay, stop it. Calm down."

Skye turned and waited, face squished up with defiance.

Iz pinched the top of her nose, where a headache threatened to flower. "I've got classes, but … uh … you could come inside and stay in a practice room for now. We'll figure it out."

Skye's eyes hardened. "This isn't a trick, right? You're not going to call them as soon as you get a chance, are you?"

"No, I won't call anyone."

"Not *ever*," Skye said.

"Come on. We'll go around the back."

"*Say it.*"

"I can't promise I'll never call anyone again!"

"You won't call DCC." Skye looked poised to run.

Iz was about to completely lose it on the little girl. She fought to make her voice calm. "I don't have time to call anybody because I'm *late for classes*. Come in and hang out for the next little while, and we'll try to decide what to do."

At last, Skye followed Iz around the side of Métier. They threaded through the trees and then onto the path that led to the tables and benches at the back of the school. Iz opened the door and peeked around to see if anyone was nearby. The hall was empty.

She gestured to Skye. "Come on."

They ran silently up the back stairs to the second floor. Iz opened a practice studio door and Skye slipped inside.

"Lock it," Iz said. "And keep out of sight of the window. If anyone tries to get in, like, make some noises on the piano so they know the room's taken. I'll come back and check on you in a while."

Skye nodded, sat down on the piano bench. "And remember your promise."

Iz fought the urge to yell something at Skye that would surely not help the situation at all.

"Just, you know, keep quiet," she said.

Closing the door, she wheeled around to sprint along the hallway to her first class.

But instead she froze.

Teo was striding in her direction, obviously in a rush himself.

He halted when he saw her. "Hey …"

"Hi." The word croaked weirdly out of her throat.

They stared at each other.

"Beaufort ..."

"Uh, yeah?"

"Could we, like, talk about all of this? Clear the air here?" He looked miserable.

Iz's heart sped up. She thought back to Gisele's words. *You can fix this.* She opened her mouth to put everything right again. To show him she was not some weirdo screaming in his face—

Crash!

The sound came from the practice room. It sounded like a piano bench falling over, maybe because someone was standing on it. A voice distinctly bellowed, "Ow!" and then, "I'm fine!"

Iz lunged forward, driving Teo back. He looked utterly bewildered.

She blurted, "I can't! Not this minute."

"Well ... is there some other time?" He looked miserable. "I admit, I don't feel great about what happened."

"I-I don't know when I can talk! This is turning into a complicated day. Maybe, maybe it's going to be a complicated week." That was an understatement.

"What's so complicated?"

"I can't—I don't want to talk about it. It's private."

The words came out harshly, completely opposite from the effect that she wanted. She instantly knew she'd made everything worse.

A bunch of emotions flitted across Teo's face—disbelief, frustration, anger, followed by a kind of calm resignation.

"Okay," he said. "You don't want to talk about it." He nodded to nobody in particular. "So ... we won't talk. That's fine."

"I want to, but I just don't know *when*." She couldn't handle any of this when it was all happening at once. She could solve either the problem of Skye or of Teo. But the two together were too much.

Teo barked out a laugh.

"It's okay," he said. "I get it."

He flung his glossy hair back like he couldn't care less. "Hey, it was fun. A couple of minutes in there, anyway. But I'm good. I can take a hint."

Iz stared in horror.

Teo added, "And since we were never officially together, I guess this isn't a breakup so much as a see you around. So, hey, see you around, Beaufort. No hard feelings. Sorry it didn't work out."

His voice was as even and rich as ever, but she noticed his hands were trembling.

He walked away from her. And this time she knew it was for good.

Chapter Nineteen

At lunch, Iz took Skye some food from the cafeteria. She knocked and whispered, "It's me. Open up."

Skye unlocked the door and Iz slipped inside.

"Here," she said. "It's just a ham sandwich, nothing too exciting. Are you okay?"

"Better than you," Skye mumbled around the food.

"What are you talking about?"

"I heard you guys in the hall."

Iz grimaced, dug fingernails into her palms so she wouldn't cry.

Forcing her voice to be firm, she said, "Yeah, uh, so … we have to figure out what to do with you. I have an idea … There's this guy called the ombudsman … he helps foster kids with problems they can't solve on their own … I found out about him when—"

"Sure," Skye said. "Avoid the topic."

"This *is* the topic. We phone the ombudsman's office, or maybe we even go there … and we tell him you don't like—"

"That's a nope." Skye crossed her arms. "I'm not going anywhere near that guy, whoever he is."

Iz exhaled, trying not to flip out. "So, then, what are you proposing we do when it's the end of the day? I can't just leave you in this practice room."

"I'm going to your place," Skye said stubbornly.

"I already told you, I can't just show up with you and say, *Oh, by the way, this is Skye and she's staying.* Not to mention, Vito and Gisele will call DCC right away to let them know you're safe."

"Relax, I have it all worked out."

Iz closed her eyes. "Oh, yeah? What's your grand solution?"

"I go in when they're not looking or something. I hide in your bedroom closet. You know it could work." Skye spoke like Iz had zero imagination.

"And then what? Tomorrow?"

"I go back to school with you."

Iz was getting more frustrated by the minute. "*This* is the master plan? You spend the rest of your life hiding in my bedroom closet at night and locking yourself in a practice room during the day?"

"Works for me," Skye said.

Iz shook her head. "No."

Skye tilted her head to one side. "Okay, let's make a deal. One night. I stay one night at your place. And tomorrow, I'll do whatever you want. You can call DCC or even that Bud Man."

"Why don't I believe you?"

"Please ... If I have twenty-four hours to get used to the idea, I can do it." Skye closed her eyes, looking all at once very small and alone. "I could tell you about a whole lot of times I didn't think I could do something. But then, when I had time to think about it, turns out I could."

Iz knew she was being played.

But Teo's voice just kept echoing in her ears—*Since we were never together, this isn't a breakup so much as a see you around.* It tangled up her thoughts, messed with her ability to make a reasonable plan.

She said, "How am I supposed to trust that you'll let me call someone tomorrow?"

"Pinky promise." Skye held out her hand.

A few hours later, Iz entered the apartment via the back stairs from the alleyway behind the restaurant. She peeped around for

Vito and Gisele. The place was empty. Creeping back down the stairs, she opened the door, beckoned to Skye.

Meanwhile, her brain screamed, *What are you even doing?*

Skye scuttled inside, followed Iz up the stairs and into her bedroom. Iz closed the door, heart pounding like it was attacking her from the inside.

But Skye seemed serene. "This is nice." She put down her garbage bag and walked around the room, appraising everything Gisele and Vito had put on the walls. Photos, a painting of a young girl with a lute. A pennant that said, *Métier Athletics,* which was funny because Métier's focus was not on anything remotely athletic.

"Iz!" Gisele's voice echoed up the stairs from the restaurant. "Did I hear you come in?"

"Uh," Iz said, panicking. "That's my foster mom. You'd better get in the closet."

Skye settled comfortably in there, sitting cross-legged. Iz closed the closet door, then rushed out just in time to meet Gisele in the hallway.

"H-hey!" Iz tried to look calm and unflappable like a dependable foster kid.

Gisele was looking anxious. "Cara, do you have a minute?"

"Uh . . . sure. Kind of."

Gisele ushered Iz into the kitchen, where they sat at the table.

"I-is something wrong?" Iz said, trying to sound casual.

Gisele shook her head lightly. "Oh, no. Nothing. Nothing is wrong."

"Okay . . ."

"It's just . . . I was vacuuming your room, cara."

"I'm sorry. I should have done that. I—"

"No, no, cara." Gisele looked like she hated to go on. "I . . . saw under your bed."

Alarms went off inside Iz.

"Oh!" she said.

She started blushing furiously.

Gisele said gently, "I cleaned it out. Some of it had gone rotten."

Iz shook her head, her whole face unexpectedly going fuzzy. This was the worst thing ever. Finally, she stammered, "I-I'm sorry."

"No, cara! No need to apologize." The kind wrinkles under Gisele's eyes spread out like a spider web of worry, and the corners of her mouth drooped with sadness. "It made me think about everything you've been through. It made me wonder … did you … were you …"

Gisele seemed to have trouble forming a question.

That Place entered the room and sat down at the table with them like some shrouded figure.

"Huh," Iz said, beyond stricken. "I just … It's only just … It was just in case … and it doesn't even make any sense … I am so, so sorry. I'm sorry it rotted. I am disgusting."

Then tears started coming down. Everything, everything was ruined. Every single important part of her life. She'd wrecked the mentorship with Skye. She'd destroyed the friendship with Teo, or whatever else it had been. And now she'd shown Gisele the disgusting Iz who lay under the perfect surface. The thief. The hoarder.

The universe seemed to be saying, *Look how easily all your good intentions got ripped down. They were as flimsy as paper, weren't they?*

Gisele took her hand and patted it. She said softly, "Cara, you will always have enough food here. I can promise you that."

Iz said nothing.

"But maybe old habits die hard. If you want … if it helps … I can give you something to keep in your room. Something nonperishable. We can make you a little shelf of things."

"Okay … okay … sure, we could do that."

She tried to stay calm, but her brain and body weren't paying attention to the commands she sent them. With the last of her shell shattered, and the bad things exposed, she felt almost like she was right back there in That Place, an insect being dissected in front of everyone.

Still, she grasped at words that would show she wasn't a complete mess. "I'm going to try to do better. Please don't give up on me."

Gisele pushed Iz back to arm's length, eyes flying wide open. "Oh, Iz, we will never give up on you. This is your *home.*"

She clasped Iz tightly again.

A muffled thud came from the bedroom.

Iz scraped her chair back. "Thank you. Thank you. So, if it's okay, I'm just going to—"

"One other thing," Gisele said.

What now?

"Yeah?" Iz tried to sound cool.

Gisele's eyes shone with almost impossible warmth. "I have so many family recipes, handed down over generations, from my great-great-grandmother all the way down to me. And now I want to share them with *you*."

"You do?"

"Yes! You're part of our family now," Gisele said. "So, I've taken the night off! They'll be fine downstairs, but if there's an emergency, I'm nearby. Iz, let's *cook!*"

Iz fought the urge to say that this was a terrible time, that she had a foster kid hiding in her closet. But she'd already destroyed one relationship today by saying she didn't have time for something. She absolutely could not spurn Gisele's kindness, although every atom in her body was shouting that she did not deserve it.

She smiled at Gisele like the steadiest foster kid imaginable. "I'd . . . I'd love to."

Chapter Twenty

Everything was totally surreal.

Iz stood there in the kitchen beside Gisele as they made spaghetti alla puttanesca, which Gisele said meant "spaghetti in the style of a . . . *fallen woman.*"

"Why did they call it that?" Iz asked as she chopped garlic into the tiniest pieces she could and tried not to think about whatever was going on in her bedroom.

"Ah." Gisele laughed a little. "There's one story that it got originally served in a . . . not so nice establishment."

Iz laughed too, but her thoughts went from fallen woman to courtesan, to Violetta, and finally to Teo. Then she was remembering the opera, picturing him showing her everything excitedly. And pizza afterward.

Her heart felt unbearably heavy.

If anyone had fallen, it was Iz.

She'd fallen away from the best friend she had ever known. She'd been numb when he first walked away, in shock. But now she was starting to experience the painful loss all through herself, from the follicles of her hair to the bottoms of her feet, like the pins and needles you got when feeling was starting to come back.

She'd fallen from *herself,* too, from her resolution to do better. *No more shenanigans,* Claudia, her social worker, had said when she'd brought Iz to live with the Santoro's, and Iz had agreed. But right now, this minute, Skye was in Iz's bedroom. Skye was at once a terrible secret from Gisele and a vulnerable kid who Iz was doing the opposite of protecting. DCC *removed* children from people who stuck them in closets.

Gisele was talking. "In Napoli, we don't do anchovies or oregano like they do in Rome. The ingredients are very simple, just tomato sauce, olive oil, garlic, capers, black olives from Gaeta, which is a little town between Naples and Rome."

"And spaghetti," Iz said.

"And spaghetti, of course."

Gisele got out a frying pan. "Pour in a bit of olive oil. Then we'll sauté the garlic till it gets golden."

"How much is a bit?"

"Just a little," Gisele said.

Iz poured some in.

"A bit more. Then we let it heat up before we put in the garlic."

"How do we know when it's heated up?"

"Roll the pan around. The oil will get runny."

Iz tried this. After a few minutes, the oil ran easily across the surface, coating everything.

"Do I put in the garlic now?"

"Yes! Stir so it doesn't stick or burn."

Iz stirred and stirred, guiding the minced garlic around the frying pan. A glorious aroma began to fill the kitchen.

Gisele opened a tin of tomato purée. She gestured to the label. "San Marzano. From Campania."

"Where's that?"

"It's the region Vito and I are from. Teo's family too."

Teo again. Iz's breath froze, as the grief shot through her once more.

Gisele glanced over at her. Gently she asked, "Have you ... talked to him?"

Iz stuffed down the pain. "Not yet. I've been trying to get him alone, but ..."

Gisele nodded, but Iz had the feeling that her foster mother could see right through the falsely bright lie.

"So, what do we do next?" she blurted.

Gisele smiled. "Here, pour the tomato into the frying pan. We'll heat it up, and after that we'll add the olives and capers. I'll just find them."

She reached into a cupboard, started moving jars around.

A movement caught the corner of Iz's eye. Skye was peeking around the kitchen doorway, exaggeratedly sniffing the air like some cartoon character.

Panicking, Iz gestured at her to go back to the room.

Instead, Skye did an insolent, little sashaying dance. She grabbed her stomach, staggered around miming intense hunger.

Iz ferociously waved Skye away.

"Be right back," she said to Gisele.

"Okay," Gisele was still looking in the cupboard.

Iz marched Skye along the hallway back to her room. She closed the door behind them. "You have to *stay in here.*"

"But I'm *starving,*" Skye said plaintively.

"You should have thought of that before you made me bring you." Then she relented. "I'll get you some food soon. But you can't leave the room and you have to be quiet."

"Fiiine."

"I'm serious."

"So am I."

Iz closed the door and sprinted back along the hall to Gisele.

"Found them!" Gisele said. "Here, try chopping the olives, Iz. But watch your fingers. Do it like this."

Iz took the knife tentatively and followed Gisele's example. Before long, she had a small untidy nest of olive pieces.

"Perfect," Gisele said. "Put them in."

Next, they dropped in the small round capers that smelled like pickles.

"Now we simmer," Gisele said. "And we get the pasta ready."

They heated water in the large pot that lived under the counter. When it began to bubble a little, Gisele dropped dry pasta in and turned the element down slightly. "I do a few in each direction like this. And then as it cooks, we'll just stir gently for the first several minutes so it doesn't stick."

Iz dragged a spoon through the pasta as it softened in the boiling water. She wished everything in her life could so easily relax and give way.

"I used to cook this in our family restaurant in Napoli," Gisele said. "It was barely a hole in the wall in the Via Benedetto Croce. And Vito started coming in everyday at midday. He hardly said a word, but he ordered this very dish each time. And then, at long last, we talked."

"What did you talk about?"

"I don't even remember! But we got to know each other. And I started looking forward to seeing him. Then he convinced me to go out one night." Gisele smiled at the distant memory.

"Was he *romantic*?" Iz said.

"Not in the least!" Gisele's laugh bounced through the kitchen. "But on our first date, he told me he was going to give me my own restaurant one day. Mind you, I made fun of him for it."

"And now look," Iz said.

"And now look!" her foster mother repeated.

When the pasta had cooked, Gisele dipped a measuring cup into the water. "This is full of starch, so we can use it to thicken the sauce."

She drained the pasta and poured it into the pan that contained the tomatoes, garlic, olives, capers, and parsley. She added a bit of the pasta water and began to stir. Sure enough, the sauce began to firm up.

"This," Iz said, "smells *ridiculous*."

"It's not just food, you see," Gisele told her. "It's my family. It's how Vito and I met. And now it's your story too, the first thing I ever taught you how to make."

She eyed Iz seriously.

"And I want you to know, Vito and I want to always be there for you. And we want to build memories with you. To the best of our ability, we will always try to make sure you have *everything* that you need."

Iz couldn't answer, she was so moved by Gisele's words. She nodded, sort of leaned in, put her head on Gisele's shoulder. Gisele squeezed her tight.

When the dish was ready, they ate together in the little kitchen.

"There's lots of extra," Gisele said, as they cleaned up after. "I'm putting it here in the fridge. Whenever you want some, you come and get it. Oh—and here, *this* is for you to keep in your room tonight." She handed Iz a small bundle. "Just a couple of biscotti from the restaurant. If you're hungry, eat them. It not, we'll swap them out for something else tomorrow."

Someone knocked softly on the apartment door. Gisele opened it. One of the sous chefs said something in a low voice. She nodded. "Coming." She said to Iz. "I've just got to go down and do something for a minute, cara."

"Of course!" Shyly, Iz added, "Thank you . . . thank you for teaching me today."

"It was my great joy," Gisele said, eyes crinkling at the corners.

When Iz was sure Gisele was gone, she scooped some spaghetti alla puttanesca into a dish, grabbed a fork, half ran along the hallway and slipped into her bedroom.

Skye was lying on the floor with her feet halfway up the wall, gazing at the picture of Manifesto all eating together in Festa. "Where's this from?"

"The restaurant downstairs," Iz said. "It's from the night of my scholarship concert."

"What's a scholarship concert?"

Iz put the food on her desk and pulled out the chair for Skye to sit down. The little girl began hungrily inhaling the pasta.

"I had to make a video of, like, me playing and singing, so these judge people could decide if they were going to give me a scholarship," Iz said. "A scholarship is, basically, a fancy way of saying they'll pay for me to go to school."

"Did they pay?"

"Yes."

There was a pause. "But why don't you recommend it?"

"What?"

"The first time you came to Eastbourne you said you didn't recommend how you got into your school. Into The Métier School."

Iz blinked several times, then remembered the conversation she and Skye had had on the opening day of the outreach program. She tried to choose her next words very carefully. "Remember, uh, how I said I didn't tell my foster mom I was auditioning?"

Skye nodded.

"When I got in, I kind of just . . . kept not letting her know. But it sort of started to be complicated. And then everything got bad for a while there."

"Why did it get bad?"

Iz let out her breath slowly. "I just kind of broke some laws. And—" She stopped before she could tell the worst part.

"*And?* Come on, you have to tell me."

"I don't have to tell you anything."

"Well, you *should*. Always answer kids' questions because otherwise, how are they supposed to learn stuff?" Skye paused. "Did you kill someone?"

"What? No!"

"Then what?"

"Ahhh." Iz flushed, mortified. "I maybe stole some money to pay for school."

"But you had a *scholarship*."

"Not then, I didn't. Only . . . after."

"After what?"

Iz sighed. "After I got caught." She swallowed. "I-I had to go to juvenile detention and court and stuff. And Métier kicked me out, and I had to re-audition."

Skye was staring with huge eyes at Iz. "Coooooool."

Iz shook her head in disbelief at the little girl. "It's not cool. I actually don't want to be doing *any* bad things anymore."

"Too late," Skye said. "'Cause right now, right here—this is probably like abduction or whatever."

"Yeah, probably," Iz said miserably.

She'd tried so hard to put all the dishonesty behind her.

Now it was back and she was completely out of control.

Chapter Twenty-One

When evening had crept into darkness, Skye started rolling around on the floor and yawning. She rubbed her eyes with her fists.

Iz's mind raced. Skye needed to sleep. But where? The safest thing would be to make her a bed in the closet, but putting a little kid in there for the night felt wrong. At last, Iz turned down the quilt on the bed. "Here. Get in."

Skye barely argued. She crept into the bed and curled up. She was out almost instantly.

Then Iz sat in her desk chair, hugging her knees and watching the little girl.

What were they going to do about all of this tomorrow? And in the meantime, how would she manage to keep Vito and Gisele from walking in tonight and discovering Skye?

She felt like she was on a Ferris wheel forcing her to circle back into her old life of crimes and secrets.

How had she ended up here again?

Finally, Iz set up a nest for herself in front of the bedroom door. If anyone tried to open it, they'd smash right into her and, hopefully, she'd make some loud, startled noise that would wake up Skye and send her running for the closet. If they asked Iz why she was sleeping in front of the door, she could make up something about how she was feeling anxious. Gisele would accept that explanation after finding the food and everything.

Iz took spare blankets from the closet shelf and laid them on the floor. She placed her backpack at the top of the makeshift bed to act as a pillow. Then she switched off the lights and lay down.

The apartment was quiet. She tried to make her brain calm down, but it remained on high alert. Also, she was incredibly uncomfortable. At last, though, she stumbled into a very shallow sleep.

Suddenly, her alarm was beeping. She shot upright. Sunlight streamed in the window. Iz looked around blearily, trying to figure out why she was lying on the floor. Then everything rushed back. She and Skye had made it through the night without getting caught.

Iz dressed quickly, then gently shook the little girl awake.

"What?" Skye said loudly.

"Shh!" Iz crouched down so she was close to Skye's face. "It's morning. I'm going to go get breakfast. I'll bring some back soon. You can get ready but stay in here."

"I didn't even change out of my clothes," Skye said, sitting up. "So, how am I supposed to get ready?"

Iz ignored this, just slipped out and closed the door behind her.

Gisele had put a plate of shell-shaped pastries on the table. "Sfogliatelle! I made them this morning. I'm putting together a container for you to take to school. If you see Teo, you could give him a couple. I know he loves them." She smiled at Iz. "Pastries can smooth over a lot."

"Okay …" Iz said. Tears pushed on her eyes at the thought of him. She gulped some orange juice, kept chugging till the whole glass was gone. Her stomach churned as she stood up. "I'm kind of behind. I was supposed to get to school early today. I'm just going to get ready."

"What about breakfast?"

"I'll, like, eat some of the sfogliatelle."

"When you see the kid, tell him the awning's still good," Vito said.

"I-I will."

Iz fled to her room.

She said to Skye, "I'm getting some pastries, but we'll eat them at school."

"How are we going to sneak out past those guys?"

Iz frowned. Skye was right—Vito and Gisele were sitting right there.

An idea came to her.

"Count to thirty … and then run as quietly as you can right past the kitchen door and down the front staircase, okay?"

Skye nodded.

Iz raced back to the kitchen and leaned against the sink. "So, I have a question about the restaurant. How do you figure out how much food to get? So you don't run out or, like, have too much left over."

They both shifted to face her, backs to the hallway now.

"I was just thinking about how that must be really hard to do," Iz added. "And how bad it would be if you ran out of stuff or, I mean, wasted food."

Vito frowned like she was insane. Iz resisted the urge to gulp loudly.

"We get to know how much we need," he said. "We buy based on how much we've used before. We can judge from past purchases."

"Oh, good! I was just … concerned."

Gisele eyed her with a worried expression. "Cara, there will always be enough. Don't worry. We've been doing this a long time. If you want, I can show you the books—"

Skye scuttled by the doorway.

"Oh, uh, sure." Iz nodded about a thousand times. "That would be great. Okay, well, I should probably head out." She grabbed the container of sfogliatelle and edged toward the kitchen doorway. "Thank you for this! Bye, then!"

She sprinted along the hallway and downstairs to the back door, hating herself for deceiving those two good people.

But at least this was the end of it. Skye would not be back tonight. The whole experience would soon just be a bad memory.

At Métier, the two of them snuck in the back door again. Iz set Skye up in the same practice studio as before.

"I'll come and bring you some lunch. And then, after school"—she spoke firmly—"We'll call the ombudsman. Right?"

"Yeah ..." Skye shoved a sfogliatella into her mouth.

Iz frowned as she closed the door. Was Skye agreeing or just saying what Iz wanted to hear?

She spent the rest of the day willing everything to be okay.

When she walked late into the Manifesto rehearsal after school, everyone was gathered in a circle while Dr. Perlinger talked seriously. Teo glanced up and away again like she meant nothing.

"Ah, Iz, come join us," Dr. Perlinger said. "I'll just recap what I was saying. The Eastbourne Centre reached out to me." He gazed at her with a worried expression. "One of the children is missing. She disappeared yesterday from her foster home. It's Skye Hill."

"Oh no!" Iz's stomach clenched.

"Did she say anything?" Dr. Perlinger's tone was serious. "Any hint about where she might have intended to go? I know you've started to build a relationship with her ..."

Iz shook her head, looked away, despised herself for lying to him.

During the rest of the rehearsal, she barely heard Becky telling about how she'd coded twelve notes to generate an enormous number of possible images and short videos depending on their order and the frequency with which they were played. She hardly noticed when everyone explored variations on the notes and exclaimed at the images and videos the combinations unlocked.

As soon as the rehearsal ended, Iz grabbed her things and fled back to the practice studio. She knocked and whispered. "It's me."

Skye opened the door. Iz hurried inside, pulling it closed again.

"Okay." She gathered all the commanding confidence she could find. "Let's go call the ombudsman."

Skye stared at her. "Uh, yeah ... about that ..."

Anger welled up in Iz, though she tried to control it. "You said you would. It's time."

"Right ..." Skye hopped back onto the piano bench. Her face was full of unspoken things.

"You promised!"

She absolutely would not take Skye back to Vito and Gisele's.

Skye pulled up her knees and buried her face in them. "I changed my mind." After a minute, she added, "I want to go to your place again. I like it there."

"Well, that's not an *option*," Iz snapped, feeling like a horrible person. "We have to go and solve this."

"No!"

Iz opened the door wide. "Skye, get out here *now!*"

Then she gaped.

Dr. Perlinger stood there, expressionless.

Chapter Twenty-Two

This wasn't happening.

Everything was fine.

"Hello," Dr. Perlinger said in an amiable voice. "I wanted to chat for a minute, but I can see you're in the middle of something." He gazed directly at Skye. "And hello to *you!*"

The silence was horrible.

"I already told her," Skye said. "I'm not going back. You can't make me. I'll take off."

She stood up, clutching the garbage bag. Her whole body looked poised to run.

Dr. Perlinger got still. The very air seemed to calm right down with him, like he had the power to settle storms. "Tell me. Tell me about it."

Skye glared at him. "I hate that place and I'm not going back. I'm going to Iz's house again."

Iz's heart sank as Dr. Perlinger glanced quizzically at her. "It was just for one night," she said in a low voice. "We were going to call the ombudsman today—"

"Except," Skye interrupted, "I changed my mind. And if you try to make me—"

"Yes, you're going to take off," Dr. Perlinger said.

Skye frowned at him and said nothing. She crossed her arms.

"I think I need a seat," Dr. Perlinger said. "Excuse me."

He opened the practice studio next door and lifted out a folded chair. Then he took another from the studio across the hall. "Iz?"

"Thanks . . ." She sank into it.

Dr. Perlinger slid into a slouch on his chair. He clasped his hands in his lap.

Everyone waited.

"So," Dr. Perlinger said in an inviting sort of way to Iz. "What did your foster parents say when you brought Skye home?"

"They . . . they didn't know." She spoke in a low voice.

"Didn't know," Dr. Perlinger looked impressed. "That must have been very difficult to pull off."

"It wasn't *that* hard," Skye retorted. "I just hung out in her closet, and she went and cooked stuff. Then I slept in her bed."

"I slept behind the door," Iz muttered.

He nodded. "And then this morning, you both came *here*." To Skye, he added, "Were you in this practice room all yesterday and today?"

"Yeah, except when I went for some walks."

Iz blinked.

"Oh? Where did you walk?" Dr. Perlinger seemed very interested.

"I went around and looked at stuff. Then if someone came along, I just hid." She glanced scornfully at Iz's appalled face. "Relax. It was fine."

"And what about food?" he asked. "Did you eat anything?"

"Iz brought me lunch."

"Ahh." Dr. Perlinger smiled pleasantly at Iz.

Iz closed her eyes.

She really just couldn't handle much more.

"So tell me," Dr. Perlinger said to Skye after a while, "if you do *take off* . . . where do you plan to go?"

"Wherever," Skye said.

"Ah. You will go around and look at stuff . . . and if someone comes along, you will hide."

Iz opened her eyes to see Skye's response.

The little girl shrugged with elaborate hostility. "Maybe."

"And as for food . . ."

"I can figure out food."

"Good. Yes, of course." He gazed up at the ceiling. "And when you get older?"

"I'll get older," Skye said, like Dr. Perlinger was completely dim.

He nodded, clasped his hands behind his head.

There was another long pause.

"I can't help thinking about your song," he said at last.

Skye scowled at him. "Huh?"

"The one about standing up to that person with the snake mind."

"So?"

Dr. Perlinger smiled pleasantly at Iz then back at Skye. "Do you remember how Teo said it reminded him of a character named Violetta from the opera *La Traviata*?"

Iz's stomach turned over at the sound of Teo's name. Again his voice invaded her head—*See you around.*

"What about it?" Skye's voice was getting more belligerent by the moment.

"I've thought about Teo's interpretation quite a lot since then," Dr. Perlinger said. "Because it turns the whole opera on its head, you see. In the original version, Violetta is told to go away forever by a cruel man who doesn't see her goodness. Who judges her."

Skye shrugged and looked away. "This is boring."

"So she does go away. And she suffers and she dies." Dr. Perlinger paused. "But . . . in your song, she just outright *refuses* to do what he's telling her to do. She doesn't feel like being controlled, does she?"

"What are you even talking about?" Skye said.

Dr. Perlinger seemed not to notice Skye's rudeness. "Maybe she's decided there's no particular future in being *silent and invisible.* Maybe she's made the decision that she is going to speak up and face him and say exactly what she isn't going to tolerate anymore."

"I already tried telling them," Skye said. "They didn't believe me."

Dr. Perlinger spoke so quietly he could scarcely be heard. "Can you tell *me*?"

"No." Her voice was like a hammer hitting metal. "I'm not telling anyone anything anymore."

Dr. Perlinger nodded, fingertips together.

There was a long silence.

"If—" Dr. Perlinger said, "and I stress that this is just hypothetical—*if* we were to contact Dominion Children's Care, I could sit with you while you tried again. Back you up, so to speak."

Skye frowned at him. "How do *you* know I'm not lying?"

"I'd assume," Dr. Perlinger said, "that you would want to speak what feels truthful to you. Anything less would not be worthy of *that song*, of your powerful way of seeing the world."

Skye stared.

Iz held her breath.

"Nah, I think I'll just go back to Iz's place," Skye said.

Something dark and furious ballooned up inside Iz. Dr. Perlinger had just handed Skye everything that Iz herself had always longed for in the past. Support, belief, a voice standing up for her. And Skye was doggedly spurning it. She was choosing to make Iz's life infinitely complicated instead.

"Well, I don't want you there! You just showed up and pushed your way in." The angry words spat out of Iz. "You're not, like, my sister or something. And if you think that running away is going to solve anything, you're crazy. There are a lot of bad people out there. Just stop being a baby and go face DCC. Leave me alone!"

She was panting now, gripped by memories of her own haunted experiences.

Skye's face withered in the silence.

Dr. Perlinger just sat there watching.

As Iz's fury subsided, panic and guilt took over. Her words had just punctured every bit of good she'd wanted to do at the Eastbourne Centre.

This was the worst volley imaginable.

She whispered, "I'm sorry."

But Skye didn't even seem to hear her.

The little girl drew up her limbs, shutting Iz out.

Chapter Twenty-Three

They all sat in Dr. Perlinger's office while he talked on the phone. First, he spoke to Dominion Children's Care. Then he called Vito and Gisele.

The whole time, Skye kicked methodically at her chair legs, refusing to look at Iz.

Iz had only a hazy sense of what was happening. Long ago, during and after That Place, she'd learned to wrap fog around her when what was happening was too awful.

While they waited for people to arrive, Dr. Perlinger got some cookies from the cafeteria, which Skye hungrily devoured. Iz tried a bite, but her mouth was too dry and her tongue too thick to eat it.

When Vito arrived, he looked like a thundercloud. No, more like a hurricane about to lay waste to everyone and everything.

Iz scarcely heard his staccato words or Dr. Perlinger's smoothing, legato responses. All she knew was, she had let Vito down horribly.

She had let Skye down.

Claudia, her caseworker, came gusting in next, all flapping and worked up.

No more shenanigans.

Iz listened to the three voices interjecting, agreeing, arguing. They were like a trio in an opera, three characters whose angular melodies fought for dominance.

"All right, come on, we're going home," Vito said to Iz, looking away. His voice was flat, like he had never met her before.

Iz trembled to her feet, hoisted her backpack, picked up her guitar.

Dr. Perlinger said something to her in a pleasant tone that suggested he did not remember how horrible she had just been to Skye.

Iz and Vito walked out of the office. Some other people came toward them along the corridor. Iz pressed to the wall to let them past.

But one of them brushed up against her.

"Sorry about that," a man said.

At the sound of his voice, Iz's whole body started reacting. Her hands shook. Her jaw shuddered of its own accord. She thought she was going to be sick.

The Man walked on. But then he stopped, turned around, and smiled at her. "Nice to see you, Iz. How've you been?"

Those unreadable eyes hadn't changed, even though a few years had passed.

Iz couldn't speak. Couldn't move.

The Man smiled again, then walked into Dr. Perlinger's office. Iz heard Skye shouting "I'm not going back to That Place, so don't even try."

"Oh!" Iz gasped, bending over and clasping her heart.

Was THAT where Skye had been living?

"Come on," Vito said to Iz grimly.

Iz stumbled along behind him, thoughts in fragments. She heard the click of Dr. Perlinger's door as it closed, shutting her out and shutting Skye in with The Man.

The whole way home, she was a solid hunk of useless meat that did not have the capacity to think or feel. Vito, driving silently, was apparently the same.

After he parked the truck, Vito unlocked the door to the apartment. He waved her in. "Let's go."

Iz fell up the stairs, defying the laws of gravity.

At the top, she took off her shoes, placed them neatly side by side on the rubber mat.

"Come back when you've put your stuff away," Vito said.

Iz set her backpack and guitar softly down in her room. She stood there for a while, her heart beating out of control.

Finally, she crept back out to the living room where Vito was waiting.

Gisele was there too now. Her face was not as stern as Vito's but still Iz could hardly bear to see the questions in her eyes.

"Have a seat," Vito said.

She sank shakily into a chair, looked down at her knees.

Nobody seemed to know what to say next. Nothing could properly express how much she had betrayed them.

"Cara," Gisele said at last. "Tell us. From the beginning. Tell us what happened."

Iz's lungs weren't taking in enough air. She gasped, "I … I just—"

Then it all started coming out, everything that had happened with Skye. Trying to befriend her. Learning that the little girl didn't like where she was living. Offering to help.

"But I wasn't very clear," she whispered. "I didn't mean she should come and live with me."

Vito harrumphed.

Iz flinched.

"Go on," Gisele said, her voice kinder than Iz deserved.

So Iz's mouth started talking again. She told about how Skye had threatened to run away. She recounted how she had agreed to bring the girl home for the night if Skye would let her call the ombudsman the next day. She described how she had snuck Skye into the apartment and kept the secret from them.

"I'm so sorry," she whispered.

"So how did you both get caught? Tell us that part." Vito didn't even acknowledge her apology.

Miserably, Iz clasped her hands and explained how Dr. Perlinger had found them. How he'd talked Skye into facing DCC by saying he would back her up.

But she absolutely could not tell them about how she'd shouted at Skye.

And she could not say a word about The Man. Not to Vito and Gisele, not ever.

Nor could she reveal how guilt was shredding her insides like cruel claws. If she'd known Skye was in That Place, she would have moved heaven and earth to protect her.

She'd betrayed Skye.

When Gisele spoke at last, her words were not so much accusing as sad. "I wish you had trusted us. What makes you think we wouldn't have tried to help, like Dr. Perlinger?"

Iz shrugged, all darkness inside. "I . . . didn't want to put you in that position."

"So instead you put us in *this* position," Vito exploded. "We get a phone call saying you've been hiding this kid in our home. How are we supposed to trust *you* again? Not that it'll matter because they'll probably take away our license."

Iz burst into racking, painful tears.

Gisele aimed a torrent of Italian at Vito. He raised his hands like he was blameless, just saying what needed to be said.

Then Gisele turned her attention back to Iz. "I understand this came from a place of wanting to help."

"But you went about it all wrong," Vito added.

"This can't happen again," Gisele said. "No secrets. You have to come to us, talk to us. We have to be open with each other."

Gisele's words were fair and reasonable. But all Iz heard was *danger, danger, danger.* She knew her time at the Santoro's was nearly over.

As if agreeing, Vito hissed like a pressure cooker whose lid had come blasting off.

He ran a hand through his silver hair. Then he got up abruptly and left the room.

Chapter Twenty-Four

The next several days were horrible.

Vito barely spoke to Iz. He could hardly stand to be in the same room with her. She felt the heavy weight of his disappointment and disapproval. Gisele, on the other hand, deserved an academy award for her performance of foster-mom-pretending-everything-was-okay.

Then there were the visitors. Various people from Dominion Children's Care and a few lawyers came by and talked with her. They spoke with Vito and Gisele too, voices mumbling ominously in the kitchen while Iz hid in her room covering her ears. After a while, though, they stopped coming. Maybe they'd decided that Iz had used bad judgment but had been mostly talked into it by Skye. And maybe they'd concluded that Vito and Gisele could not be held responsible for not knowing a secret Iz had taken pains to keep from them.

School should have been a relief from the tense atmosphere at home, but it wasn't.

Teo had completely moved on. Iz actually had to sit there one day in the cafeteria while he and Chloe Farrington FaceTimed one table away.

She distinctly heard Chloe say "See my earrings? Custom made!"

"No way! They're beautiful!" Teo boomed.

"I know, right? It's Violetta and Alfredo! I had them done after the summer to commemorate our amazing time with *Traviata*."

Iz couldn't help peeking over to see a girl with thickly tumbling, dark-red hair and the most beautiful green eyes ever. She looked away again quickly, feeling completely without substance. She wished she could just vanish away like steam or something.

The only good thing was that nobody at Métier seemed to know what had happened with Skye. When Becky asked Dr. Perlinger for an update, he said only, "Thankfully, she's been found." So Iz ended up doing almost as impeccable an acting job as Gisele, pretending that this whole disaster had not happened.

Still, for the first time ever, she skipped her Special Projects tutorial and two Manifesto rehearsals. She couldn't bear to see Dr. Perlinger, knowing he had witnessed her unconscionable behaviour. And she could never sit in the same space with Teo ever again.

She thought about skipping Eastbourne too.

But on Wednesday morning, Dr. Perlinger caught sight of her in the library and she wasn't able to scurry away fast enough.

"I missed you this week," he said.

"Uh . . ." Iz stared at him, unable to think of any suitable words.

He gazed back agreeably at her. "You'll be at the outreach after school?"

She nodded like a puppet flapping its head back and forth.

"Good! We've made a commitment, after all." He eyed her as if there was a lot more he could mention. Like about how she'd shouted at Skye and undone all the good work she'd tried to do. Finally he said, "You've had a bad week. Don't let that impact the positive. Consider going back over your reasons for starting the outreach. For being at Métier, in fact."

Iz flushed. She nodded.

"See you there," Dr. Perlinger said cordially.

She spent the rest of the day dreading the outreach. She wasn't sure she could face Dr. Perlinger again after their talk. She was terrified of seeing Skye.

Everything, everything had become so much more personal and invasive than she'd ever wanted. And underlying it all was the sick nausea of that moment when The Man had slid up against her.

When she'd turned right back into that powerless, manipulated, exploited kid trapped in That Place.

After school, she ran out the doors alone, not wanting to walk with anyone. She just wanted the hour to be over.

But Becky's voice rang out. "Iz!"

Iz flew around. Manifesto were all coming up behind.

Her heart sank. "Uh, hi!"

"Where've you been this week?" Becky said.

"Yeah, we missed you at the rehearsals. Everything all right?" Bijan's eyes held questions.

Iz shrugged, flushing. "Uh, just sort of tired. Feels like I'm running all the time. I needed a break."

Jasleen slipped in on the other side. "I get that way too. Métier's overwhelming sometimes, right? All these big expectations and even bigger personalities—"

"What do you mean, bigger personalities?" Teo grabbed Jasleen's hand and pulled her forward. He twirled and dipped her, while she yelled with laughter. Iz felt like a dry husk. He was doing this on purpose.

Jasleen shrieked, "What is *wrong* with you?"

"Wrong with *me*?" Teo retorted. "You're the one stepping on my feet, Singh."

Jasleen's eyes flicked at Iz, confused.

Iz forced a huge laugh out so everyone would know she thought Teo and Jasleen dancing together was hilarious.

When everyone reached the centre, she hung around at the back of the group while they lugged equipment up the stairs. She managed to always have someone blocking her view of Dr. Perlinger.

Inside, Poppy and K'Nesha tackled Teo like always. He twirled them in a circle while they fanned out like they were on a carnival ride.

Iz crossed her arms tightly, trying to ignore him, while also keeping an eye out for Skye.

The little girl was nowhere to be seen.

She told herself she was relieved. She didn't actually want to see Skye anyway. What could Iz possibly say to make up for her horrible words?

But then The Man's snake voice slithered into her memory for the thousandth time, reminding her she was responsible if Skye was back in That Place.

Nice to see you again, Iz.

Iz shuddered involuntarily. Memories rushed into her head of nameless people watching from the shadows, twisting her music—her precious guitar—into a vehicle for crass ugliness and horrible shame.

If she had only tried harder to come up with a solution, been less selfish, not so wrapped up in her own pain, she might have figured out how to help Skye in a way that could have worked.

But keeping secrets from Vito and Gisele had been more important than helping Skye.

She hated what a monster and a coward she was.

Chapter Twenty-Five

By the time that the equipment was set up and everyone had come to the circle, Iz was on the verge of suffocating under the weight of her worry and guilt. She wasn't sure she would be able to string two thoughts together.

But the kids didn't know that. They were relentlessly enthusiastic.

"This is a trophy." Devanch held it up.

"Look at my necklace." Shemar swung some chain at her.

Everyone shouted over each other and brandished objects.

"Uh … nice." Iz frowned. Why were they shoving all this stuff in her face?

Daniella held up a book with a clasp and bellowed, "It's my sister's. I swiped it. I've been trying to pick the lock."

Teo burst out laughing, throwing his head back. Dimly Iz could tell that Manifesto and Dr. Perlinger were laughing too.

"Yeah," Iz said, trying to pull herself together. "But, like, *why*?"

"Because I want to know what's in it."

"No, I mean, why did you bring it here?"

Daniella looked at Iz like she had sprung extra eyes or something. "You told us to."

Iz rummaged through her memory. Finally she remembered the end of their last session, when she'd asked them to look for silent objects that held a secret story.

"Ahh," she said. She peered at the book. "Is it, like, her *diary*?"

"No, look at the cover. It says *Thought Book*. She writes thoughts in it, I guess. She doesn't know *I* know she keeps it in the box under her bed."

Bijan said carefully, "Do you think she would want you reading her thought book?"

Daniella shrugged. "I just want to know what's in it."

"What do you *think* is in it?" Kwame asked.

"I don't know. It's probably boring. Like, don't forget to pick Daniella up from school and get more milk and pay the electrical bill and put gas in the car and stuff like that."

"A to-do list," Will suggested.

"Why would she want to keep a to-do list *secret?*" Rina said.

"Maybe she doesn't want me to know how boring she is."

"Sounds like you already know," Teo said.

Everyone laughed.

"So does your sister look after you?" Ahmed asked.

"Yeah, since my mom left with her boyfriend. Basically, my sister does the grown-up stuff, I do the kid stuff." Daniella spoke matter-of-factly. "Like, now she works at this warehouse. She says she doesn't mind because all she ever did in school was read her book while she waited for everyone else to finish their work."

There was a short silence.

"She sounds smart," Teo said.

"So let's crack it open," Daniella said, rubbing her hands.

"No, I don't think so," Dr. Perlinger said quickly.

He looked over at Iz, who huddled there miserably. "Iz, your thoughts?"

"Uh." She forced her creaky brain to move. "We ... we can imagine what's inside though."

Voices burst out.

"If she's smart, she probably writes smart stuff. Like, E equals MC squared."

"I have zero idea what that means."

"Maybe she's inventing things. Like robots."

"Maybe she's figuring out solutions to mysteries."

"Maybe she's planning for the future. Like, what she wants to do with her life."

"Maybe she's writing a chapter book or some poems or, like, songs."

Fuzzily, Iz realized that Ahmed had stood up with a marker and begun writing down their ideas as they shouted them out.

Then Teo's voice rolled out again like faraway thunder. "How would you describe a person who writes all these cool ideas?"

"Kind of awesome," Ezekiel said.

"*Yeah,* kind of awesome," he said. He grinned at Daniella. "And you thought she was boring!"

Daniella waved her hand dismissively at Ahmed's list. "Nothing you guys are saying is true, though. The one time I saw her writing, she was just sitting there crying and blowing her nose."

Everyone got quiet.

"Maybe," Shemar said after a while, "she misses going to school."

"Giving things up," Teo said in a clear voice. "Losing things. That hurts."

Iz absolutely could not look at him. She crouched there while Ahmed wrote Teo's words on the paper.

Other voices chimed in tentatively.

"Maybe they're mean at her job. My mom's boss is a jerk."

"Maybe she's still doing learning, but she writes it in her book because she can't *really* do it in school."

"Maybe she pretends she's somebody totally different who's, like, an explorer. And she writes about everything she discovers, and her challenges and everything. Close escapes. It's, like, a diary for a completely different person. Then she doesn't think about being sad." Ezekiel's voice was enthusiastic.

"So," Dr. Perlinger said softly, "looking at all of these possibilities we've talked about, and knowing there are so many more that we haven't even thought of, that little book sounds like a very important space for your sister. A sacred space." He nodded his head at Daniella. "Thank you for bringing it in to show us. Now, I would like to challenge you to put it back where you found it, so you can honour *whatever* big thinking she does in there."

After that, one by one, the other kids shared their objects.

Kateryna introduced them to the stuffed bunny she had brought from Ukraine. Shemar showed them the necklace he'd been given by his grandmother in St. Lucia. He explained how it helped him remember that she was always nearby even though there was an ocean between them. Ezekiel brought out the trophy his brother Devin had won in soccer. It was still on display in Devin's bedroom, even though he had died in a fight a few years earlier. Poppy showed a beaded purse and told how her aunt had taught her some Cayuga words while they worked on it.

Ahmed wrote and wrote, till he had covered several chart pages with their thoughts. He and Manifesto taped up the papers on the walls. They stood back.

"These objects," Jasleen said, "Have a lot to say."

"Don't they?" Dr. Perlinger agreed.

"It's like," K'Nesha said, "when you have the TV turned down really low and you have to get up close so you can hear it."

"It's like when you're looking at a seashell and you're like, this is just a seashell," Shemar said. "But you stick it up to your ear, and it makes this shh-shh-shh sound."

"That's the ocean," Devanch told him.

"Yeah." Shemar waved his hand, trying to put the words right. "But you wouldn't even know the ocean was in there unless you stuck it to your ear. You have to ... pay attention or something. You have to actually lift it up."

"And ..." Poppy's voice was slow. "Nobody else is going to know unless you tell them. Like, they'll just walk right by it unless you say, lift it up like this."

One by one, the kids volunteered their thoughts while Iz sat there miserably.

She was a silent object herself.

So was Skye—so silent she was missing.

"Are we going to make a song about all of our objects?" K'Nesha's voice pierced through Iz's thoughts.

Iz blinked. "Uh . . . yeah. Sure. Of course."

But her brain protested like some rusty and damaged machine. She heard herself giving a weird rasping gasp like she was drowning.

"Let's write some lyrics. Call out your ideas! They don't have to be perfect." Teo's sonorous voice rumbled into the conversation like a life raft Iz didn't deserve.

"No rules, people!" Daniella shouted.

Everyone started talking at once. Ahmed scribbled everything down as fast as he could. Will grabbed more paper as needed.

Iz forced herself to nod and smile like she was totally invested in what they were doing but really, she was imprisoned in a jail of self-loathing. She had erased herself and erased Skye, and there was nothing she could do to fix it. What was more, The Man kept disrupting her thoughts so she couldn't even string them into something useful.

When she couldn't stand the pain any longer, she drifted toward the door and slipped out. Guilt consumed her at abandoning everyone. She could hear Dr. Perlinger saying, *we made a commitment.* But this was too much, too much.

She ran all the way home, stumbled into the restaurant, burst into the kitchen.

Everyone turned to look at her, faces alarmed.

Gisele rushed over. "Iz! What is it? What happened?"

But Iz's words were gone, replaced by roaring sobs of despair.

Gisele held her. "It's all right. It's all right. It's all right."

Iz tried to imagine the whole world was made of Gisele, that Gisele was stronger than everything.

But The Man's face swooped in again, smiling.

Sorry about that.

Iz grabbed at her head, desperate to get him out. But she didn't know how to do it. She didn't know how to do anything.

She was nobody.

She was vanishing right in front of herself.

"Would it help to talk to Meredith?" Gisele spoke with infinite humanity.

Iz trembled and wept and finally nodded.

Chapter Twenty-Six

Gisele was able to get Iz an appointment the next morning.

After breakfast, they drove over together, while Vito handled the deliveries and oversaw the kitchen prep. They parked in the familiar parking lot. They walked in together.

Iz pushed open the office door that said *Meredith Danes, Individual and Family Therapy.*

She was aware of Gisele's hand lightly on her shoulder.

Meredith popped her head out of the inner office, with that air of dishevelled benevolence. "Iz! How are you?"

"Fabulous," Iz said automatically.

Gisele was patting her. "Should I stay or go? What would you like?"

"I …" Iz blinked. "If it's okay … I just want to …"

Gisele nodded. "I'll wait in the car, tesora." To Meredith, she added, "Thank you again so much for seeing her quickly."

"I will always make room for Iz," Meredith said warmly.

When Gisele had gently closed the door behind her, Meredith ushered Iz into the inner office. Iz sank onto the couch and gathered as many cushions as she could comfortably reach.

Meredith sat in her usual chair and then she did that trick of turning herself into a safe haven. It was something to do with her eyes, or with her steadiness. Everything became quiet and watchful and protective.

"Tell me," Meredith said. "What's been going on with you?"

It was such a simple question, but the answer was not so easy. So, Iz burst into tears for the millionth time, her sobs like a savage melody whose notes were stabs of pain. Meredith handed her tissues and leaned forward, sharing the tears.

Finally, Iz subsided into hiccups and ragged breaths, the shredded aftershocks of grief.

"So," Meredith said softly. "Big feelings."

"I wrecked everything. Like ... *everything*."

Meredith nodded and waited.

"And because of that, I've ..." Iz forced herself to say the horrible truth. "I've hurt a whole lot of people. Vito and Gisele. My friend Teo. And a little kid. I-I've done like *real damage*."

"What makes you say that?"

Iz flinched. "I mean, I don't even know where to start. It's all tangled up in my head."

Meredith smiled a little. "Then why not let it come out tangled? You and me, we're pretty good at undoing knots."

Iz weighed Meredith's words. "Okay," she whispered at last. "Here's what I *wanted* to do."

It all spilled out.

About creating the Eastbourne outreach because she was desperate to provide a creative and challenging music program that was everything she had not had. About how she'd wanted the program to inspire kids in the present while also doing right by the aching little girl she had been.

"It sounds," Meredith said, "like a really wonderful idea. A beautiful idea."

"Yeah ... but it all went wrong." She looked anxiously down at her hands clutching the pillows. "There was this one kid ..."

She heard herself telling Meredith about the rocky way she and Skye had started to build a relationship. About that horrible night when she'd hidden Skye in the bedroom and deceived the kindest people in her life.

"Ahhh." Meredith nodded. "I see. I see."

Iz mumbled miserably into the pillow, "No, you don't."

"Tell me?"

Slowly, disgustingly, the horrible truth came out.

Iz's cruel words.

Skye's face crumpling.

The Man.

That Place.

She buried her face in the pillows.

"A lot to untangle." Meredith's voice was a universe of empathy. "A lot to carry."

"And now she's missing, and ... I don't know where she is. Like, maybe she's in That Place. Or maybe she's run away again. Either way, I totally let her down." Her voice quivered. "And I let Vito and Gisele down. I ruined their trust."

The pain swirled around her, amorphous and confusing.

"But, like, I keep trying to figure out what would have been the right thing to do," she whispered. "Like, I *couldn't* have told them. They would have turned her in. They'd have had to."

A long silence went by.

"And ... I mean ... I was really scared of ..."

Meredith waited.

"I don't know," Iz said sadly. "Like, I was scared of being too much of a pain, you know? So ... I was selfish. I put my own needs ahead of Skye's."

"Selfish. That's a loaded word."

"But it sort of fits ... right?"

"Looking after *yourself* ... it's literally the first rule of survival." Meredith let that sink in. "Sometimes, in fact, we give ourselves *lots* of rules so we can get through traumatic or scary situations. "*Do* be easy to deal with. *Don't* say anything that will offend anyone. Does this sound familiar?"

Iz nodded, pillows practically covering her face.

Meredith went on gently, "So maybe ... is it possible that some part of you was scared to tell Vito and Gisele about Skye because it would inconvenience them, and they would want to get rid of you?"

"Well, *I'd* get rid of me. I mean, it would change the whole way I looked at me."

There was a pause.

"That's your rule, though," Meredith said. "It might not be theirs."

Iz glanced up.

"When we make survival rules, we're often little people at the time," Meredith went on. "They're a child's rules. They're designed to protect us, to keep us safe. But when we grow and change . . . they can hold us back. Like being in a box that's too small."

". . . Yeah?"

Meredith continued, "Your rules don't leave any room for other people to have their own thoughts or opinions. They may not see the situation the same way as you because they haven't had the same experiences you've had. They may bring compassion where you expect only judgement. Kindness, empathy—those are real things. People feel them. They act based on them."

"Yeah, I just never met too many of those people." Iz barked a laugh.

"Well, you have some in your life now. Think about this: After everything last year, and even though you hid Skye under their very noses, they *haven't* sent you away, have they? They've tried to understand."

"Vito can't even look at me."

"Maybe he has some childhood rules too. Maybe if you two talked, you could get past those rules together."

Iz muttered, "I don't actually talk to people. Not, like, *talk.*"

"Maybe that's another rule that hurts more than it helps now. People might surprise you if you shared a bit of yourself with them."

Iz thought about Teo's lion voice calling her *Onion Girl.* Pain welled up all over again, as she thought of how she'd pushed him away.

"I had this one . . . friend. He said he was, like, there to listen to anything I wanted to say," she whispered. "But I didn't know how. Underneath the rules, I'm just this ... this mess of *nothingness*, you know?"

"Mess of nothingness. That reminds me of our very first session together, when you said you felt like you didn't exist."

"So I've made zero progress, then." Iz's laugh was bitter.

"You," Meredith said warmly, "have made lots of progress. But let's go back to that first session for a minute. Do you remember what I asked you?"

"You asked what my songs were about."

"And what did you say?"

Iz cast her mind back.

"I said my songs were angry about kids being mistreated by adults. They were like trying to shine a light on it. To speak out."

Meredith nodded. "And I asked you to name that voice. Do you remember what you called it?"

Iz remembered very well. "A ... fierce voice."

"A fierce voice," Meredith repeated. She looked right at Iz. "Fierce Voice."

Iz shivered.

"Imagine," Meredith said softly, "if Fierce Voice was sitting here with us right now. Imagine telling Fierce Voice about all the yucky things inside you. Would Fierce Voice say you were disgusting? Would Fierce Voice send you away?"

"I ... don't know."

"Think about it."

Iz did.

She whispered at last, "Fierce Voice would be really angry on my behalf. It would say I should never have been in That Place. It would say I didn't deserve it."

She pictured Fierce Voice in her mind, huge and warm like a friendly dragon, breathing fire and standing between herself and That Place. She imagined it wrapping strong, scaly arms around her.

She swallowed. "It would maybe give me a hug. It would want to make sure Those People never got to hurt me or anyone else again."

Skye's song sprang into her mind, about people standing up and fighting back.

Her voice rose. "It would say, *Those People don't get to decide who I am*. It would say to them ... *You're finished, I'm naming you, I'm right here in front of your face.* It would say, *I'm changing the story and I'm kicking you out of it.*"

She stopped, startled at herself.

She shrank from those words ringing in the air.

She felt ridiculous.

But Meredith didn't seem to think she was ridiculous. Meredith's eyes were almost glowing with appreciation for Iz's outburst. She said, "I have an idea for you to try."

Iz flinched. "Uh ... okay ..."

Her therapist spoke slowly and carefully. "What if, this week, you grabbed a tangled thread of all that stuff underneath the *rules* ... and you shared it with Fierce Voice? You already know Fierce Voice will *get it*. Fierce Voice protects kids. Fierce Voice protects *you*."

Iz shuddered at the thought of talking about all the dark things, even with an imaginary dragon.

"I don't know. It ... seems kind of weird."

"It doesn't have to make sense," Meredith said. "It doesn't have to tell a logical story. It could be feelings. Fierce Voice won't care. Fierce Voice has *no rules*." She paused. "And one day, maybe, when you're just walking along the street or whatever, you'll start to feel that same Fierce Voice pulsing inside you. Because Fierce Voice is really you, isn't it?"

"Uh," Iz said. "I don't know. Maybe."

She felt the furthest thing from fierce at the moment.

Chapter Twenty-Seven

She thought about Meredith's words all the way home.

When Gisele had parked the car, Iz went up to her room, closed the door, and lay down in the middle of the floor.

Feeling like an idiot, she whispered, "Hey, Fierce Voice!"

Not surprisingly, nobody answered.

"Yeah, forget it." She sat up, totally embarrassed. This was not her thing at all, having a conversation with an imaginary dragon.

Meredith's words came into her head then.

It could be feelings. Fierce Voice won't care. Fierce Voice has no rules.

Feelings, okay, those she could do.

Iz sat cross-legged, placed hands on her knees, breathed slowly to relax, just as she'd been taught by Meredith.

She closed her eyes, let her mind drift amid the slow breaths.

After a long time, her imagination stirred.

Behind her closed eyes, the outline of something appeared. It was enormous, as tall as the sky, all crimson and golden, with eyes that were wild, bottomless oceans of fire.

Fierce Voice bent down, and they stared at each other. Iz saw herself reflected in its eyes. Then the dragon lay down beside her like a mighty and loyal dog.

Iz leaned against Fierce Voice, trying to absorb some of its strength.

They sat like that for an eternity while she simply breathed.

Slowly, she started imagining that with each inhalation, she was taking in Fierce Voice's power. The air felt like flames going into her lungs. She began to fill up with Fierce Voice's steadiness and courage.

Inhale, exhale.

Fear out, fire in.

She was scared, scared—

But she reached her arms into the darkness.

Slowly, slowly, fragments of nightmarish memories came to her.

you're always playing that guitar
come on, show me
don't be scared, I don't bite
you've got a real talent
other people should hear you
I'm having a few friends over
new faces
changing faces
disgusting drinks that made her feel weird
playing strings with trembling fingers
finally wearing nothing, nothing but her guitar
He took requests
songs and other things
she's beautiful, isn't she?
prettier than the last one
and when she refused
ropes swishing then slicing
the Woman's cigarettes burning
scalp screaming
banging on the box
apologizing
begging
promising
offering
anguish
fog

For what felt like hours, the images oozed through her mind. Beside her, Fierce Voice's eyes flicked back and forth across them all too.

Fierce Voice somehow knew how much she had hated herself then, how much she still hated herself now, how she had wished in those days she did not exist, and how she had not really existed properly ever since.

She could see that Fierce Voice was getting angrier and angrier at everything it saw. The dragon opened its mouth full of teeth, took in a mighty breath, and blasted out a great, flame-filled roar. Iz imagined the noise, the heat, the fire. She watched That Place get entirely consumed.

Then a weird thing happened.

Fierce Voice's anger somehow became her own.

Her rage rose up, violent and shocking and infinitely dangerous.

It threatened to consume her.

"Oh!" Iz gasped, terrified.

She forced her eyes open, scrambled to her feet.

Immediately, the dragon vanished. But the horrible nightmares, freshly excavated, refused to leave. And her rage was still there.

She panicked, whipped her head back and forth, trying to get the scary things out.

Quick! Floor is sturdy. Quilt is soft. Photo of Manifesto is from that wonderful night last June. Your notebook is on your desk. You are here. You are real.

Her notebook!

Iz threw herself into her desk chair, opened to a new page, gripped the pen as if it were a life preserver. She scrawled words on the page, trying to exorcise the memories.

I want blazing summer in my brain
To shake this foulness from my back
Kick off the last of the excrement

She imagined that Fierce Voice was nodding. *Yes, yes, go on.*

Iz started scribbling down random words then, like she'd done at Eastbourne when the kids were calling out ideas. Each word was part of a roadmap to the place she might go if she could find the courage to throw out all rules. Each word was a signpost pointing to what her life would be like if she wasn't always worried about what might happen if she opened up to anyone.

Sharing the bad stuff
Talking
Actually trusting someone
Screaming
Smashing the silence

TELLING

She stared at the last word.

Recoiled.

"No," she whispered.

Meredith's words came into her head again.

Maybe that's another rule that hurts more than it helps now.

Iz imagined that Fierce Voice was lying down beside the chair, tail wrapped around her legs, wing unfolded over her shoulders. She told herself she was bundled in a protective quilt made of Fierce Voice.

She doodled around that nightmarish word so it was less scary. She drew a zigzag circle all around, like the sun's rays going out.

For the first time in ages, an original tune rose up in her.

It was a hissed whisper at first, spiky and discordant. It was a staccato knock at a door. Then it grew until it was pounding, slamming, insistent. It was a storm that wanted to smash that door down.

Iz's fingers began to move of their own accord as she listened to the demanding, driving melody in her mind. The notes, jagged like lightning, illuminated the unthinkable. They spattered out a catastrophe, a worst-case scenario.

Nothing about the notes was playing by any rules.

Words swarmed at her, screaming, refusing to be shut away anymore in her mind. She scribbled them down as fast as she could.

Been silent too long
Scared to be heard
Words too searing
Burning my skin
But I'm tired of being careful
Angrier than I know
Harder to stay quiet
Than to scream
Fierce Voice rising
Fierce Voice rising
Fierce Voice rising
Fierce Voice rising
Shouting down the darkness
Reaching to you
Lifting you up
Lifting us up
Screaming our story
Words bawling
Melody howling
Fierce Voice rising
Fierce Voice rising
Fierce Voice rising
Fierce Voice rising

Iz shouted it over and over. Slapped out primal chords.

As she did, she thought of Skye, of Kateryna, of Daniella's sister, of all the children whose stories were right there waiting to be heard, deserving to be known. All of those silences were desperate to be broken. All of that pain waited to be acknowledged, to be shared, to be carried.

She thought of Verdi shackled by the horror of losing his whole family—of how hard it must have been to put voice to that nightmare at last. But he'd somehow done it. He'd looked it in the face, and he'd walked right into the pain. He'd turned his grief into some universal thing that spoke to everyone.

She heard Daniella saying *Moral of the story is, tell people! Then they'll know!*

Not even planning to, Iz put down her guitar.

She stood there shaking as if someone was violently swinging her about.

This was insane.

It was impossible.

It would destroy everything.

But she locked eyes with Fierce Voice, who blew a smoke ring that was at once comforting and a harbinger of what could happen if anyone crossed Iz again.

She imagined Violetta nodding at her like she was on the right track.

Iz opened the bedroom door.

Her brain was screaming, *what are you DOING?*

Chapter Twenty-Eight

She walked downstairs to the restaurant.

Gisele was doing ninety things in the kitchen with a halo of steam all around her. In the dining area, Vito chatted with regulars at a table. They were both so busy that Iz almost turned around and went upstairs again.

"Are you going to play tonight?" One of the diners was smiling at her.

She croaked, "Uh … maybe later."

Vito looked up at the exchange. He and Iz stared at each other. His eyes were emotionless.

Iz blinked, ignored the pain of that. Tried not to think about how she had let him down, or to consider how hard it would be to ever gain back his good opinion.

Instead, she imagined she wasn't standing there alone because a dragon was curled around her. "Vito, do you have a minute?"

He glowered, nodded.

Iz walked back into the kitchen, dizzy with the enormity of what she was thinking of doing. She kept picturing Fierce Voice circling her, purring in a calming, protective rumble.

"So?" Vito said gruffly.

"Uh, I h-have something to say," Iz said loudly. "To you and Gisele."

Gisele heard and hurried right over. "What is it, cara?"

"Uh … can we go somewhere quiet? Somewhere private?"

Vito and Gisele exchanged glances.

"Let's go upstairs," Gisele said.

Iz hardly noticed climbing the steps to the apartment. The next thing she knew, Gisele was filling the kettle, plugging it in, getting down three mugs and three teabags.

Finally, they sat at the table.

Iz stared down as the contents of the tea bag slowly transformed the water … just as her words were about to transform everything between the three of them.

"So," Vito said at last.

"I just have to tell you about something that happened," she said, in a tiny voice.

They were silent.

Then tears started rolling out and it was completely weird because she was not involved in creating or feeling them at all. The tears seemed to have made the decision all on their own to make an appearance. Part of Iz was slightly fascinated by that. It was like she was split off into two people, one who was observing herself and another who was about to speak.

"Yeah … I … I was in A Place … a bad foster home …"

She could hardly believe she was actually saying the words. But as they kept oozing from her, she registered the way that Vito and Gisele got very still and grave. She could see Vito's eyebrows joining to make an ominous shelf over his eyes. She noticed how Gisele's own eyes got wet and how Gisele wiped them over and over.

Iz could barely keep going, knowing how acutely she was disappointing them. But she thought about Fierce Voice, about no rules. She reminded herself that she wasn't telling for herself only. She was telling for Skye, for all other kids.

And so, she imagined dragon wings supporting her while she told them about The Man, the brush against him in the hallway, the terrible, terrible revelation that *Skye was in That Place.*

She heard Gisele breathing very loudly.

Vito scraped his chair back, lumbered to his feet. He stared down at Iz and Gisele for a minute.

Then he walked straight out of the room for the millionth time.

Iz heard him thump heavily down the stairs to the restaurant.

She sat there in disbelief and shock.

She whispered at last, "What do I do now?"

Gisele didn't say anything for a long time. Then she muttered in a low, ferocious voice, "Cara." She enveloped Iz in a hug that Iz did not deserve. "If you want to go after Them, I will help you."

Iz looked away. "I already tried to tell, twice, and my worker didn't believe me. I asked to be moved but they kept me there. Until I broke The Woman's nose."

Understanding dawned in Gisele's eyes. "I read about that in the notes."

Iz flushed.

"And now," Gisele said with anger, "I know exactly why you did."

Abruptly, she got up from the table, left the kitchen.

Iz was scarcely breathing.

Both of them were gone now.

But Gisele returned a minute later with her laptop. She put it on the table between them.

"What's this for?" Iz said.

"I know in the training they told us about formal complaints," Gisele said fiercely.

"F-formal complaints?"

"There's a process. I'm going to find it again."

Iz hunched over and studied the creases in Gisele's forehead as her foster mother frowned and blinked and typed. Iz got so caught up in the infinitesimal shadows and changes in Gisele's face that she almost forgot what Gisele was doing.

So, she was half-startled when Gisele said "Here! I knew it."

Iz looked at the screen. "What's this?"

"Internal complaints review, it's called." Gisele scrolled. "Every foster care agency has to have one. We can make a complaint about That Terrible Place so it can be investigated."

"W-we can?"

"Yes." Gisele leaned close, reading some more. "There's a form to fill out. Then, within seven days, they have to let you know if they're going to have a meeting."

"A-a meeting?"

Anxiety fluttered through Iz.

Gisele got very quiet. She poured more hot water into Iz's mug. The teabag began magically to turn it into tea again.

"We don't have to do anything," Gisele said quietly. "It's up to you." She paused. "But if you decide you want to do something about this ... This *Man* and This *Woman* and This *Place*, I will support you. I will go with you. I will sit in that meeting with you, if you want. And if anyone, *anyone* dares to question one *piece* of what you have to say ..."

Iz's whole chest started aching. The ache was fanning out from her heart. It was made of terror but also of intense love for Gisele.

Still, she couldn't help asking, "Do you ... do you think, you know, kind of ... *less* of me now?"

Gisele regarded her with incredulous fury. "I could not adore you more."

Iz let out the breath she'd been holding.

Fierce Voice purred, wrapping its tail around her.

Iz had broken all of her own rules, had told the worst secret in the world ... but the world had not ended.

Gisele was right here.

Vito, though.

Vito was a different story.

Chapter Twenty-Nine

"You can take someone in with you," the young woman said.

Iz gazed at Gisele, whose nervousness and determination reminded her of a sheep dog on its first day protecting a flock. "My foster mom's coming," she whispered.

"Okay. You can follow me, then."

The young woman led them along a hallway.

Everything in the last few days had moved really fast. Iz had filled out the form. Gisele had taken it to the Dominion Children's Care main office and handed it in. Shortly afterward, an email had arrived asking them to attend a meeting on Wednesday afternoon at four o'clock. Iz was half-relieved that the meeting was at the same time as the Eastbourne outreach, since she didn't feel quite up to walking in there again just yet.

They entered a small room with a table in the middle.

"Just have a seat," the young woman said. "They'll be here in a minute. Can I get you anything? Tea or coffee? Maybe a soft drink?"

"No thanks," Gisele and Iz said at exactly the same moment.

After the woman left, they sat in there alone.

Gisele squeezed Iz's hand. "I'm right here, cara. If you get scared."

Iz nodded.

But weirdly, she wasn't scared. She actually felt like she wanted to do battle. Which was bizarre, considering how long she had spent trying to hide the terrible secret of That Place. The difference now was the fact that Gisele was sitting beside her. Iz could feel Gisele's rage simmering on her behalf.

A dragon was sitting right here too.

The door opened and two women walked in with files and laptops.

They smiled very warmly.

"You must be Isabelle," said one. She extended a hand for Iz and Gisele to shake. "I'm Fiona."

"Hey," Iz said edgily.

"And I'm Kiki. Nice to meet you!" The second woman shook their hands too.

"This—this is Gisele," Iz said.

"Gisele Santoro." Gisele's voice was loud and formal. "I am the foster mother. Foster-to-adopt. I'm here to support."

"Of course."

When everyone had settled at the table, and the laptops were open, Fiona said brightly, "I think we're ready!" She smiled at Iz. "It's very scary to come here and talk, I know. We are going to try to make it as comfortable for you as we can, okay?"

Iz nodded.

"So . . ." Kiki scrolled on her screen. "Just so we have our facts straight, I'm going to confirm some basic details. Is that okay, Isabelle?"

"It's okay."

As Kiki went through a checklist of questions, Iz answered them mechanically.

"And . . . can you share with us why you're here today?" Fiona asked.

Iz took in the deepest breath ever. She imagined Fierce Voice doing the same, then exhaling smoke and flame all over the room, just like Iz's words were going to do.

This was it.

"I want to make a complaint," she said, "about a foster home I was in from the age of ten to twelve."

Fiona nodded encouragingly.

Gisele gripped Iz's hand with both of her own.

And so, Iz started talking.

As she told Kiki and Fiona everything, her voice actually didn't shake. She had expended a lot of the emotion of the memories by sharing them with Fierce Voice and then telling Vito and Gisele. Now, weirdly, there were only the facts left, dry like the abandoned exoskeleton of an insect.

Fiona and Kiki wrote everything down.

Every so often, they asked a soft question to clarify.

They passed a box of tissues across the table for Gisele.

And Iz glared the memories down in her mind, brain utterly bent on its task.

Telling.

Protecting.

Fierce Voice.

"There's another girl—Skye Hill—in that house," she said. "At least, she was. I don't know if she is now. And I'm worried about her. That's why I'm here. Because nobody should ever be in That Place again. And I want to know where she is and to make sure she's safe."

"Oh . . ." Kiki looked at Fiona. "We can't give out that information right this minute."

"But I—"

"Tell us," Fiona said, "about your relationship to her. How do you know about her being in that foster home?"

Hands in fists, Iz launched yet again into the story of the outreach and of Skye.

Fiona's eyebrows went up as she typed.

"It wasn't a good choice, hiding her," Iz said. "I'm trying to fix it today. I'm not hiding anymore. Not hiding me and not hiding anyone else. I'm . . . I'm *telling.*"

Fiona typed some more.

"Iz is a good girl. She made a mistake, that's all." Gisele's voice boomed out.

"So, you met Skye at the Eastbourne Centre, when you were there with your school band."

"Manifesto," Iz said.

"And your school is ..." Fiona scrolled back up. "It's a private high school for music, is that right?"

"The Métier School. Yes."

Kiki said encouragingly, "You must be very talented."

"I don't know."

"She is," Gisele said firmly.

Kiki flipped through some papers and Fiona looked on.

"M-maybe it says in there about, like, how I got into Métier," Iz said. "I didn't make the best choices on that occasion either. But I paid for what I did, and I got a conditional discharge and I re-auditioned and they gave me a scholarship." Desperately, she pretended she was burying her head in shining dragon scales.

"It's in the past," Gisele added.

Fiona nodded slowly, looking at the pages and typing into her laptop.

Iz sat there feeling more and more resentful, like they were judging her, like her history and her reputation were getting all mixed up with her complaint. Like she was Violetta or something.

Except, she reminded herself, Violetta had never had Fierce Voice on her side. Fierce Voice was the ultimate secret weapon.

Emboldened, she said, "How I got into Métier isn't actually part of this, right? I'm here to talk about That Place—that foster home."

"Of course," Fiona said immediately.

"And I want to know," Iz said, "if Those Two are going to be investigated."

"Well, that's part of this process. After we finish talking with you, we're going to do an internal investigation of our own. Then, we'll let you know if we're going to proceed to a formal investigation."

"How long will it take before we know?" Gisele asked.

"Not long. A week, maybe two. We'll be in touch, I promise, one way or the other."

"Well, you *have* to formally investigate them," Iz said, "because I'm telling the truth. And because no other kid should be in That Place." Her hands were in fists.

Fiona nodded. "We are going to leave no stone unturned, I promise. Every complaint gets taken seriously, so please don't worry."

Kiki added, "And now, I just want to go back and clarify a couple more details, if that's okay."

Iz sat like a rock and answered everything. Beside her, Fierce Voice simmered with righteous anger and a refusal to be ignored.

Finally Fiona said, "Do you have anything else you'd like to add?"

"Yes," Iz snapped. "I want to know if you are going to remove any other kids in that house while you investigate These People. Because if you leave anyone in there with them, it's-it's like abusing those kids *yourself*. It's like assault. It's like attempted murder."

She knew she sounded overly dramatic, but she didn't care.

"I asked my caseworker *twice* to get me out of That Place, but she never took me seriously. I am here today being as serious as I know how to be. S-so you need to hear me. You need to shut them down. You should just go over there right now and do it."

"Don't worry. Any child in the house would be removed during any investigation." Fiona's calm voice sounded like she was using the de-escalation training Ms. Sole had given Manifesto.

Iz let out a ferocious breath and nodded. "Good."

Gisele was patting her on the back. She said to Fiona and Kiki, "We will be waiting to hear from you."

"As soon as we can," Kiki promised her. "And, Isabelle, thank you so much for your bravery today. It takes a lot of guts to come in here and make a statement."

Then everyone stood up and smiled and shook hands again.

The meeting was over.

Iz and Gisele walked out to the car. Silently, they got in and Iz put on her seatbelt. Gisele started the engine. They drove slowly out of the parking lot.

Iz was suddenly aware of how quickly her heart was beating and how shaky her hands were.

"Cara," Gisele said. "You were superb in there. I am very, very proud of you. You did a good thing, not just for yourself but for other children too."

"I don't know if they're going to take it seriously."

"They will. They said they are going to do an internal investigation."

"That doesn't mean they'll go to a formal investigation."

"They will," Gisele repeated, like a soothsayer who could see into the future. She said it with such confidence that Iz actually felt calm wash over her, as if everything might actually end in a fair way.

Unexpectedly, her spirits rose a little.

"Let's get ice cream," Gisele said. "Ice cream makes everything better."

Chapter Thirty

On Thursday, Iz stood in front of Dr. Perlinger's door.

She wanted to knock and at the same time she didn't. They were about to have a totally uncomfortable conversation. She needed to apologize and to explain, and the explanation was going to take her to some really personal places. This was going to be on a whole other level from the big talks they'd had together in the past. But she had to do it. She needed him to understand. And then she needed to ask a huge favour.

Iz swallowed, steeled herself, imagined a dragon, and knocked.

"One minute!"

There were some scraping sounds, like heavy things were being moved, and then the door opened.

"Ah! Iz! Come in! Just had to get these away from the door." He gestured at several large boxes that were pushed to the walls.

"What's all that?" Iz asked shyly.

He waved his hand. "Supplies. New instruments. Research. Please, sit down. I've been thinking about you."

"Ah. Huh. I bet you have." Iz perched anxiously on the edge of the armchair.

He sat down opposite, just like always. But today everything felt tense, heavy.

"How are you?" he said gently.

Iz crossed her arms. "Okay … sort of …" Then she imagined Fierce Voice's confidence and protectiveness wrapping around her. "So, I have to tell you about something. And then I have to *ask* you something."

He regarded her with the gaze that could see right inside a person. "I'm all ears."

"First," Iz said, "I am sorry about everything that happened. Hiding Skye. And yelling at her. And then not coming to Special Projects or the Manifesto rehearsal." She paused. "And running out on that really horrible outreach last week … and not even *making* it to Eastbourne this week."

"I was worried," Dr. Perlinger said. "I debated calling you. But I didn't want to make it worse. And I hoped …" He looked right at her. "I hoped you might come and talk to me when you were ready."

She nodded. "That's why I'm here. I have to … explain a whole lot of things, actually."

He said nothing, just waited.

"So," Iz said brightly. "Some stuff has been going on."

She gathered courage, felt the warmth of Fierce Voice beside her.

She looked right at her beloved teacher.

She began to speak.

As Iz told him almost everything, her brain was interested in how That Place diminished with each telling while she herself grew larger or something. If they kept going on this trajectory, maybe soon she'd tower over the horrible memories and they would cease to have any meaning or power at all.

But Dr. Perlinger's face seemed to sag.

"Oh, I do see," he said softly.

His eyes filled with compassion.

Then they *flashed.*

"Oh, Iz."

"Yeah," she said.

Dr. Perlinger kept shaking his head. When he spoke, his voice was thick. "Such a heavy burden to carry. I am so, so sorry."

"It's okay," Iz said awkwardly. "I just wanted you to know." She gathered courage. "Because … I sort of need some help."

"What kind of help?"

"It's about Skye. I need you to tell me what happened in that meeting in your office. Did they send her back to That Place?"

"Ah," Dr. Perlinger said, still looking shattered. "No, I don't believe they did. She was so upset … they seemed to make the decision not to send her with her foster father after all. I think they arranged emergency housing."

"Really?" Relief burst over Iz.

Here came the big ask.

"Dominion Children's Care won't tell me where she is. I-I feel responsible for her. I know I'm not, but …"

Her voice trailed off.

"I understand," Dr. Perlinger said.

She nodded rapidly. "Yeah … so … I have an idea. You're the head of our outreach program. Can you call DCC to find out where she is? You could be worried because she missed the class this week. And then you could, like, phone her foster parent to say she needs to come back."

He regarded her.

"There's nothing even *wrong* with that. It's not, like, lying or *anything*." Iz could hear the pitch of her voice rising.

At last, he said slowly, "I could make some inquiries."

"Oh, thank you!" Iz exploded with relief.

He levelled her with his kind and intelligent eyes. "Iz, I don't even know how to find words to … express my pain about what you've told me, and I know it is nothing compared to yours. Anything I can do to help, please know I will do it. And I am deeply, deeply humbled that you trusted me enough to tell me about it. I promise, this story shall remain between us."

"Thanks." Iz paused. "So—when are you going to make the call?"

He laughed like a ghost that scarcely remembered how. "Perhaps I'll wait until the sun's properly up, at least."

"Okay, fine, but the sun *is* up."

"I'll phone this morning." He smiled.

"Good. All right then."

"And now," Dr. Perlinger said, "what about some tea?"

Iz looked at him and at the cluttered little office where she had spent so many hours working on her Schubert project last year. Gratitude swelled in her like a tsunami, not unlike how she'd felt when Gisele had been a pit bull on her behalf at DCC.

She and Dr. Perlinger were back on track.

"Sure," she said. "Tea would be great."

They sat there chatting in a way they hadn't in a while. They talked of the kids' epiphanies at the Eastbourne Centre, of their remarkable ideas about learning to listen to silent voices and coaxing overlooked objects to speak. Iz told him about how her room at Vito and Gisele's was filled with photos from Métier. He described how his daughters were going through a phase of being obsessed with complicated and slow-moving and frequently unsuccessful magic tricks. She walked him through the steps for making spaghetti alla puttanesca and he wrote down notes.

Chapter Thirty-One

When Iz finally headed out of Dr. Perlinger's office, she sprinted toward her next goal—Teo.

He was in the cafeteria, drumming on a table, surrounded by instrumentalists who all happened to be girls. They were jamming to something raucous with a driving folk-rock beat.

He caught her eye across the room, his mouth wide with laughter. Turning to the instrumentalists, he said something.

They started a new melody that sounded a bit like bluegrass. He started singing.

I wish
to cleanse myself of such a stain.
I have called you here as witnesses
that I have paid her all I owe.

Iz stiffened. She knew that song. It was from *La Traviata*. It was the scene when Alfredo yelled at Violetta, insulted her in front of everyone, accused her of only having been interested in his money because he did not understand why she'd left him.

Iz figured that Teo was saying she was just like Violetta. He was saying Iz was not loyal.

But he didn't know the whole story.

Iz wanted to run out of the cafeteria, but she imagined a dragon's head nudging the small of her back, stubbornly pushing her forward to complete her mission. So she walked toward Teo.

As Iz drew closer, she heard him teasing the girl to his left. "Yeah, you pretend to be so quiet, but I heard your composition in Theory this morning. That thing was a torrent of fire. Sorry, but your secret's out."

"Hey," Iz said loudly.

He glanced up at her. "Beaufort."

His voice was so impersonal. She pushed on anyway. "Do you, like, have a second?"

"Not really. We've got a presentation this afternoon."

"Rockabilly *Traviata*!" One of the girls broke out in laughter.

"Oh." Iz stood there feeling like she should leave them alone. But then she remembered she was supposed to be getting rid of rules that didn't help. She imagined Fierce Voice towering behind her, backing her up. In a strained but clear voice, she said, "I-it's important. It'll only take a minute."

She was scared but determined not to run. She wasn't going to cry either. She was just going to clear the air, and then she would deal with whatever came afterward.

Something crossed his face, a ghost of concern.

He said to the others, "Be right back, okay?"

Iz led him into the hallway.

Teo said, "Yeah, so . . . ?"

She'd sort of rehearsed how to say things, but now her mind went blank. Then she remembered Meredith saying it was okay if things came out tangled.

"When I said I couldn't talk . . . I really *couldn't* talk," she blurted. "Skye was like right there in the practice room and she wanted to come live at my house, and I literally didn't know what to do . . ."

"What?" Teo looked bemused.

The words kept rushing out of her. "But I'd been *really* wanting to talk to you, I wanted to apologize for everything because I was so sorry about that fight when I got kind of all messed up over some stuff and I took it out on you. I mean, you're not responsible for whatever Chloe Farrington said, and I shouldn't have gone all nonlinear. I guess I just sort of freaked out because she was totally right about how horrible I was in the summer for ghosting you, and I felt so ashamed."

She hunched her shoulders while her eyes filled with tears.

"I hate how everything's wrecked," she whispered. "Because, I mean, you are . . . or at least you were . . . basically my best friend."

He frowned, sorting through her words. "Sorry, just for a minute, can we go back to the part where Skye was in the practice room?"

"She . . . showed up and said she was going to live with me. And then *you* appeared at, like, the exact same moment." She winced, remembering the awfulness of that day.

Understanding dawned on his face. "Was this when she went missing?"

Iz nodded. "She came to find me. She said she didn't like where she was living, so she was going to live with me. We got caught by Dr. P and then there was this whole horrible thing . . . and I don't know where Skye is now . . . It's like, *so complicated*."

Teo regarded her. "Why am I not surprised by *that*?"

"I know. Complicated . . . it's kind of my specialty."

Relief coursed through Iz. She was so grateful to be talking to him again, even though the whole world was turned upside down.

"I just . . ." she said, "I want you to know that I was really desperate to talk to you. It was *all* I wanted. And then you came along right *then* and I couldn't."

She hoped he'd say something, but he just stood there looking at her so she babbled on. "I get it if you don't want anything more to do with me, after I yelled at you and then wouldn't even talk—but I just, like, miss you so much—and I *really* want to talk. Like, name the time and we can talk. Right now, tomorrow, next week, whenever."

He just kept gazing at her though.

"Whatever . . ." She nodded, shook her head. "Like, if you'd rather just not talk, that's cool too. I mean I screamed at you . . ."

"Beaufort." Teo raised his chin like he was also going to face something head on.

"What?"

His unhappy eyes were on her. "I get it."

"Y-you do?"

"I figured … you were done with me. And so then I was angry, and I've been going around doing everything I could to make you jealous. I didn't even try to figure out what was going on."

Grateful tears pressed against her eyelids.

"I don't know how to make it up to you," Teo said miserably.

"I don't know how to make it up to *you*."

"This is what we call a stalemate."

Iz said in a small voice. "We could talk … now."

They started walking aimlessly along the hallway.

Teo said at last, "Chloe …"

"She's a little territorial though," Iz said. "You have to give me that."

"She doesn't *know* you," he retorted, "except for anything I said from the summer."

"And you told her I was a monster," Iz said, trying to make a joke.

"I told her I was totally in love with you."

Iz's eyes widened.

Her jaw dropped.

"Ah, no, never mind," Teo said quickly, seeing her reaction. "Forget I said that."

They walked silently again.

At last, Iz looked up at him. "You said it though."

Then they were staring at each other, standing in front of Lecture Hall B.

"I don't …" Teo said, "want to scare you or rush you or anything." His eyes flitted back and forth across her face. "I know … I know there's stuff in your past …"

She stiffened. Even though she'd told so many people about That Place, she didn't want it to pollute this moment. Right now, there was only room for herself and Teo, nothing else. She imagined

Fierce Voice whipping its scaly tail back and forth, sweeping everything else away.

She said at last, "Yeah, there's ... stuff. And one day, I mean, I'll tell you about it. Like, in some tropical place with butterflies and warm breezes and flowers."

Teo nodded, smiling in that way that made her heart swell. "So, we're going to Hawaii?"

She couldn't help laughing out loud. "Yeah, let's go to Hawaii."

"And," Teo said, eyes twinkling, "we won't invite Chloe. I mean, then her boyfriend would have to come along, and it would be a whole thing."

"Oh right, this mythical boyfriend I keep hearing about."

"He exists, trust me."

"I'll believe it when I meet him."

"That can be arranged."

The bell rang to indicate the end of lunch.

They stood there, reluctant to go to class.

"Uh," Iz said. "Do you want to ..." She gestured aimlessly. "I mean ... you could come over to Festa tonight ..."

He shoved his hands in his pockets and hunched over, looking down at her. He was still miles taller. "Do *you* want me to?"

"I wouldn't have asked if I didn't."

He smiled slowly. "Okay then."

"Okay!" Iz said. Suddenly she felt better than she had in days.

When they got to Festa after school, the door flew open. Vito bellowed at Teo, "Hey, look what the cat dragged in! Haven't seen you around here in ages!"

It was more than he'd said in Iz's presence for days.

Gisele hurried up behind. "Come in! Come in!"

"You going to sing for us?" Vito said. "And Gisele's got beautiful osso buco tonight."

They bustled Teo inside like he was some kind of prodigal son. Iz followed behind.

For the next couple of hours, the two of them sat at a table together and laughed and teased each other. Gisele kept bringing out more food until Teo said he was going to explode. Then, Vito set up the microphone and a couple of stools.

When they sat down, Iz drew out her guitar. "So, what should we sing?"

"*Traviata*?"

"Sure, except I don't know how to sing opera."

"Just sing it your way."

"My way is, like, rough and everything. Dr. Henderson says I sound like a psychic wound. You don't want me to wreck Verdi, do you? I thought you were like some kind of opera purist."

"Nope. Rockabilly *Traviata*." He smirked.

She laughed out loud. "Okay. Let's sing the part where he's trying make her believe he's in love with her."

"And she's just so brittle and untrusting," Teo said.

Their faces were getting quite close together.

"Light good?" Vito boomed, head appearing between them from behind.

Chapter Thirty-Two

In some ways, things were so much better after that. Each morning, Iz hurried to school, where Teo usually accosted her as soon as she entered the building. They bantered most of the day. They could hardly take their eyes off each other. She was so relieved not to be fighting with him anymore.

But there was still plenty to worry about. Each afternoon, she arrived home hoping and fearing that the internal complaints review had come to a decision. She kept going to Dr. Perlinger's office to find out the result of his phone call. But Dominion Children's Care was silent, and Dr. Perlinger turned out not to be there any of the times she tried to find him.

So, she just trudged on, telling herself she was wrapped in Fierce Voice's warm wings, trying to be brave and determined in the face of things she couldn't control.

Which was definitely not easy.

On the day of the next outreach, Iz ran up the steps hoping to see Skye there. But the little girl was not under the table or behind the coats or in the area with the garbage can and recycling. She wasn't anywhere else either.

Dr. Perlinger came into the room then. He held up crossed fingers.

Adrenalin shot through Iz. Did he mean he'd made the call? Was there a chance Skye might still be coming?

"Let's get this party started," Ezekiel shouted.

Heart pounding with equal parts worry and hope, Iz called, "Yeah, come on, let's join the circle."

As they all ran to sit down, Iz kept her eyes peeled on the doorway. She sent pleas to the universe to make Skye walk through it.

"Where were you last week?" Shemar asked her curiously.

"And why did you take off the week before?" Ezekiel added.

"Ah, I was going to talk to you all about that. I'm really sorry." She looked around the circle, then locked eyes with Teo for a second. She exhaled a fiery breath. "I was kind of dealing with some stuff. I promise, I'll never walk out on you again."

"What stuff?" Daniella asked.

"Hmm." She wasn't going to tell them about That Place, obviously. An idea came to her. "You know how you were writing a couple of weeks ago about silent things talking? It was a little bit like that. I needed to . . . to speak up about something, and I was scared to do it. So, I-I ran away. But now I'm back."

"What did you have to speak up about?"

"Long story." Brightly, she changed the subject. "Did you finish your song about the silent objects? Do you want to show me now?"

Their voices overlapped with excitement.

"We did *so much!*"

"Kwame made the rhythms, Kwame, show her."

Kwame sat down at the drum set and began pattering out a complex pattern. As he did so, Ahmed and Will taped up the papers from the last two weeks. The scribbled words and arrows and crossed out parts and different colours were testament to exactly how hard they had all worked.

The song was raw, it was rough. The kids were bellowing it more than they were singing. But when Iz looked at their faces and saw them all engaged in this thing together, she found herself shaking her head in amazement.

She's got a thought book
Keeps her tears inside
Left her school to look after me

My brother won an MVP
That's what he was to me
He's gone, left behind his trophy

My grandma gave me a necklace
She said it meant the miles didn't matter
I run it through my fingers like it's water

Bunny, you look so quiet
But you've crossed an ocean, away from a war
My explorer and best friend

Beautiful beads, in my auntie's hands
She sews them into paths, shows me how
We walk along old and new ways . . .

As Iz listened, her heart swelled.

She said softly, "You wrote all this in the last two classes?"

They yelled over each other.

"I came up with the part with her tears inside and Rina said it was *magnificent!*"

"We used some of the same tune as last week, but Ahmed showed us how we could change it up—"

"Jasleen said, 'Pretend you're the bunny. How would it be feeling?'"

"The necklace looks like water when you run it through your fingers, and then Bijan said, 'What would water sound like?' And see we made the tune go up and down sort of like waves, and then LaRoyce added the piano part that sounds sloshy—"

"It was," Dr. Perlinger said to them quietly, "a really extraordinary collaboration between all of you."

Iz could scarcely believe it. "Th-this is . . . beautiful. Not just the songs. Not just the words. But . . . the *ideas*."

"Do you love how we were telling everyone about the quiet things?" Poppy said.

"Like, we were standing up and saying, *People! Eyes here! Pay attention!*" Daniella's voice was commanding.

An image flashed in Iz's mind—Fierce Voice roaring fury and encouragement on the night she'd made the excruciating decision to tell Vito and Gisele about That Place.

She said softly, "Reminds me of a song *I* wrote this week."

They clamoured for her to play and sing it.

Finally, she sat down on a stool, tuned her guitar.

She changed the feel this time. It had originally been a savage scream, a diatribe against the universe. But now, she made it slow. She lingered over every line. And as she repeated the chorus, she deepened the words each time. Made them echo. Made them stick.

Fierce Voice rising.

Fierce Voice rising.

At the end, there was an uncharacteristic silence.

"Hey," said a voice.

Iz's head flew around. A brazen little figure stood in the doorway.

"Skye!" Iz shouted. She ran over, picked the girl up and swung her around.

"Careful!" Skye roared.

"Where've *you* been?" Devanch asked.

"None of your business," Skye said. Then she added, "Just kidding. First, I was hiding in a practice room at Iz's school, and then I was staying at her place, and then I was hiding in a practice room again. And she brought me these pastry things, but after that they made me go to a new foster home with *Winifred*."

There was a short silence.

Iz couldn't look at anyone.

Their voices erupted.

"You were staying at *Iz's* place?"

"Can we stay at Iz's place too?"

"Can we go to a practice room at her school?"

"No," Iz said quickly.

A woman came running into the room.

"Skye, you can't take off like that," she said. "I was parking the car, and you just jumped out—"

"You knew I was coming in *here*," Skye said. She turned to Iz. "This is Iz."

"It's nice to meet you, Iz," said the woman, still out of breath. "I'm Winifred, Skye's foster mother."

"Uh, nice to meet you too."

Iz tensed for whatever was coming next, but Winifred's next words were seemingly without innuendo. "I've heard a lot about you from Skye. It sounds like you've been very kind to her."

Iz flushed. She'd been anything but kind. But she was going to fix things.

"Winifred has a piano," Skye broke in. "Like an actual piano with strings, not a fake one like *that*." She pointed at the digital keyboard LaRoyce had just been playing.

"Nice," LaRoyce said.

"And she does, what is it, amateur musical theatre. At an actual *theatre*."

Winifred shook her head, downplaying Skye's words. "I just have a small part with the little company in our neighbourhood. Skye came to a rehearsal."

Dr. Perlinger walked up to them, holding out his hand. "Aaron Perlinger. It's very nice to meet you after our phone chat."

Winifred looked flustered. "Yes, thank you for that. I've been completely disorganized the last couple of weeks. I was meaning to bring her back, and it's just—"

"Of course, very understandable." Dr. Perlinger smiled down at Skye. "And now you're here! Are you ready to get started?"

In response, Skye skittered to the circle, then lowered herself slowly. "Elevator going down."

Manifesto all laughed.

And Iz sat there surprised at the change in the little girl.

She said to everyone, "Let's perform your song for Skye. Come on!"

They all shouted their agreement.

As Kwame played the intro on the drums, Iz couldn't help smiling at how intensely Skye's head moved back and forth as she took in their performances.

When they were done, Shemar said, "So what do you think?"

Skye shrugged.

She made them wait.

Then she said, "It's ... *okay*, I guess."

"What's wrong with it?" Devanch demanded.

"Well." Skye sighed like she was annoyed at having to explain herself. "I mean ..." She pointed at Shemar. "It would be better if, like, your *necklace* was talking." Her finger singled each of them out. "And your *book* ... and your *bunny* ... and your *beads* ... and your *trophy* ..."

She scrambled out of Iz's lap and started storming around the inside of the circle, voice rising. "And, see, they're all under a *spell* so they can't talk. They're all, like, stuck in the attic."

Manifesto eyed each other with little smiles of anticipation.

"But maybe a kid finds them," Skye intoned. "Maybe the kid's *hiding* in the attic. Maybe she's mad or sad or something, which is why she can hear them ..."

She stopped, frowned.

"At first, the kid's, like, *What are all these things, and why do they all have these weird little calling voices?* The kid finally decides to talk back to one of them. Like the necklace or something."

The kids were silent, listening.

"The kid holds the necklace up like this." Skye lifted her hand slowly. "She asks, *Why are you making this little song?* The necklace is having trouble talking, but the kid helps it. Little by little, the necklace whispers its story about the grandma over the ocean ..."

Shemar beamed.

"And the kid takes up the song, and sings it, and then some magic happens, and the kid breaks the spell on the necklace. And the necklace is able to tell the kid about this curse on these things, how they've all been, like, separated from the rest of the world, how nobody's been able to hear them."

Skye clapped her hands at everyone like they needed to wake up. "So the kid and the necklace go to find all the other silent things. One by one, they listen to these little whispered stories, and they raise them up, and the spell is broken. And in the end, they work together to break the spell that got put on them."

There was a silence while they all stared at each other.

"And how do they break the spell?" Daniella asked.

"Duh." Skye pointed right at Iz. "With *her* song."

Iz blinked. "'Fierce Voice Rising'?"

"Yeah. They work together to write it and sing it, and it breaks the spell." Skye swung around at Teo. "It's like *you* said."

"What did I say?" Teo looked startled.

"This is an *opera,*" Skye told him.

"I said this was an opera?"

"No. You said an opera is a story with a bunch of songs. Which is what this is."

"We could do *acting,*" Ezekiel exclaimed.

Skye roared, "Okay, you stand here, and you stand here." She started bossily pushing people into position. "And we need to figure out who's going to play the kid who finds them."

Everyone looked at everyone else and started laughing.

"What?" Skye said.

Iz and Dr. Perlinger gazed at each other. She burst into an enormous grin. Because Skye had just made the hugest volley possible. She had elevated everything they were trying to do.

Iz thought back to the day Skye had brought in her song, that heart-stopping howl to the universe proclaiming her right to stand up and fight back. Skye's song had led to so many things, complicated and painful and much more personal than Iz had bargained for.

But maybe Skye's song had been predicting this exact moment.

Maybe Iz's own pain and ragged past had been too.

Chapter Thirty-Three

At the end of the hour, Iz and Skye sat together on the floor.

"I shouldn't have yelled at you. I was stressed but that's no reason. I'm really sorry. None of what I said was true." Iz looked the little girl right in the eyes, being as direct and truthful as she could. Summoning a dragon to help make things right.

"You were mean." Skye paused. "I was mad."

"I don't blame you."

"But I'm not mad now. I talked with Winifred."

Iz said in an undertone, "I . . . made, like, a complaint about your foster home. I went into DCC and did an interview thing."

"You did?"

"Yeah." She paused. Gathered her nerve to say the next words. "Because I was there too. In that same Place."

She waited to see what Skye would say to that. But Skye stayed quiet, so Iz stumbled on. "I-I didn't want to tell anyone about it for a long time. Not even *think* about it. I sort of had, like, a rule about it in my head."

"Same." Skye spoke so softly Iz barely heard the word.

"B-but then my therapist helped me start thinking that keeping it a secret wasn't actually, like, helping. Not helping me, not helping you or any other kid. So, I told." She paused. "And, I mean, I hope they're going to shut That Place down. Maybe even get the police involved. We'll find out any day now."

"They won't do anything," Skye said.

Iz frowned. "I'm pretty sure you're wrong. This was like a formal complaint."

"I know I'm right, and I'm just a little kid."

Winifred showed up then. "Skye! Are you ready?"

Skye scrambled to her feet. She looked down at Iz while Iz looked up at her. Then the little girl unexpectedly squeezed her arms around Iz's neck. "See you next week."

She walked out the door with Winifred and didn't look back.

Iz sat there a minute longer in the empty room.

She looked around at the stacked chairs, the chart stand. To a stranger, it looked like any other room. Nobody could know how much creativity had taken place in here unless someone told them about it.

Finally, she gathered her stuff and walked out of the Eastbourne Centre. She hoped Teo would be waiting there.

He was, leaning against the railing. When he saw her, his face burst into teasing sunshine that stood out against the darkening sky. In a fake-anguished voice, he exclaimed, "Oh, I can't do it. This outreach will be terrible."

"What?"

He laughed, flashing those teeth. "You. Remember?"

It took her a minute to realize he was referencing their talk at Giovanni's restaurant that night after Dr. Perlinger had emailed to say Eastbourne was really happening. It felt like a million years ago.

She couldn't help smiling. "What's your point?"

He fell in beside her as they walked. "Did I ever tell you about Dr. P's fiddle leaf fig tree? We stole it, and then we sent him postcards for weeks. That fiddle leaf fig tree went on a huge round the world musical tour. It made its debut at the Grand Ole Opry with the viral single, 'She Severed My Roots with Her High-Stepping Boots.'"

Iz burst out laughing. "That's utterly ridiculous."

His arm rested lightly around her shoulders, which she totally noticed. "We sent him clues to find his plant. The whole school was in on it at this point. And when he showed up, we had a huge reunion party." He twinkled down at her. "We wouldn't have done that for just anyone."

"Well, I mean, Dr. P is *Dr. P.*"

"Exactly. Amazing teachers inspire outrageous creativity." He leaned down, smiled meaningfully. "Teachers like *you*."

"Ha," Iz said, flustered. "Whoa. No. Not even remotely."

"Yeah, okay, whatever."

When they reached Festa, Teo said, "See you tomorrow, Onion Girl."

"See you tomorrow, Opera Boy."

She ran into Festa, glowing.

Gisele looked up as Iz blasted into the kitchen on her way upstairs.

"Hey!" Iz said. "Smells amazing!"

"Sweetheart. Do you have a minute?" Her usual smile was slightly crooked.

"Uh . . . okay. I mean, sure."

Gisele led Iz back out into the restaurant and toward a table in a dark corner. "Come sit down."

Iz lowered herself cautiously into the chair. The table was covered with delicate wine glasses, gleaming cutlery, crisp white napkins. Its perfection made her uneasy. She felt like something imperfect was about to happen.

She conjured up Fierce Voice, kept her eyes trained on the dragon.

"So," Gisele said, patting Iz's hand.

"What?"

"We heard from Dominion Children's Care today."

Iz didn't even have to be told. She could see it in Gisele's compassionate expression.

"They aren't going ahead with a formal investigation, right?" she whispered.

Gisele's expression hardened. "They said there was insufficient evidence. And—" She caught herself.

"And what?"

Gisele clearly didn't want to speak the next words out loud. "Unreliable. They said that."

"That I'm unreliable."

"I'm going in tomorrow to have a talk with them," Gisele said darkly.

Iz thought about everything she had done to get into The Métier School. Lying, stealing, identity theft, and the rest of it. She thought about how she had hidden Skye.

"I . . . I *am* unreliable," she said in a tiny voice. "Why should anyone believe me about anything?"

"Because you're telling the *truth*," Gisele said with flashing eyes.

Horrible awareness dawned on Iz now. "And That Place, it's probably going to keep being a foster home, right? So, everything I've done has been useless. Life is still going to be completely unsafe for some kid who . . ."

"Cara, we'll fight it. We'll go above their heads. We'll—"

Iz shook her head, eyes blurring. "There's no point."

The door to the restaurant opened, and a couple walked in. They chatted with the greeter, who led them to a table not far away from Iz and Gisele.

The man said to Gisele, "Beautiful place."

Iz stiffened. The hair on her arms stood up.

She knew That Voice.

"Thank you," Gisele said.

Iz gathered the courage to look at him. The Woman stood there too.

The Woman wriggled her fingers in greeting. "We read about this place in the newspaper article they did about you, Iz, and we've always wanted to come and try the food." She put a hand to her heart. "Today, honey, we were just so happy to have this misunderstanding behind us that we thought, this is the time. Fresh start. And if that beautiful aroma is anything to go by, we're in for a real treat."

Iz's heart started pounding so fast she genuinely thought it might give out.

She scrambled to her feet, brain short-circuiting, alarms pealing in her head.

Foggily, she heard Gisele saying "Iz!"

"Huh! Ha!" She skittered backward, away, away from the table, while The Man blinked at her as if she were completely crazy.

"What's wrong?" Gisele cried.

Shaking uncontrollably, Iz pointed at The Man and The Woman. "It's—Them. From That Place."

"I'm so sorry," The Man said. "I didn't mean to upset you, Iz. We just wanted to try your foster parents' restaurant."

"Get out," Gisele said.

"I think there's been a miscommunication." The Woman smiled at Iz. "Honey, we're so glad to see you."

Iz's brain flooded with panic. She hardly knew where she was or who she was. Her thoughts were jagged, nonlinear screams.

Vito and Gisele's place had just been invaded.

It had become profoundly unsafe.

She banged into the chair of another diner, muttered an apology, scrambled as fast as she could to the door, and flung it open.

Like an animal, she took off racing down the street.

Chapter Thirty-Four

Lungs ripping—

Feet stumbling—

Arms and legs throbbing—

Heart shuddering—

Iz's body had completely taken over her mind.

She ran in no particular direction, breath raw and hacking. Occasionally, she stopped, leaned over, and panted until The Man infiltrated her head again. Then she shot forward, propelled by unthinking terror.

The sun went down. The stars came out.

Much later, sometime in the middle of the night maybe, rain fell. The drops came sporadically at first, then harder and harder. Iz was soon soaked through. Her heart and brain started fighting, a battle between primal fear and the practical need to stop running and find somewhere dry.

She came across a little park tucked behind some trees. On impulse, she pelted across the grass and crawled under the stairs of the slide. She hugged her knees, buried her face, made herself as small as possible, and just breathed.

After a while, fragmented thoughts fluttered back into her brain.

Had she just run away?

Yes. She had run away.

And she couldn't go back now that Those People knew where she lived.

Festa wasn't safe anymore.

Into the clanging terror now came a profound sense of grief.

Iz sat there and wept for hours. She wept about the loss of Vito and Gisele, of The Métier School, of Dr. Perlinger, of the Eastbourne Centre. She wept about the loss of her own bravery, about the destruction of her best intentions.

And she wept about Teo, about the beautiful night at *La Traviata* when they had sat there together in the darkness watching that doomed girl, Violetta.

As the rain fell all around and the night grew colder, her brain started getting confused. The dividing line between herself and Violetta blurred. She was both of them at once, banished from her home by voices more powerful than her own. Life could not possibly be the same now. Every choice was gone. Here, under this slide, was the catastrophe at the end of their stories.

I did warn you she was going to kick it.

She clung to the memory of Teo's voice. She curled up in a ball. At last, at last, she gave herself to the darkness.

When Iz awoke, grey dawn surrounded her. At first, she had no idea where she was. She sat up, stretched out her aching neck, rubbed feeling into her frozen legs. Then everything came swimming back. She pressed hands to her heart, which ached at the loss of her whole world.

But another feeling was there now too. It pumped through her veins alongside the grief and confusion and fear. It simmered through every pore.

Anger.

How dared Those People come to Festa? How dared they kick her out of her own home, her own life?

She was angry at herself too.

What had happened to Fierce Voice?

She'd forgotten about the dragon as soon as Those People showed up. In that horrible moment, Fierce Voice had fallen apart like a botched magic trick. Fierce Voice had turned out just to be a way to mislead her brain into thinking she was braver than she was. When she had really needed the dragon, it had been of no use at all.

And now, here she was, alone, sitting under a stupid slide while rain poured down.

Iz clutched her head while images and memories ran through her mind. Playing her guitar in her little bedroom at Vito and Gisele's. Sitting at the breakfast table while espresso filled the air and opera played softly. Debating with Dr. Perlinger and collaborating with Manifesto. Starting the outreach program at Eastbourne.

Her anger grew.

It was a life she'd fought for. And it was a life that wasn't just her own now. She was part of Vito and Gisele and Festa and the little apartment upstairs. She was part of Métier. She was part of the Eastbourne kids and their outreach program. She was part of Skye coming out from under a table.

And—

She was part of Teo, whatever their friendship was.

Totally in love with you.

Iz breathed in sharply. She raked at her hair.

Finally, she crawled out from under the slide, unfolded her cramped muscles, stood up in the sleet.

She was scared, scared.

She was entirely vulnerable and exposed.

Iz whispered, "What do I do?"

Chapter Thirty-Five

A few hours later, she stood in front of a green door.

It belonged to a house on a street dominated by tall trees that were all fading yellows and oranges and reds. The sidewalk, covered with crunching leaves, gleamed with the sheen of rain.

She was slightly scared to knock, so just stood there remembering the last time she'd been on this porch. Closing her eyes, she saw a table groaning under the weight of many dishes. She heard everyone singing at a grand piano. The memories warmed her half-frozen body.

A bench beside the door was covered in yellow and blue cushions. "Just sit down for a minute," Iz muttered.

She sank onto it, allowed her head to fall back against the pillows, closed her eyes.

Sometime later, a car pulled into a driveway. Doors slammed. Feet thumped on the porch. Someone called her name and shook her awake.

Iz opened her eyes to see Teo's face close to hers. There were golden specks in his eyes.

"Hey!" she said curiously. "Are your eyes brown or yellow?"

"Ah, Iz." Teo's voice was strained. "Everyone's been so worried!"

Teo's dad knelt at her side, his face so much like Teo's. "Sweetheart, we've all been out looking for you. Where have you been?"

"Oh!" Iz sat up. "I—like—I'm so sorry. I don't know. I was under a slide. I kind of, like, got . . . scared. This thing happened at Festa."

"We know." Teo looked really sad.

"You do?" She cast her mind back, trying to remember when she had told him.

Teo stroked her hair, and it was actually sort of nice. He said, "Gisele told us a little bit about what happened."

"You wouldn't like Those Guys," she said.

"You're right." His yellow-brown eyes flashed. "I hate them."

"They kicked me out of Vito and Gisele's. It's not safe there anymore. I can't go back. So, I came here."

He growled in his lion's voice, "It *is* safe there. Nobody's kicking you out. You're not alone. We're all here for you. Nobody's going to be allowed to hurt you." Suddenly he was hugging her. "Ah, Iz, I'm so glad you came back."

"Me too," Iz said, realizing she was.

The green door opened, and Teo's Nonna appeared. She leaned down with worried eyes and spoke to Teo and his father in Italian.

"Let's get you inside," Teo's dad said.

Iz walked into the house with them, then found herself descending onto a soft couch.

Teo plonked down beside her, face crumpled with worry.

"I'll call Vito," his dad said, picking up the phone.

Nonna said something sharply.

"Yeah, and Juliana too."

Mr. Russo walked into the next room, and Iz heard his voice. "We came home, and she was sitting here on the porch."

A bit later, Nonna materialized with a mug. She pressed it into Iz's hands.

"What's this?" Iz said.

"Hot milk," Teo said. "Nonna's specialty. It's good."

Iz lifted it to her lips and sipped it. "It *is* good!"

"Iz." Teo's caramel voice shook. "I'm really sorry."

"Why are *you* sorry?"

"I mean . . ." His eyes filled with actual tears, which was kind of fascinating. She saw herself reflected in them. "I'm sorry they didn't listen to you when you went to make a complaint. I . . . I wish I'd known you were doing that. I would have gone with you. I would have *made* them listen."

"It's because of everything I've done. I'm not reliable," Iz explained.

Nonna said something sharply.

"Exactly," Teo growled, brows drawn.

While Teo's dad kept walking around talking on the phone, Iz drank more and more of the hot milk. It was the creamiest, most beautiful thing she'd ever tasted.

The whole time, Teo sat there looking more distressed than anyone she'd ever seen before.

"See, I *am* an onion girl," she said, trying to make him laugh and agree.

She felt safe and warm. Her eyes kept closing, but she forced them open again in case this turned into a dream that wasn't real.

In the end, though, sleep won.

Chapter Thirty-Six

The walls were covered with yellow and white wallpaper. She had never seen this room before in her life.

Rising on one elbow, she muttered, "What's going on?"

"Iz," said a familiar voice. "You're awake."

Gisele leaned forward, clasped Iz's hand in both of hers.

"Hey," Iz said, completely disoriented. "Where are we?"

"The spare bedroom at the Russos'. You fell asleep and Teo's dad brought you in here." As Iz stared with horror, Gisele began to weep. "My darling, never, ever run away again. I can't bear it. Promise me. We will help you. We will always help you. Please, please trust us, cara."

"I-I'm sorry," Iz whispered, horrified. "I just, I got scared. I didn't think."

A little shiver ran through her, remembering that moment when The Man and The Woman had come in. How they had spoken so pleasantly, but with such frightening intent. That had always been the way of them. From the outside, nobody had ever suspected anything.

"We got hold of everyone and we all looked for you. And we called the police." Gisele's voice got stony. "We should have just called them in the first place, instead of making that complaint with DCC." She paused. "Cara . . . the police want to talk to you."

Iz's eyes shot open. She scrambled to a sitting position. *"What?"*

Traumatic memories flew into her mind.

Sitting in the back of a car, wearing handcuffs.

Being in juvenile detention and then in court.

Listening to a judge talking about all the bad things she'd done to get into The Métier School.

Panic surged in her. "No, no, I can't talk to the police."

Someone tapped softly on the door. Teo's head poked around it. His face lit up with a brilliant smile when he saw her. "Beaufort! Finally! You're awake!"

"I am indeed." Iz felt totally awkward all of a sudden. She had a jumbled memory of sitting on his porch or something. Or maybe his couch.

What had she said to him?

She started blushing furiously.

"Are you hungry?" Teo said. "Nonna's made pastina. I can get you some. Or you can, like, come out to the table."

"Uh." Iz was starting to feel profoundly weird about sitting in the bed with the two of them looking at her, especially since she was sure she looked like some ragged urchin, rained on and mud spattered. "I'll come out."

She followed Teo and Gisele into the little kitchen, where a huge pot of soup steamed on the stove. Nonna hugged Iz, filled a bowl and placed it on the table. She and Gisele headed out of the room, leaving Iz and Teo alone.

"Try it!" Teo watched eagerly as she lifted the spoon to her mouth and swallowed.

"It's so good!" Iz realized how ravenous she was. For the next several minutes, she devoured the soup, while Teo sat there easily across from her.

When the pastina was completely gone, she felt warm and full. Somehow, sitting with Teo in that comfortable kitchen, she was able to utter the fear that was on her mind.

"Gisele says, like, the police want to talk to me."

She shivered, thinking about the idea.

"That's okay." Teo leaned close and said in a mysterious voice, "You have a secret weapon."

"Uh, I do?"

He nodded. "Juliana. My cousin. She's a lawyer and she's going to help. And believe me, she's a pit bull."

"Wait, what?"

Her alarm was growing.

"Don't worry," Teo said. "You get the family-and-friends rate. Which is, like, *zero dollars*."

"Why do I need a *lawyer*?" She was shaking now. Was she in trouble for making the complaint? Or for running away?

"Iz, Iz." His voice was like syrup pouring over her anxiety. "Juliana would just be with you when you talked to the police, as your supporter or whatever. She'd make sure you got *heard*, you know?"

Iz gripped her hands together. She was suddenly back in that meeting room at Dominion Children's Care, getting asked questions about her bad choices in the past. She whispered, "It won't make a difference. They won't believe me."

Teo's forehead wrinkled like he was trying to figure out how to say something. "But they might, with Juliana's help ... I mean ... it's *okay* to let people help you."

He ladled more pastina into her bowl and placed it in front of her again.

"Like, when the car crash happened with my mom and sisters, you remember how I told you I stopped talking, right? And Nonna moved in." He paused. "I mean, the whole family was around us, all nine million cousins and everyone. They were basically relentless. And Nonna played me opera after opera and talked about the storylines, and little by little I started talking again."

Iz was silent.

"What I mean is, dad and I couldn't do it on our own. We ... we *needed everyone*." He looked across at her with his tawny eyes. "And right now, you sort of need everyone. And we want to help. And hey, you are *totally* brave, Beaufort. You can do this."

"Well, but I just have some issues with the police."

"I know. This is different, though." His eyes were on her. "This is you getting a chance to speak up. Like in your song. 'Fierce Voice Rising,' remember?"

"Uh. Clearly, I do *not* have a Fierce Voice. I ran away at the first sign of trouble like some kind of fool." She thought of that stark moment in the rain when she'd realized the dragon had not helped, was not real.

Teo began twisting a paper napkin around his fingers.

"You're wrecking that," Iz said.

"So, you got scared. You're allowed to be scared. But, like . . . you *came back.*" His eyes darted across argument points she couldn't see. "Not only that, but think about all those outreach classes, of the kids talking about how things are silent until, like the right people hear them and help their voices to be heard."

Iz sucked in her breath at that.

Helpers.

Dr. Warren.

Verdi.

All at once, she was thinking back to those lectures that seemed like they'd happened a thousand years ago. Verdi had been given an education by a wealthy benefactor. Someone had handed him a manuscript that broke through his pain and grief, helped him write again.

Teo's voice interrupted her thoughts. "And, okay, here's another perspective. I mean, *La Traviata.*"

Iz blinked. *Had he somehow read her mind about Verdi?*

"Like," Teo said, "if someone had stood up for Violetta, had stood *with* her and helped her speak back, maybe she wouldn't have been driven away from her home and her new life. Maybe she might have had a totally different ending to her story."

Iz stared at him, taken aback by the passion in his face, and by the fact that it was on her behalf. Suddenly she remembered Dr. Perlinger saying something similar to Skye. *I could sit with you while you tried again. Back you up, so to speak.*

"We're standing with *you*. We're raising our voices for *you*." Teo's voice seemed to make the very air vibrate, but he looked anxious and abashed, like he'd probably gone too far. "I mean, obviously only if you want."

It's up to you. Gisele had said the same thing before they made their complaint to Dominion Children's Care.

Iz weighed his words, weighed all their words.

She wasn't actually used to asking herself what she wanted. It felt weird, like she was peeking through the window into an unused room in her mind that she hadn't even known was there.

She said, "I think . . ."

Teo waited.

"I mean . . ."

She imagined opening the door to that little overlooked room in her head. She walked in and gazed around at all of her own silent, hopeful things that had maybe been waiting a long time to be asked what they wanted. Fierce Voice was huddled there too, banished into silence after that terrible night.

Sorrow flooded her, seeing the dragon so rejected and alone.

Tentatively, she reached out a hand.

Fierce Voice inched forward.

After that, they clung to each other, joined in the memory of how terrifying that night had been, how alone she'd felt, how stripped of bravery, without the imaginary dragon that had given her strength to do things she could never have imagined.

Then—

Iz opened up her heart to the dragon.

Fierce Voice crept inside.

"You okay?" Teo said.

Slowly Iz nodded.

She whispered, "Fine, I'll do it."

Chapter Thirty-Seven

Gisele had brought a change of clothes. Iz changed into them gratefully. Then she hung out with Teo all morning, both of them staying home from school.

In the afternoon, Juliana came over, dressed in jeans and a chunky sweater, with her hair up in a messy bun.

"This is Juliana," Teo's dad said to Iz.

"Uh, hi." Iz felt unable to meet Juliana's eyes.

"We'll leave you alone." Mr. Russo ushered Teo and Nonna out and closed the kitchen door behind them. Iz, Gisele, and Juliana sat down at the table in front of a plate of pastries and mugs of tea.

The door opened again. Vito stumped in, sat down heavily in an empty chair, glared over everyone's heads.

Iz's whole body tensed. This was the first time she had been in the same room with him since waking up in the Russos' spare bedroom. He was probably over-the-top livid about her taking off. The rift between them at this point felt unfixable.

"Well, Iz, I've heard so much about you from Teo." Juliana's voice was bright. "She's so talented and so smart and so gorgeous. Flowers spring up wherever her feet touch the earth. When she breathes, angels sing cantatas in heaven above."

Iz snorted.

Juliana burst into laughter too. Her wide grin was a lot like Teo's. She had a slightly impish quality.

"So you're, like, a lawyer or something?" Iz said shyly.

"I'm a human rights lawyer."

"Oh, okay."

Juliana's eyes twinkled. "Do you know what that means?"

"No."

Everyone laughed.

"Well, a simple way to put it is to say that I stand up for people's human rights. Like yours, for example." Juliana took a long sip of coffee. "Ahhh, this is perfect. It's been a long week." She glanced at Iz with eyes that had the same drooping lids as Teo's. "You know that feeling?"

"... Yeah."

"Yeah," Juliana said. There was a wealth of meaning in her word. "How are you feeling?"

"Okay," Iz said. "Ish."

"That's good." Juliana's voice was deliberately casual. "Well enough to talk to the police if I call them to come over?"

"Uh." Iz drew up her knees and hugged them. "I don't know. Maybe." She struggled to say the next thing. "See ... but last year there was *this thing*, and I actually got arrested ..."

She couldn't look at Juliana.

Teo's cousin's voice was warm. "Yes, I know. I know about that."

"Y-you do?"

"Yes. You got a conditional discharge. That's over, Iz." Juliana spoke with confidence. "It's not connected to this."

"But ... what if the police don't believe me either? What if ... *they* say I'm unreliable?" Iz let out an unhappy breath. "I *am* unreliable, you know."

Vito's voice burst out like a thundercloud, making everyone jump. "*If one more person says that ...*"

They all stared at him.

Vito glared up at the ceiling like it had personally offended him. "This girl, this girl ..." He gestured at Iz, his voice growing louder. "They don't know her. They don't know anything about her. I mean, yeah, she's done some stuff she shouldn't have. But that's not who *she* is. They should be over there arresting Those People—and I use the term *People* loosely . . ."

Everyone was silent.

Vito bellowed, "They're supposed to *protect* our kids." He clambered to his feet, started pacing. "I can hardly stand it. This girl—*my* girl—they were supposed to protect *her.*"

Iz stared at Vito with fascinated shock.

Nobody had ever spoken like that on her behalf.

All those days when he had walked out of the room, unable to look her in the face, was this what had been going through his mind?

"Come sit down," Gisele said to him in a soft voice.

After he did, there was a silence.

"If anyone," Juliana said with complete conviction, "approaches Iz with the slightest prejudice, you can be assured I will go after them. And I am extremely good at that, let me tell you." She flashed Teo's lion-hearted grin at Vito.

Iz whispered the scary thing in her mind. "But, like, what if That Guy is mad because I'm talking to the police?"

"Don't worry about *him.* We're going to get a peace bond," Juliana said.

"What's that?" Gisele asked.

"It's like a restraining order. If the police think there's enough evidence, they'll send it to court, and the court will contact Those People to sign it. And then they won't be able to harass or intimidate you."

"Wh-what if they don't want to sign it?" Iz whispered.

"I'm betting they won't put up a fight." Juliana smiled grimly. "Because if they refuse, there will be a hearing and they'll have to come to court and prove why they shouldn't have to. And then it will be a public thing. Most people just sign."

Iz hugged herself protectively. She hugged Fierce Voice too, who was safely held in her heart. ". . . Okay."

Juliana phoned the police.

When she hung up, she said, "They're sending a couple of officers here. Shouldn't be too long."

Iz nodded stiffly.

A battle raged in her head. Part of her wanted to run away again. But the other part remembered her conversation with Teo about helpers who added volume to your voice and gave you the strength to tell your story.

She was also thinking about that surprising little room in her mind where she could examine her own ignored wishes and try to figure out what *she* actually wanted to do. She pretended she was walking in there again. She imagined consulting with the parts of herself that had been silent, while her heart pulsed with Fierce Voice.

When the doorbell rang later that afternoon, Juliana answered it and talked to people in the hallway.

She led two female officers into the kitchen.

One of them held out a hand, with a smile that wasn't as horrible as Iz had expected. "How are you doing, honey?"

"... Good ..."

"Don't be scared," the officer said in an actually kind way. "We're here to help. We're your friends, okay?"

Iz exhaled slowly. She didn't quite believe it, but she nodded.

For the next few minutes, the officers asked her about herself—how she liked living at Vito and Gisele's and what she was learning at The Métier School. But after that, somehow, they snuck into getting her to talk about when The People had walked into the restaurant. She told them how her brain had short-circuited till only one thought remained—to run as fast and as far as she could. She said, sheepishly, it had been sort of a stupid thing to do. Juliana spoke up then, pointing out that the timing of Those People's arrival in Festa had been clearly purposeful, given that Iz's complaint had just been struck down. She used words like *harassment* and *intimidation*.

After a while, the police started tiptoeing into Iz's history in That Place. They didn't ask about it in one big question, but rather through lots of little queries. Iz tried to answer everything the police asked, although they crept deeper and deeper into painful memories. She locked her mind's eyes on Fierce Voice the whole time, drawing strength from the dragon that lived now in her heart.

Juliana told the police about the internal complaint Iz and Gisele had made to Dominion Children's Care and how DCC had decided not to pursue it further. Iz heard Juliana saying, *conditional discharge*, and *conflation*, and that maybe there was no such thing as a perfect victim.

Next, they were all talking about the peace bond.

Juliana brought out a paper and showed it to the police. As voices bounced back and forth in messy counterpoint, the police began to write things on it. Juliana's tone was clear and firm. She directed a lot of what was put on the form. Everyone seemed to be agreeing about next steps.

Further investigation.

Interview other children.

A little while later, the police stood up and shook everyone's hands. One of them said to Iz, "You did great, sweetheart."

"Thanks," she mumbled.

After they were gone, Juliana said softly, "How are you?"

Iz blinked at her.

How did she feel?

She hardly knew.

Scared. Shaky.

And . . .

"Maybe okay," she whispered.

Chapter Thirty-Eight

"Imposed on your hospitality long enough," Vito rumbled to Mr. Russo after the police had left. "Should get this girl home."

"Nobody's imposing," Teo's father smiled at Iz. "She's always welcome."

"Hopefully next time under better circumstances," Teo added.

Without thinking, Iz wrapped her arms around him. She hung on and felt his arms hug her back tightly.

"Okay, okay," Vito said.

Gisele had brought Iz's coat. Iz wrapped herself in the warm fabric, feeling as though it was like an embrace from her foster mother.

Everyone came out into the driveway to see Iz off. Nonna held her close for a minute.

"Thank you," Iz said shyly.

She didn't know exactly what she was feeling, but thought it was mostly love wrapped in a blanket of embarrassment.

As if he could tell what was inside her and wanted to lighten the mood, Teo suddenly dipped Iz backward. He smiled down at her. "Thanks for choosing our place to crash at."

Iz found herself laughing. "Yeah, I apparently like to inconvenience people."

He leaned close, whispered, "Anytime, Beaufort."

Then he gallantly opened the door to Vito's car and gestured for her to enter.

As Iz settled on the seat, she flashed back to that horrible moment when she had gone running into the icy night. She'd felt so lost, isolated, and banished from the world. But now, here was Teo closing the door and leaning in the car window like a member of the family.

Was it possible that the act of running away could somehow draw everyone closer together? That didn't make any sense, and yet ... weirdly, it was how Iz felt.

"Drive safe," Teo said to Vito, deadpan.

Vito waved a hand like Teo was an insect he was batting away. "Been driving over thirty years, thanks."

Teo nodded compassionately. "And it's easy over time to forget the rules of the road. I'm doing my beginner's in a couple of weeks. So, if you want any pointers—"

Vito's bushy eyebrows crawled toward each other. "You're too young to write a driving test."

"No, I'm not."

"You have to be sixteen."

"I *am* sixteen."

Vito stared with an almost comical expression. "You're *sixteen?*" He glowered at Iz like she was personally responsible for Teo being older than he'd thought.

"Well, I'm almost fifteen," Iz said defensively.

"All right, all right," Vito growled. "Stop leaning on the window. We're leaving." But the affection in his voice was unmistakable. "Don't be a stranger at the restaurant, son."

As Vito drove, Iz gathered her nerve and said brightly to him, "So are you happy *that's* over?"

Vito just grunted.

As the silence continued, her heart faltered. Why was he still refusing to talk to her? He'd been having conversations with everyone else, even joking with them. And she'd sort of felt like his explosion at the Russos' house had been in her defence. But now he was like a stone again.

When they got home, Gisele put on the kettle for tea. Iz sat down at the table and waited to see if Vito was going to sit down too.

But he muttered, "Going to do the receipts." He opened the door to the restaurant, passed through, shut it behind him.

Iz went cold all over, watching him go. The closed door seemed to represent the barrier between them.

Gisele set tea in front of her. "It's hot. Be careful, cara."

Iz blew into the mug, and steam shot up into her face. The heat of it made her think of Fierce Voice.

Iz breathed in and out. She imagined her breath turning into curling flame.

She stood up and said to Gisele, "Be right back."

When she arrived downstairs, Vito was behind the bar.

"So, are we rich?" Iz gestured at the receipts. She sat down on a bar stool and eyed him.

"We're doing okay."

"That's good."

There was a long silence.

She gathered her courage.

"But *we're* not doing okay," Iz said. "You and me."

Vito blinked up at her from under his bushy eyebrows.

Iz swallowed hard. "I'm here to have it out."

Vito put down the paper in his hand. He stood up straighter and met her gaze. "Oh yeah?"

"Yeah." Iz was cowed by his granite face, but what she wanted was stronger than what scared her. "I've already apologized a bunch of times for hiding Skye here, but here's another one. I'm sorry."

Vito huffed like an angry goose, flapping his hand like the matter was long closed.

Iz ignored this gesture, stumbled on. "And I know you're really, really upset about Those People and about That Place and I-I am too. But you keep walking out of the room, and you won't talk to me, and it's not like *I* am responsible for That Place. I'm a kid. *They* were responsible. So I'm starting to feel judged, to be perfectly honest."

"Not judging anything," Vito growled.

"Well, you kind of are, because—"

"Not. Judging." Vito blew out the hugest breath ever while looking over Iz's head. He rubbed his mouth and chin and scraped back the hair on his head. He closed his eyes.

When he opened them, Iz was startled to see that they were wet.

"Never mind," she said hastily. "Forget it."

Vito spoke slowly in a voice that didn't sound like him at all. "A year after we were married, Gisele lost a baby. *We* lost a baby. And I couldn't do a thing to fix it. Couldn't help either one of them."

Iz sat there in shocked silence.

"She couldn't have children after that. I never thought we'd have another kid of our own. But then you came along. And you were stubborn and pushy and talked your way into working here, and after a while I couldn't imagine the place without you." He looked up at the ceiling. "Couldn't imagine *us* without you."

Iz gripped the counter. "But now ..." she whispered.

"But now nothing. You're our kid. And someone did ... *that* to *my kid*." He pushed the palms of his hands into his eyes. "And I can't go back in time to protect you from it. Dads are supposed to protect their kids. That's how it works."

Iz gaped.

"So." Vito looked down at the accounts again.

Iz said after a minute, "Oh Vito, I'm so sorry."

What should she do?

What did real people do when someone they loved shared a really sad, horrible thing?

She remembered the moment at Eastbourne when Chanti had told everyone about going to a homeless shelter. Iz had agonized about how to honour the little girl's devastating volley. Now, Vito's words were like a volley too—broken and hurting.

What could Iz possibly volley back that would ever be worthy of her foster father's painful revelation?

Meredith's voice came into her mind. *Maybe Vito has rules too.*

Iz thought about that.

At last she whispered, "You're not supposed to be able to fix what happened back then. You're not the king of time and space."

Vito shrugged and turned over an invoice.

"But," Iz said, thinking of the dragon inside her heart, "that doesn't mean you can't be a dad to me *now*. And, like, protect me if you want." Voice shaking a bit, she added, "Hey, I can protect you too."

Vito grunted. "*I* don't need protecting."

"When you're like a thousand years old you will," Iz said. "You'll need me to carry you around in a bucket and fight off predators."

She wasn't sure, but she thought she might have heard him snort.

Iz got off the bar stool. She marched around the back of the bar, stood behind Vito, grabbed his shoulders and shook him. It was like doing battle with a boulder.

"Hey, hey, okay," Vito said.

"I'm still stubborn and pushy. And I'm going to shake you until we fix things between us," Iz said.

She kept trying to shove him around, until he finally growled, "What is wrong with you?"

Audaciously, Iz wrapped her arms around him. She squeezed as hard as she could.

"Remember," she said in his ear, "how mad you were when I was playing outside the restaurant on the street and I knocked your plant over? And I said you should give me a job and you laughed at me and told me to go home. And now I *am* home." She summoned the Fierce Voice inside her. "At least, I want to be . . ."

Vito hugged her back. "Idiota. This is your home."

Gisele's voice broke in softly. "And on that note, I have a proposition."

She stood in the doorway of the restaurant's kitchen.

"What are you, a cat?" Vito said, wiping his eyes. "Tiptoeing around."

"I didn't want to disturb you." Gisele sat down on a bar stool.

"What's your proposition?" Iz said.

Gisele reached for Vito and Iz's hands and squeezed them. Suddenly Iz realized Gisele's eyes were moist too. "We're a family. Nobody wanted to rush you, Iz. We wanted to make sure you were comfortable. And you can have all the time in the world, and you can say no too, and we will understand." She paused. "But if you want … if you feel like you might be ready to go ahead …"

Iz held her breath.

"Foster to adopt. We're ready," Gisele said, looking at Vito with love in her eyes. "Aren't we?"

"I was ready from the beginning," he said gruffly.

Iz looked back and forth between these two kind people.

Love threatened to explode inside her.

Softly, she said, "I'm ready too."

Chapter Thirty-Nine

On Monday, the doorbell rang.

"Go get that," Gisele said to Iz with a smile.

Teo stood there grinning when Iz threw the door open. "Chaperone service."

"Hey! Come on up, I'll get my stuff."

As she gathered her guitar and backpack, she could hear his toffee voice bantering with Vito. She was actually sort of relieved Teo would be at her side as she went to school today. He'd announced he'd be there every day, actually, as long as Those People were at large and the peace bond wasn't finalized yet.

When she walked back out into the kitchen, he lounged easily at the table, munching toast and sipping espresso. "You took so long, Gisele had to give me sustenance."

"I'm sure you didn't need much coaxing," Iz shot back.

Walking into Métier was slightly weird after everything that had happened. She felt like she was different somehow and that surely everyone must be able to see that.

But as soon as she got to her first class, all worries were replaced by tremendous relief at being able to put her brain to the interesting task of learning again.

She watched eagerly as Dr. Warren entered the room, strode down to the front, climbed on her desk as usual, and swung her legs.

Everyone fell silent in appreciation for whatever dramatic thing was to come.

Dr. Warren clicked her remote, and a picture came up on the screen. It showed a stony face with closed eyes. Words at the bottom read *Death Mask of Giuseppe Verdi.*

Iz stared at the picture. A shiver trickled down her spine at the thought that she was looking at someone who had died. She felt a sense of personal loss too. This man who'd written *La Traviata* had in a weird way become her friend. He and his opera had sustained her this term in so many ways.

"Now we come to Verdi's last days," Dr. Warren said quietly.

Not a sound could be heard. Iz leaned forward so as not to miss a word.

"He had a stroke, lay dying in his home. The whole city, the whole world, was holding its breath, united in grief."

Afraid to exhale into the darkness. Iz knew exactly what that was like.

"And in this painful time," Dr. Warren went on, "helpers reached out again. People did something extraordinary. An act of love."

Iz held her breath.

"Straw. They put straw on the streets around his home." Her teacher's voice was barely audible. "And why? So the clattering of the cartwheels wouldn't disturb him."

It's okay to let others help you.

Without warning, Teo's words from his kitchen popped into Iz's head.

Unexpected warmth flowed through her as she thought about the people in her life. Meredith was right—kindness and empathy had risen to meet Iz when she needed it, once she had begun throwing out her own rigid rules, once she had invited a dragon to live inside her.

When Wednesday arrived, Manifesto headed over to the Eastbourne Centre. As they walked, the boys kept running straight at the girls, only to swerve right or left at the last minute.

"Just ignore them. They're cavemen. Here." Jasleen handed Iz the bag of candy they were all sharing. Iz popped another one in her mouth, and the sweetness of it transformed everything into bright colour.

"Think fast!" Teo zoomed up at Iz.

"Okay!" She grabbed his hand. He stumbled backward, shouting with surprise. Then he wrapped his arms around her, lifted her up, swung her around. Everyone was laughing. Iz felt grateful in every pore to be among these friends.

When they arrived at the Eastbourne Centre, Dr. Perlinger was beginning to unload instruments onto the pavement. As Iz picked up things to carry inside, he said in a low voice, "And how are *you*?"

Iz knew Vito and Gisele had reached out to him that night when she'd been missing. "Uh ... okay. It's been an interesting couple of days." She quickly told him what had happened with Juliana and the police. "So we're just, like, waiting now."

His face filled with great kindness and understanding. "And while we wait, let us never forget that our Iz Beaufort is of rare, tremendous value. We can't do without her."

Iz blushed. "I can't do without"—she gestured around—"*this*. I'm kind of ... not a whole person on my own."

Then she felt like a complete fool.

"Well," Dr. Perlinger said, walking with her up the steps. "You are certainly a whole person. The magic of this outreach, and indeed of Métier in general, is when *whole people* come together to do something powerful and creative. All of those vibrant voices together, you know. It's hard to ignore them."

When everything was set up, Iz called everyone to the circle. Teo sat down beside her and was immediately ambushed as usual. Smoothly he hoisted up Poppy and swung her over to Iz's lap. "Here. Take this."

"Nooo!" Poppy squealed and crawled back onto Teo.

A creature practically dive-bombed into Iz's lap, stretching its feet out and leaning its head back onto her shoulder.

"Ahhhh. That's better," it said.

"Hey, Skye." Iz's voice was muffled by the little girl's hair.

"Mine," Skye announced.

"Huh. Okay." Iz sat there almost completely still, afraid to move, not wanting to break the spell. She caught Teo smiling down at her like he totally got it.

The hour was packed with work, as they began to write songs to be sung by each silent object that was under a spell. The room rang with a cacophony of rising and falling voices, people singing little snippets, Manifesto weaving a through line of questions and suggestions.

At last, they had roughed out the first song, which would be sung by Ezekiel's brother's trophy.

I'm the trophy
For a kid who played a sport
Smart and brave
Big brother
Gone too soon
He deserved a trophy
For being who he was
So that's me
And I want to tell everybody
That he was an MVP

Then Skye's voice rang out as she looked right at Iz. "I wrote a song for the beginning. It's about how lonely the girl is when she's hiding in the attic, because she feels like nobody cares about her. And I put stuff in it about listening, because this opera is about *listening.*"

A smile crept across Iz's face. "It is," she said.

Skye began to sing.

Hey, I'm in a statue
I'm in a statue
Need somebody to hear me
To hear me

Chip away the stone
I don't wanna be alone
I want you to hear me
Can you hear me?

Tears sprang into Iz's eyes.

"You like it?" Skye stared at Iz without blinking.

". . . I love it."

When they got to the last song in their opera, "Fierce Voice Rising," Iz sang alone before Manifesto and the kids joined her. The sound of their voices seemed to fill the whole world with courage and determination. She could feel the dragon inside her stirring in response.

Meredith's words came into her mind then.

Maybe one day you'll figure out that Fierce Voice is you.

Iz stared at Devanch and Ezekiel, at Poppy and K'Nesha, at Kateryna and Chanti and Daniella, and at the gentle and deep-thinking Shemar. She looked at the members of Manifesto dotted among them. She saw the smiles and the way everyone was interacting with everyone else.

"We should perform this somewhere," she said softly. "Like, when it's all finished."

"A very, very good idea," Dr. Perlinger said, from where he was sitting and watching. "So where?"

If their voices had been noisy before, they were ear-deafening now.

"YouTube!"

"TikTok!"

"In the mall!"

Dr. Perlinger laughed out loud at their excitement. At last, he held up a hand to quiet them. "What about The Métier School? It has a concert hall with lights and microphones, and there's room for lots and lots of people to come and see you."

He gazed at Iz with shrewd eyes. "I do think it's time to reveal what our outreach has produced so far. The quality of songwriting.

And more than that, the quality of *thinking*. We've thrown ourselves into imagining how we can help others be heard. That is a tremendous accomplishment."

"When are we going to do it?" Daniella demanded.

He rubbed his hands together. "The Winter Concert is coming up in December. I think we should perform our opera then. It'll be a wonderful chance for people from all over the place to see our little ensemble."

"What's an ensemble?" Shemar asked.

Dr. Perlinger waved an arm. "It's *us*."

At the end, while everyone packed up, Iz quietly said to her beloved teacher, "I mean, when I think back to that first meeting, when they were all out of control, I can hardly even believe … this."

"They weren't out of control." Dr. Perlinger smiled. "They just didn't know where to aim their volleys yet."

She grinned. "Well, now they're writing an opera. And apparently Skye is in charge."

"This is when you know it's *working*. When they begin to volley amongst each other. Iz Beaufort, you played a big role in getting them here."

"Uh … I mean … thanks." Warmth spread through Iz.

Teo's phone rang. He pulled it out, strode into the foyer. His voice carried clearly into the meeting room. "Farrington! How are you?"

He left the building, closing the door.

Iz stared after him. The good feeling in her evaporated. In its place was a weird, roiling mix of feelings she couldn't disentangle.

Closing her eyes, she willed her brain to slow down. She was tired, tired of extremes of anger and jealousy. She was exhausted by feelings that took her over.

Teo could talk to anyone he wanted. Even if he chose to go outside so nobody like Iz could hear.

Her hands just kept doggedly helping to clean up. When she was done, her feet carried her to the door. Somehow she pushed it open. She forced herself to walk calmly into the autumn sunshine.

"Oh, yeah, I call her Onion Girl, ha ha," Teo was saying cheerfully. Then he saw Iz and turned away. "Gotta go. Talk to you soon."

Iz inhaled sharply, hurt flowering into anger.

Somehow, she forced her feet to keep walking down the steps.

"Hey, Beaufort! Wait up!"

With every ounce of strength, every bit of control she possessed, Iz swallowed what she wanted to say. She told herself getting furious was kind of like running away from her better self. She didn't want to run anymore. She was trying to stand her ground, figure out what she was feeling, act on that without blowing up. She was choosing audacious, fierce discipline over some knee-jerk reaction.

The trouble was, she had no idea how to sort out her emotions at this exact moment. So she gave Teo a crooked smile as he fell in beside her, then did some of her best acting ever to pretend that everything was fine. He seemed oblivious to the mighty battle flaming in her.

When they got to the restaurant, Iz forced herself to smile, to say goodbye with dignity. She entered Festa, planning to race up to her room as quickly as possible.

But someone beckoned from a table at the back. Vito, Gisele, and Juliana were sitting there looking serious.

"Iz!" Gisele pulled out a chair. "Come. Sit."

"Uh . . . yeah?"

Whenever Gisele asked her to sit down, it never seemed to lead to anything good. Iz started trembling. But, summoning more of the extraordinary acting ability she hadn't known she had, she forced herself to sink onto the seat.

You are Fierce Voice.

Whatever this is, you can handle it.

You're not going to run.

You're tired of running, remember?

If she said it enough times, maybe it would be true.

There was silence.

"They signed it," Juliana said. Her face burst into that grin so much like Teo's.

Iz stared, barely comprehending. "Th-they did?"

"I told you they would," Juliana said with satisfaction. "They didn't want to go to court."

"Also," Gisele said gently, "Juliana's going to help us get things rolling with the adoption."

"Oh! Good!" She tried to sound happy and excited. But Teo's mocking words to Chloe undercut any joy or relief Iz was feeling.

I call her Onion Girl, ha ha.

"Everything okay?" Vito's voice was gruff. "Something happen?"

"Oh, uh, no. I'm just like tired from the outreach today."

"Get you some hot chocolate." Vito lumbered off.

"You know," Gisele said, "I think we're going to have a little get-together to celebrate. We could use one. What do you think, Iz?"

"Oh! Yeah! A get-together sounds great."

"Maybe," Gisele said to Juliana, "you'd like to come. And the Russos."

"We'd love to," Juliana said.

Chapter Forty

Every day, Teo picked her up in the morning and brought her home after school. He filled their walks with cheerful stories and exuberant remarks, like nothing had happened.

At first, Iz struggled to respond.

But after a while, as he kept loyally being there, doubts crept in about what exactly she'd heard.

Maybe he'd been talking about something totally unrelated to her. Or maybe he'd just been running off at the mouth as usual.

So she asked herself—

Can you be confused and hurt but also move past that because it is not helpful to hang onto those hard emotions?

Choosing to put down wounded anger was one of the most difficult things she'd ever attempted. Every ounce of her Fierce Voice had to fight to do it over and over again, every time the painful feelings came back.

But gradually, gradually, she felt better.

On the morning of the gathering, she and Gisele rose early and baked together. The cozy apartment felt warm and safe, with gorgeous smells coming from the oven and opera playing loudly.

Then, out of nowhere, Vito came looming. "You should go do your homework."

Iz blinked at him. "Uh, I don't really have any."

"Nothing?"

"I mean, I guess I could work on this math project thing, but it's not due until—"

He gestured to her room. "Get to it."

"Well, but, it's not even due for—"

"You must have practising to do too," he rumbled. "Haven't heard you working on that Bach for a while."

"I was just playing it last night."

"Stop arguing."

Frowning at how illogical Vito was being, Iz shrugged and looked to Gisele for backup. But Gisele was very busy chopping candied fruit.

"Fine," Iz said. She trailed to her room and closed the door. She took up her guitar and ambled through the Bach piece several times. She practised scales. Then she found herself plucking through Skye's song and softly singing along.

I want you to hear me.
Can you hear me?

Those words resonated so much with Iz now. She was working so hard to hear *herself.* To be brave and to figure out how she felt. To face her fallible and confused heart. The process required every ounce of fierceness inside her. But somehow it also felt good and strong . . . like she was on the right track.

Sometime later, a knock came at the bedroom door. Gisele peeked around. "Iz, can you help me with something for a minute?"

"Okay." She followed her foster mother out into the hallway.

Her jaw dropped.

Balloons and streamers hung everywhere.

A banner spanned the wall in the living room, displaying the words *Happy 15th Birthday, Iz.*

The table was covered by a tablecloth decorated with images of music notes and instruments. In the centre was a huge bouquet of red roses.

"Wh-what . . . ? I thought this get-together was like about the adoption or whatever . . . ?"

"That too. But the main thing is your birthday! We've been keeping it such a secret." Gisele's face was pink.

"Oh . . . wow . . ." Iz was speechless. Nobody had thrown a birthday party for her before. November 5th was pretty low on her radar, on everyone's radar.

"It's not till Thursday next week," Gisele said anxiously, "but we thought we'd have it this weekend so people could come. Is that okay?"

"It's perfect." Iz's eyes darted everywhere. She could hardly process what she was seeing. Later, maybe, in the privacy and silence of her own room, she'd go over it piece by piece.

The doorbell rang.

"Go greet your guests," Vito said with a flourish, like Iz was some kind of superstar.

Iz skittered down the stairs. When she opened the door, the Russos exclaimed and hugged her. They were carrying wine and food and flowers and gift bags.

"Surprise!" Teo grinned down at her.

Iz led them up into the apartment. Gisele and Vito hustled around putting out food and getting drinks for everyone. In addition to everything that Gisele had prepared, Nonna had brought homemade meats, cheeses, and cannoli.

The little living room filled with the sound of people chatting partly in Italian and partly in English.

"Iz is helping to make the dinner," Gisele said proudly. "Spaghetti alla puttanesca."

"Gisele taught me the recipe," Iz added shyly. "It's pretty much the only one I know right now. But I'm going to learn more. I'm going to learn all the family recipes." She looked nervously at Gisele. "I mean, if you still don't mind showing me."

"Mind?" Gisele laughed out loud.

Nonna's smile spanned out like a welcome mat. She said something in Italian.

Teo said immediately, "You're right. She is."

"I am what?" A little flutter of anxiety ran through Iz.

He laughed. "Don't worry, Onion Girl. Nonna likes you a lot."

"Ah," Iz said. "Ha ha. Good."

Onion Girl.

For a fraction of a second, her memory shot back to him standing on the steps talking to Chloe on the phone. Hurt and confusion and shame flooded her all over again. But then she reminded herself she had made the decision to let those things go.

So she looked at him right now with his face full of goodwill and his hair curling in all directions and his tawny eyes fixed on hers. And she chose to remember how he'd been so compassionate, so loyal, so supportive over the last several days.

Not only that, but he really looked good tonight.

She started blushing. "Just a second. Gotta check on the sauce."

In the kitchen, she leaned against the counter.

"Hey, smells beautiful in here." Teo was suddenly standing there, so tall he almost reached the top of the cupboards.

"Oh, uh, g-good. Hope it's, you know, okay."

He lifted the lid of the saucepan and inhaled deeply. "Ahhhh." Then he noticed the tray with the tin foil over it. He reached over to lift the foil up.

Iz said quickly, "No, that's a surprise."

His eyebrows flew up. "A *surprise*!" Cajolingly, he added, "I won't tell, I promise."

"It's for *you*, though," Iz said, her whole face beating.

"For me!" His eyes sparkled. "Now you *have* to let me look. I mean, it's cruel to keep people in suspense ..."

Iz regarded his glowing face. "Fine," she said at last.

Teo reached out his hand but drew it back like he was afraid of being bitten. Finally, he lifted up one side and peered underneath.

"Sfogliatelle! My favourite!"

"Yes, I believe you've told me that a thousand times."

"Did Gisele make it?"

"No." She flushed even more. "I ... I did."

He stared. "*You*?"

"Well, I mean, Gisele showed me all the steps. We basically hung out in the kitchen together while I was doing it this morning. It's *complicated*! All the layers!"

Teo clasped her in an unexpected hug and swung her around. "Beaufort, this is the nicest thing anyone ever did for me."

"Ha!" Iz said. "I guess people have been really mean to you then. Because this is just, like, a pastry."

"Not true," Teo said. "It's so much more than a pastry."

She peeked up at him. His tawny eyes were so magnetic she felt herself being drawn in.

She must surely have totally misheard him.

"Hey! How's dinner coming?"

Vito stood there, holding a half-empty appetizer tray. He thumped it down on the counter.

Iz and Teo turned away immediately.

"I need one of those slotted spoons," Iz blurted, opening the cutlery drawer.

"Where do you keep the measuring cup?" Teo rummaged through a cupboard.

Vito gazed steadily at them while arranging more food on the tray. "Don't forget to visit with your other guests," he said to Iz.

Afternoon rolled into evening. Iz and Gisele triumphantly carried in the dinner, while everyone exclaimed with appreciation. The little apartment rang with laughter and conversation.

After dinner, Gisele produced a cake from nowhere. It was in the shape of a guitar, beautifully decorated in browns and creams. The words, written in red frosting between the black strings, read *Happy 15th Birthday, Iz.*

"Wait, a picture," Vito said.

A bunch of people took out their phones, while Iz sat there in front of an actual birthday cake that was hot with candles that flickered and glowed.

"Make a wish!" Teo said.

Iz closed her eyes and wished as hard as she could. Then she blew out the candles.

She got all of them.

Everyone cheered.

After that, everything was a blur of plates and cake slices and ice cream and passing things around the table until everyone had some. Iz looked shyly at the people sitting there, feeling so surprised and grateful to be at the centre of something this warm and beautiful.

When dinner was over, they went out to the living room. People produced presents and began handing them over.

Nonna had sewn Iz a tote bag with her name on it.

Vito and Gisele had bought her a Métier bomber jacket like Teo's.

Juliana gave Iz a book entitled *Strong Women Who Changed the World.*

And Teo—

He said, "Mine's not ready yet. Sorry."

"Oh! Okay!" She tried to act like that didn't matter.

"But in the meantime, here's this."

It was a stuffed bear holding a guitar.

"This isn't the gift?" she said. "It looks like a gift to me."

"No, this is just the filler. You have to wait for the real thing. It's going to be a little while longer."

Iz said to the bear, "Doesn't it hurt your feelings to be called the filler?" She hugged it and looked shyly at Teo. "I love him."

"What are you going to call him?"

"Not filler." She considered it, then the perfect name came to her. "Alfredo."

"Alfredo!" He laughed out loud, all shining teeth and hair. "Alfredo Beaufort."

"Alfredo Santoro soon," Vito said.

"Or Alfredo Beaufort Santoro if you want," Gisele added.

The evening wore at last to a close. Everyone began gathering coats.

Iz finally asked Juliana the thing that had been on her mind all night. "What's happening with … you know …?"

Juliana zipped up her leather jacket, hoisted her fringed purse onto her shoulder. She regarded Iz with unflappable eyes. "They're starting to interview other kids who were in That Place."

"Other kids," Iz repeated.

Then the full meaning of Juliana's words hit her.

She thought of Skye.

"Like, but what if . . ." she said.

"What if?"

Iz could hardly put her thoughts into words. "What if . . . the kids are sort of scared to say anything?"

She pictured Skye dwarfed by two big police officers trying to get out of her what had happened in That Place. It made Iz's heart hurt to think about it.

Juliana nodded like she could see the worry behind Iz's words. Like she'd had experiences with people who might hold back from telling about a bad thing because they were scared about everyone knowing. Who thought they'd wreck the universe with their dangerous revelations.

"The police are going to be very gentle," Juliana said softly. "Like they were with you."

Iz nodded.

But she was thinking, *Skye isn't just going to trust people right away.*

And if Skye didn't confirm what Iz had said, then maybe the police wouldn't do anything. Those People would just keep on hurting kids over and over again.

Chapter Forty-One

As the weeks passed, the Eastbourne kids kept working on their opera, supported by Manifesto. They wrote the rest of the songs. They decided on the acting parts. They put in moments when each of them would run to an instrument and play a simple thing before going back into character. And they added a narrator to their storyline so it would make more sense to the people watching. Throughout, they argued, laughed, shouted, and tackled each other, volleys shooting out in all directions.

Other elements crept into the project too.

One day, Will, Ahmed, and Kwame introduced their work in progress about heavy metal Mahler. As they pounded big chords, squealed out quieter melodies on the electric guitar and careened into explosive runs, Poppy said, "It's like being on a roller coaster—up and down!"

"No," K'Nesha said. "It's like being at a movie. You know, when they have music in the background. When it gets exciting or scary or sad or whatever—"

"When are we going to have music in the background of our opera?" Daniella interrupted.

"Uh." Will looked at Ahmed and Kwame. ". . . Right now?"

On another day, Rina showed everyone her project, which was an exploration of how music and psychology were linked. She taught them about music therapy and pointed out ways that different instruments could convey particular feelings. The kids demanded to add some of these instruments into the songs.

A really big new concept came on the day Becky presented her programming project. The kids played with it for the whole hour, gleefully mixing up the note patterns to make new images and videos appear.

Then Becky softly said, "Hey . . ."

She squinted, her inventive brain working hard.

"Becky," Iz said, noticing. "Do you have an idea?"

"Well . . . I was just thinking. I could create images especially for our opera and project them onto the backdrop. We could program them to change with certain chords or melodies in each scene."

"So it's responsive . . . in real time . . ." Ahmed looked really interested.

The kids detonated with excitement at the idea.

"We could have a picture of an attic—"

"And like, it could show the shelf where she finds the necklace—"

"And the cupboard where the trophy is—"

"And you could bring back important things by playing the right notes again."

"Could we have some videos of us too?" Shemar spoke slowly. "Like at the end, maybe during 'Fierce Voice Rising' . . . showing us working on the opera."

"Of course we could!" Iz said. She added, "Becky, this is a really wonderful idea."

Becky smiled down at her hands and smoothed her jeans, looking utterly shy at the positive attention. Iz felt a sudden kinship with her. She had a weird feeling they might understand each other.

They spent a few weeks planning and filming little videos. Becky recorded them on her phone, edited everything, and then programmed the keyboard and images to communicate with each other.

On the day she presented the finished product, everyone sat there mesmerized at the pictures. One showed Devanch on the drums, supported by Ahmed. In another, Daniella tried out the oud, with Bijan and LaRoyce behind her. In a third, kids lay on the floor with markers and big paper while Manifesto kneeled there too. Finally, there was an image of the overwhelming mess of wet paper and globs of paste from the day they'd worked together to make a papier mâché globe.

After the photos came the videos.

Shemar and K'Nesha waved a sign that said *Listen to people!* while everyone slid in on their knees and cupped hands to their ears.

Poppy and K'Nesha played an acrobatic clapping game then tumbled together, joining fingers to make a heart.

Manifesto capered around with kids perched on their shoulders and lifted up letters to spell *Together*.

In the final video, everyone passed the papier mâché globe from one to the next. Some kids sent it overhand, some lobbed it from behind, and some spun it on a finger—or tried to. When it got to Teo, he was tackled by Poppy and K'Nesha. He staggered forward, lifted the girls up. They held the globe high like football superstars, while everyone else slammed into the shot, shouting and screaming.

Iz laughed with everyone else at the photos and videos. In this moment, Eastbourne felt like the warmest place anywhere.

Chapter Forty-Two

On the day of the dress rehearsal, Dr. Perlinger arranged for a small bus to pick everyone up at the Eastbourne Centre and transport them to The Métier School.

As the kids tore along the aisle, Miss Cathy called, "Walking!"

Nobody listened. They threw themselves into seats, twisted around to see where everyone else was sitting. The noise level was immense.

Somebody started singing the song about Shemar's necklace. Everyone joined in as the bus pulled away from the curb.

I'm rolling, rolling, over the waves
I'm a necklace made up of three . . .
Grandma, Shemar, and me . . .

When the bus arrived at The Métier School, the kids tumbled onto the sidewalk. They leaped around chasing each other, while Manifesto unloaded instruments. Miss Cathy kept tackling people before they ran into the road.

At last, Dr. Perlinger said cheerfully, "Follow me, everyone!"

He led them up the stairs and into the foyer. As the kids walked into the impressive space, they stared around at the beautiful carved wood, at the curving staircase.

Iz's breath caught in her throat as she watched their reactions to the school she loved so much.

"What's that sound?" Daniella said in a hushed voice.

"People are practising," Dr. Perlinger said.

Everyone listened to flutes, violins, and voices soaring up and down in scales and arpeggios.

"It's like . . ." Skye frowned. "It's like, when it's a really hot night and there's lightning."

Iz's eyes widened. Music heralding a storm. Music *being* the storm.

"That," she said softly, "is perfect."

"I know."

Iz thought then about the other storm she had wanted so many times to ask Skye about. That storm was huge and dangerous, terrifying, but it had the potential to clean the air and force a change.

Now, in this beloved space, with that otherworldly music all around, she summoned the nerve to ask, "Did . . . did the police come and talk to you?"

Skye stiffened. "How did you know?"

"I didn't. I just wondered. They talked to me. And I heard they were going to maybe talk to other kids in That Place. That's all."

Skye regarded Iz with a hint of antagonism. "I said I wouldn't talk to *them*." She crossed her arms protectively as if keeping the police out. "It's none of their business."

"Oh." Iz nodded and crossed her arms too. Then she noticed she had done the exact same motion as Skye and uncrossed them.

"Come on, everyone!" Dr. Perlinger beamed and walked backward along the hall.

As the group trailed after him, Iz's brain worked quickly. If she tried to convince Skye to speak out, would that be a good or a really bad thing to do? On the one hand, Skye was absolutely correct that her experiences in That Place were personal, painful, not for public conversation. No little girl should have to sit with strangers and talk about it. But on the other hand, if nobody spoke out, more and more children would experience those same horrible things.

As they all climbed the stairs to the second floor, Iz tried to think how she could articulate what was in her mind. Finally, anxiously, she said, "That Place ... I don't like to talk about it either. But ... I sort of *did*. Like, when they asked."

"I know. You already told me." Skye looked away.

"Yeah."

They kept walking. Iz was getting completely stressed.

She felt like she had that first day at Eastbourne, when everyone had wheeled around with uncontrolled energy. She'd been desperate, with no idea what to volley or even how to volley. Dr. Perlinger had had to help her figure out how to do it.

She could use his help now. Iz looked up at his bouncing head and silently asked, *How are you supposed to convince someone that doing a difficult and terrifying thing is important?*

At that moment, Dr. Perlinger announced cheerfully, "And here we have practice rooms! Mostly used for practising, and occasionally for other nefarious purposes."

Manifesto laughed.

Iz thought back to the day when Dr. Perlinger had caught Skye and herself in a practice room. She had lost hope of coaxing Skye out, but somehow he had convinced the little girl to let him call Dominion Children's Care.

How had he done that?

She cast her mind back over his words.

Slowly, an idea came to her. "Hey, do you remember when Teo was talking about your song? How it was about Violetta standing up to the dad?"

"Yeah."

"And then Dr. P said he liked that interpretation because it turned the opera on its head ..." She put every ounce of strength into her next words. "He said Violetta told off the dad because there was *no future in being silent or invisible.*"

"So?"

"*Telling* is like that." She willed her words to come out right. "*Telling* is like ... saying, Those People did really awful things. And if I keep silent and invisible, they'll keep doing them." Her voice grew fiercer. "But I've had enough. I'm going to speak up and be, like, a 3D person, and my words are going to bring them down."

As Dr. Perlinger merrily led them past the practice studios, Iz waited anxiously to hear what Skye would say.

After a long silence, Skye muttered, "Why do the police want to even know?"

Iz glanced down at her. "They're investigating Those Guys."

Skye marched ahead grimly.

"And … and if they get like enough evidence, they'll maybe charge them," Iz added.

"They won't get enough evidence."

Iz swallowed. "They might. I mean … they got lots of evidence from *me*."

"Like what?"

"Well, I don't have to tell you." Iz's stomach felt tight. "I mean, you lived there."

"True."

"And it might be good," Iz said slowly, hoping she wasn't doing real harm by continuing this line of talk, "to give them more evidence." She tried to speak casually. "I guess, I mean, the more evidence they get, the more likely the police can charge Those Guys. And then they can't hurt anyone else."

Skye glanced up at Iz. She looked away again.

Iz added softly, "It was hard when I told them. But … not as hard as I expected." She was quiet for a while. "The police were actually sort of nice."

"That surprises me," Skye said.

"I know. I was surprised too."

"Now have a look at *this*!" Dr. Perlinger said. He opened the door to one of the recording studios. The kids ran in. Will and Kwame started telling them about the recording equipment.

"Hey! Skye!" Shemar was beckoning to her. "Come see the soundboard."

Skye stared at Iz with eyes that were stones, then walked with a show of reluctance to Shemar.

After that, Dr. Perlinger showed them the classrooms. He let them go up on the stage in one of the lecture halls and pretend to be giving important speeches from the lectern.

He even took them up to the third floor where the library was. He led them past shelves of musical scores, as well as books and journals about theory, history, and performance.

As they walked downstairs afterward, Skye ended up beside Iz again. "I wish I could go here."

"You *could* go here, when you're old enough."

"Naw. I don't even know how to read all those squiggles. I don't know anything. I just like to write songs."

"We're going to teach you that stuff," Iz said quickly. "Trust me. We're going to help. We're just getting started."

Skye stared up at Iz. "Why do you even care so much?"

Iz's breath caught in her chest.

She thought about her own improbable route to Métier, about all the people who had appeared—almost like magic—to help along the way.

She said, "I have a friend who taught me some stuff so I could audition to come here. And . . . when I asked him why, he said *he* got helped when he was a kid, so he had a responsibility to help me. And he said if he helped me, I had a responsibility to help someone else. He called it a chain of giving."

Skye was uncharacteristically silent.

"So," Iz said. "I can help you. Then you can help someone else."

They had reached the main floor now, and Dr. Perlinger was leading them into the concert hall where they would be performing their opera during the winter concert. The kids stared with wide eyes at the high ceiling, the rows of seats, the balcony above, the stage at the front. They were uncharacteristically silent with awe. They looked afraid to move.

But Dr. Perlinger called heartily, "Everyone, up you go! Investigate!"

Finally, Daniella stomped up the steps onto the stage. "Ooh, this is cool, you can see everything."

Like a switch had been thrown, everyone followed her. Ezekiel and Poppy and K'Nesha scampered around, peeking into the wings. Shemar stared open mouthed at the hot lights. Kateryna climbed the risers at the back and stood looking out at the expanse of empty chairs. Then everyone rushed at the microphones and bellowed into them. Mercifully, the equipment was turned off.

Skye stood in the aisle by Iz's side, looking a little nervous.

"Aren't you going to check it out?" Iz said.

"You come too."

So Iz and Skye walked up onto the stage together.

"Did you do a concert in here?" Skye waved around the hall.

"No. This is going to be my first."

The little girl stared up at her, then broke into a rare grin. "Hey. Twinsies."

Dr. Perlinger clapped his hands. "Have a seat!"

Gradually everyone stopped shouting and capering. They sat down cross-legged on the stage.

Dr. Perlinger smiled over at Iz.

Iz smiled back and came to stand in front of them all. "Look at us! I mean … who expected this? We're here in this place, this amazing concert hall, and we are about to do our last rehearsal before we perform our opera to an audience out there."

Out of nowhere, Shemar said, "*We're* like the silent things."

Iz exhaled softly, transfixed by his volley. "Can you … explain what you mean?"

He struggled to find the right words. "Like … we didn't know we could write those songs until we did. My grandma's necklace … I didn't know I could tell all those things about it. I didn't know it was inside me. Or inside the necklace."

"Or inside the instruments from Syria," K'Nesha said.

"Or inside the trophy."

"Or inside Violetta," Skye broke in, looking at Teo. "Like in my song."

She spoke like it had always been her idea to put the mistreated girl in her lyrics.

Iz's heart felt like it was suspended, waiting and hoping Skye could be like a rewritten Violetta and stand up to Those People by talking to the police.

Teo grinned. "I've seen *Traviata* a thousand times, and I like your Violetta the best."

"Yeah, you saw it with Iz," Daniella teased. "On your *date*."

"Outing!"

"So," Iz said loudly, "let's try to hang onto this feeling, right now. And when we perform our opera tomorrow"—she glanced at Skye, imbued her words with all the fierceness possible—"we can help them see how important it is to help people to speak out and tell their stories."

The little girl stared back at her, expressionless.

Over the next couple of hours, they played and sang through the entire opera while Becky's images lit up the screen behind them. Up in the sound and lighting booth, Métier students experimented with levels. Dr. Perlinger frequently stopped to chat about raising or lowering the volume of the microphones.

Iz expected the Eastbourne kids to explode due to the stop-start nature of the practice. But although they flopped down and rolled around on the floor during the lulls, they snapped back into surprising focus when the next time came to sing.

As the rehearsal went on, various people opened the big doors at the back and poked their heads in to listen. Some drifted down the aisle and sat down. Iz recognized a few of her own teachers—Dr. Nguyen, Dr. Henderson, and Dr. Warren, among others. She couldn't help feeling incredibly proud of what the kids and Manifesto were doing together on the stage.

When the practice came to an end at last, the scattered audience hooted and clapped.

"Bravo!" Dr. Nguyen shouted.

The kids staggered around like they were zombies on their last legs. Manifesto was scarcely any better. Dr. Perlinger ran easily down the stage steps to the main floor, where he met with the other teachers.

Iz overheard her voice instructor, Dr. Henderson, say, "This is really marvellous, Aaron. It needs to have a life past this concert."

"Very little to do with me, you know. It's *their* project. But yes, I'm exploring other performance options."

"On that note," Dr. Warren said, and their voices dropped.

When Dr. Perlinger and the teachers had finally stopped talking, Miss Cathy helped to corral the kids out to the waiting bus. Everyone climbed on board, Manifesto included. Then they all drove back to the Eastbourne Centre.

The sky had darkened by now, and the centre was lit up from inside. Iz saw figures waiting in the entrance. As the bus pulled up at the curb, parents and guardians came out to meet it. The children tumbled onto the sidewalk, shouted goodbye to everyone, waved, and headed off.

At last Manifesto were the only ones left. Slowly they departed as well. Jasleen, Becky, and Rina trotted off laughing. Ahmed and Will and Kwame set out, talking loudly about their heavy metal version of Mahler's *Symphony of a Thousand*.

Bijan and LaRoyce left arm in arm, completely in sync, finishing each other's sentences as usual.

Watching them walking closely together, Iz's eyes underwent a strange shift, refocusing and readjusting until she saw the boys in a new way.

"Are they, like . . . ?" she asked Teo.

He laughed gently. "You only just figured that out?"

Learning to listen. Learning to look.

"It takes me a while," she said.

"Apparently."

Unexpected lightness and exultation flooded her. At Bijan and LaRoyce having each other. At people not being alone.

She and Teo strolled at a leisurely pace through the dark streets to Festa. Iz was grateful for his presence, for the way he laughed as he told her about the Awkward Flash Mobs that would ambush Métier teachers with terrible singing and dancing.

"Haha, we got Nguyen three times in one day! But then he like *erupted* into this aggressive ballet thing, and none of us knew he had all this dance training."

Iz laughed and squeezed his hand.

She tried to think about warm Festa ahead, about this loyal boy beside her, about Skye going home to Winifred. She tried not to think about Those People and about the shadows all around.

Fierce Voice. Fierce Voice. Fierce Voice.

Chapter Forty-Three

The day of the concert dragged. Not even Ahmed's electric Paganini impression at lunch properly held Iz's attention. She just kept checking her watch and thinking, *five hours to go ... four hours to go ... three hours to go ...* How were the Eastbourne kids getting through this long day? Iz couldn't help grinning, imagining them all blasting out chaotic, excited volleys.

After school, Manifesto walked over to the Eastbourne Centre. A thousand years later, the small bus arrived to take everyone to Métier for the concert.

"Slow down," Miss Cathy called as the kids scrambled everywhere to find a place to sit. She looked extremely stressed.

But Dr. Perlinger was serene. "Everyone, take a seat as soon as you can. The sooner we are settled, the sooner we can head ... to our very first performance!"

They all cheered like mad and fell into some kind of barely contained order.

It was a short ride, luckily.

When they entered the Métier foyer, pine fronds hung everywhere. Scattered among them were bells, snowflakes, red bows, and tiny white lights.

A lot of other people were already there. Some were parents and family members, waiting for the doors to the concert hall to open.

Some were Métier students, giddy and leaping around, pumped to perform.

"Let's go warm up," Iz said, beaming at everyone.

The kids followed her up the curving staircase like they owned the place. She led them into the Berenger-May Room, which would be their holding space until the time came for their performance.

Once inside, Iz and LaRoyce began to run everyone through a series of vocal exercises. Iz sang and LaRoyce played piano. Then Manifesto all picked up instruments and joined in. The kids danced all over the place while they sang the warmups. Manifesto could not help laughing. Iz couldn't either.

"Okay," she said to them at last. "You're good to go. Try not to destroy the room while we wait."

As they cheered and started to run around, she sat down to tune her beloved, unique guitar quietly, ear to the strings, picturing the notes like rubbery lines that became taut and smooth as they met the exact pitch.

"Iz, I don't know where my necklace is. It's gone!" Shemar's voice broke through her concentration, hand to his neck. "I had it on, but it must have fallen off."

Everyone started looking all over the floor.

"It could be in the hallway," Bijan said.

"I'll go look!" Daniella jumped up.

"No," Iz said quickly. "I will. You kids stay here."

In the end, several members of Manifesto fanned out along the hallway and down the stairs to the foyer, which was now almost wall-to-wall people.

LaRoyce and Bijan went outside to check the sidewalk and see if the bus was still there so they could search it. Becky and Jasleen headed to the door and started zigzagging back laboriously toward Iz. Iz began at the foot of the staircase, intending to move toward Becky and Jasleen.

The foyer was crowded and hot. A bit of claustrophobia rose in Iz. She pushed it down, tried to breathe through it.

Notice the pine boughs, the smell of perfume, the carved wooden walls . . .

But her brain began to creak out of control, and she could tell that another panic attack was threatening to make an appearance.

Everything seemed to be breaking into fragments.

Flashes of winter coats, purses. Mouths moving, laughing.

And then—

Iz froze. She rubbed her eyes, blinked, started to tremble.

No. No. There was a peace bond.

But nonetheless The Man was standing there, looking away from her toward the hallway that led to the practice rooms. Same stance, legs slightly apart, leaning back like he owned the place.

More than anything, Iz wanted to run.

But she clenched her fists. She couldn't, ***wouldn't,*** abandon the Eastbourne kids on the night of their performance.

So she stood there as empty and vulnerable as she had that night in the park, by the slide, in the sleet, when she was only her fractured self.

Except now a wild dragon rose inside her and with it, a sense of the injustice of this moment. It was not fair that he had come here, to this school, to this concert. He did not have the right to defile something so rare and wonderful. She would not tolerate it.

Iz lurched forward, boomed with a Fierce Voice that trembled but nonetheless seemed to shake Métier. "You leave me alone! Get out! Get out of here!"

As if in slow motion, The Man turned to her. "Pardon me?"

She saw his whole face then.

The room swam. Iz blinked and staggered. "I-I'm so sorry. I thought you were someone else—"

She turned and pushed desperately past people, leaving the stranger standing there looking confused.

"Found it!" Jasleen was suddenly beside her, holding Shemar's necklace triumphantly.

"Ah! G-good!" Iz stammered.

Jasleen and Becky took off up the stairs. But Iz stood in place, trying to get her head together.

"You're amazing! You're perfect!" A rich caramel-brown voice resonated out over everything. It was unmistakably Teo.

Her brain somersaulted, confused. Was he praising her for bravely confronting someone she'd thought was The Man? But she hadn't been brave. She'd yelled at some poor guy who was just trying to enjoy his evening.

Iz looked wildly around to see where Teo was. At last she spotted him standing in the alcove near the stairs.

He wasn't alone. Chloe Farrington was right there beside him. Iz recognized her from that FaceTime call in the cafeteria.

As if in slow motion, Teo wrapped Chloe in a hug. He swung her around. Their heads bent close for a long time.

Iz stood staring like a fool. At last, she made her jerky legs start climbing up the stairs.

She sank onto a couch in the Berenger-May Room.

"Hey." Skye sat down next to Iz.

"Hey," Iz said thickly.

"You need a hug?" Skye stared into Iz's face.

"Sure."

"Sit still. Incoming."

Skye wrapped her arms around Iz and squeezed tighter than any boa constrictor. She practically crushed Iz's bones. "There. Consider yourself hugged."

Then her eyes grew shadowed. "So … uh … I have to tell you something." Her voice became almost a whisper.

"What is it?"

"*You* know."

Iz frowned, forcing her brain away from Teo and Chloe. "What do I know?"

"*They* came over this morning."

Iz's jaw dropped.

When she trusted herself to speak, she whispered in a low, furious, determined voice, "What did *They* want?"

"They wanted me to tell," Skye hissed back, imitating her.

Iz blinked, bewildered. Then she realized the little girl was not talking about The Man and The Woman. She was talking about the *police.*

"Oh!" she exclaimed.

Skye climbed over the couch's arm and slid down beside Iz. She put her head against Iz's shoulder. "I … said to Winifred that I'd maybe changed my mind. So they came over and …"

Iz waited tensely.

After what seemed like an eternity, Skye muttered, "And … I told about everything."

Iz exhaled. "That was really brave, you know."

"Yeah, I know." Skye squinted up at Iz. "And … like, you were actually right."

"I-I was? About what?"

"It was bad, but it wasn't *so* bad."

Iz nodded, remembering her own conversation with the police. They had inched with her into the horribleness of That Place, never moving more quickly than she could handle.

"I-I'm sorry," she whispered. "I'm sorry you had to tell. But—"

"But maybe we can put Those Guys away. I know, you don't have to keep saying it," Skye said.

Teo burst into the room, glowing and exuberant, high-fiving people.

Painful electricity shot through Iz.

But she told herself that he did not get to have top billing in her mind right now. Skye's bravery mattered so much more than Iz's hurt feelings.

She shoved Teo fiercely out of her head.

Chapter Forty-Four

A Métier student leaned around the door. "You're next after the junior flute ensemble."

"Okay, everyone!" LaRoyce called. "Line up!"

After an impossible period of mayhem, they trooped down the stairs and into the backstage area of the theatre.

Ezekiel darted forward and peeked around the curtain at the audience. "I see my mom!" He waved and beamed.

They all started poking their heads out and gesturing at people.

"Technically," Will told them, "you're supposed to wait out of sight."

"But if we keep hiding, how are they going to know we're here?" Daniella said.

"They kind of assume we are," Kwame said.

"But what if they're *worried* we might not be? Shouldn't we try to make them feel better?" Daniella looked ready to debate to the death.

"Fair." Very deliberately, Ahmed peeked his head out as well.

Most of Manifesto took a turn.

At last, Iz gazed out too. There in the fourth row centre were Vito and Gisele, looking very proud and slightly nervous. Gisele was wearing her good dress and Vito had on a shirt and tie.

Even amid her turmoil, Iz felt a wave of gratitude when she saw them there. Vito and Gisele were like great strong edifices that could not be knocked over by the wind or shaken by the movement of the earth. They were true and they were hers.

That was something.

That was actually pretty much *everything.*

The MC's voice burst into the silence. "Next, we're so excited to welcome the Eastbourne Ensemble to the stage."

This was it.

The audience clapped and cheered and hooted with huge enthusiasm.

Miss Cathy whispered, "*Walking* to your places."

The kids found their spots in an actually measured, serious way, and waited patiently while Manifesto took up their instruments.

Dr. Perlinger walked to the podium. His voice boomed out of the microphone. "Good evening, everyone. Tonight, you have the great good fortune to witness the extraordinary results of a new partnership between The Métier School and the Eastbourne Centre. These remarkable young people have been coming together each week since early September, mentoring each other while crafting and performing original music."

He raised a hand to Iz. "It's the brainchild of Iz Beaufort here, who has been the glue running through all of our sessions. Iz, would you like to say a few words?"

Iz stepped forward to the microphone.

When she spoke, she was startled by how loud her voice was. "So, yeah, I first suggested doing an outreach to Eastbourne because, when I was a kid, I attended after-school classes there. And I knew how much it would have meant to me to have a music program there, like a really challenging one. So, I had the idea of kind of *presenting* music to these kids. But . . ."

She looked around at them.

"I didn't realize how hard it actually is to be a teacher. I figured I'd just be, like, you know, saying stuff and having everyone listen and go, *Great, thanks, that is so wise!*"

The audience rumbled with laughter.

"And I didn't realize how much of teaching comes out of listening, out of being, like, open to what the kids were saying. Dr. Perlinger calls it the volley."

She smiled at the teacher she adored. He beamed back.

"Also," Iz continued, "I definitely didn't understand how many of our big ideas would come out of, like, little moments where someone just said something on their mind and then other people took it and raised it up sort of and turned it into something so much bigger. We listened to each other. We tried to figure out how to build something, like, *good* out of all of us working together." She paused. "It was hard and it was amazing too."

The audience broke into applause, while Iz stood there flushed and amazed at their response to her stammered and improvised words.

Dr. Perlinger turned to the Eastbourne kids. "Have you enjoyed the classes?"

They exploded into loud whoops and yelling.

The audience burst out laughing.

Dr. Perlinger smiled broadly. "Now, without further ado, please enjoy our inaugural performance of *The Opera of Silent Things*."

Silence fell.

Skye stepped forward into the attic, into the spotlight, into what she was meant to do. Ahmed softly strummed chords on the electric guitar, and LaRoyce began to play the theme from the statue song.

Iz's emotions soared, primal and rapturous.

She felt all of it.

Trophies. Bunnies. Thought Books. Foster kids who wanted so hard to do the right thing. People trying and hoping, feeling and sometimes failing, falling but not about to be defeated.

Listen.

Pay attention.

Lift them up.

Chapter Forty-Five

A million years or a second later, the last notes of "Fierce Voice Rising" resolved into a soft hum that drifted over the auditorium like something elemental and infinite.

Silence fell. The audience didn't react for a moment, just sat there spellbound.

When applause erupted at last, it wasn't just applause. There were hoots, whistles, shouts of "Bravissimo!"

The Eastbourne kids stared open mouthed, then burst into gargantuan grins and cheered for themselves too. Iz stole a look at Skye. The little girl's eyes were massive as she took everything in.

Iz whispered, "Let's bow together like we practised."

Everyone joined hands and bent their heads to the audience at exactly the same time.

When the clapping had finally finished, Dr. Perlinger and Miss Cathy led them back upstairs to the Berenger-May Room. The Eastbourne kids began screaming and running around.

Skye poked Iz hard. "We were good, right?"

"We were *awesome*."

Skye looked up suspiciously like she could tell Iz was keeping something back. "Is … is the Eastbourne Ensemble over now or something?"

"Is it *over*?" Iz repeated incredulously.

"Now that the concert is done."

"The concert," Iz said, putting as much emphasis onto her words as she could muster, "was just the *beginning*."

Skye nodded and glared around like she didn't actually care. "Okay. I guess that's good."

"I guess it *is*," Iz said.

Skye's foster mother came running up. "Honey! That was *fantastic!*"

"Of course it was," Skye said smugly.

"When you sang the song about the statue coming to life, do you know that I just sat there crying?" Her foster mother bent down so she could see right into Skye's eyes.

Skye looked pleased with herself. "So can we get dessert now like you said?"

Winifred laughed. "Yes, I think we should, don't you?"

Skye tugged on her foster mother's arm, pulling her toward the door of the Berenger-May Room. But a minute later, she ran back and threw herself at Iz in a violent lunge that was part hug and part attack.

"Next week. Same time, same place," she whispered in Iz's ear.

"Absolutely," Iz said.

She watched Skye and Winifred walk away.

She told herself she felt great. She was so proud of Skye. Of all of them.

But under her deliberate thoughts, that other thing brewed.

You're amazing! You're perfect!

She winced.

Before she could think any further about it, though, Dr. Perlinger came strolling across the room toward her. He smiled and waved. Dr. Warren was walking with him.

Iz flushed to see her Profiles of Composers teacher up close for the first time. She felt like she was standing in front of some celebrity. Dr. Warren had played a larger role than she knew in shaping Iz's thinking this term.

"Iz!" Dr. Perlinger said heartily. "You know Dr. Warren, yes?"

"Uh, yeah," Iz said, all tongue-tied. She stammered, "I actually, like, love your class. *Helpers* . . . it's amazing."

She felt like a total fool.

But Dr. Warren grinned. "I'm glad! I often think of *you*, you know, while I'm teaching that class."

"Y-you do?"

"Oh, yes. Aaron and I frequently chat about you. Such an achievement tonight!"

"What? Really?" Iz was completely overwhelmed now. "Yeah, no, but, I mean, the kids actually did it. Like, I was just mostly trying to figure out how you're supposed to teach. That was my special project this term, like experimenting with some stuff about music pedagogy. I only wrote one song for this. The kids came up with the ideas and Manifesto shaped them and put together a lot of the music, and I basically just kind of . . ."

"*Helped.*" Dr. Warren and Dr. Perlinger said it at the same time.

They laughed.

Then Dr. Perlinger rubbed his hands together. "And on that subject, Iz, there's something Dr. Warren wants to run by you. An idea."

"R-really?" Iz glanced shyly at her.

Dr. Warren said, "I'm quite involved in activism related to children and musical outreach. I help a number of organizations that are working to bring music to children in crisis around the world."

"Oh!" Iz said, surprised.

But then, she wasn't. She thought of Dr. Warren's focus on people caring for each other. She remembered the lecture about how a rich benefactor had supported the young Verdi, and how the right manuscript had been given to him at the right time to help make sense of his grief and bring him back from darkness. She thought of straw placed on roads to lessen the discomfort of a beloved composer close to death.

"So, Iz," Dr. Warren said, "I wanted to mention that there's an international conference on children's rights coming up next year. It's in Rome. They've put out a call for original children's performances.

They'll select one to close the conference, from my understanding." She paused. "And I think that the Eastbourne Ensemble should submit its opera for consideration."

Iz's eyes opened wide. "W-what?"

"See, here's my opinion," Dr. Warren said, in her gritty, compelling way. "This group is a powerful voice speaking out about empathy and looking out for each other. It deserves a higher profile. It needs to be *heard*. Our hurting planet desperately needs it at the moment." She turned to Dr. Perlinger. "Am I right?"

"I certainly think so," Dr. Perlinger said. "Iz, what do *you* think?"

They both looked at her, waiting.

Iz stared back, mouth gaping.

What do I think?

Slowly, she began to make sense of Dr. Warren's words.

A million thoughts started shooting through her mind. "Uh, I mean, what would we have to do? Film or record it, I guess. And—but—if we got chosen, would we have to pay to go? Because I don't think Vito and Gisele ..."

Dr. Warren waved her hand as if brushing away Iz's concerns. "If you were actually selected, the money wouldn't be hard to figure out. The patrons have deep pockets. And we can probably apply for some funding. Maybe the conference itself would help."

Dr. Perlinger added, "The performance is already filmed. We did that tonight along with the rest of the concert."

Excitement built in Iz as she looked from one teacher to the other. "I mean, yeah ... it sounds amazing. Not that they'd pick us or anything. But still ..."

"But still," Dr. Perlinger twinkled back at her. "But still!"

"We need to share that 'Fierce Voice Rising,'" Dr. Warren added. "A ferocious song, by the way. About ripping down barriers, demanding to be heard. Without such fierce voices, what do we actually have?"

Dr. Perlinger nodded as if everything was unfolding exactly as it should.

Chapter Forty-Six

At the end of the concert, Iz wove through the thick crowd looking for Vito and Gisele.

The panicky, claustrophobic feeling started to rise again.

The Man had not been there before, but he might be now.

"No," she whispered fiercely. She was feeding herself scary stories, like some kid sitting by a campfire in the dark. There was a peace bond against Those People. They were not going to come after her again.

Still, her eyes darted everywhere and her heart raced.

When Iz finally saw Vito and Gisele standing in a corner looking pink and proud, she practically ran to them. "Hey! Hi!"

Vito unexpectedly wrapped an arm around her shoulders and squeezed.

"Cara," Gisele said. "What a performance! Those kids . . ."

Iz gripped her hand. "I know! I'm so glad you got to hear them. I mean, I'm sorry you had to miss work tonight though."

Vito said gruffly, "To see my daughter perform? Don't be sorry."

My daughter.

For a split-second, warmth completely overran her.

But then—

She saw Teo.

He was standing not far away, talking fast about something he obviously thought was funny. Another guy stood there, firing comments right back like they were in some competition of hilarity. And on the other side of Teo—

Chloe Farrington laughed, tossing her chestnut hair back.

Iz's stomach twisted painfully.

Teo glanced over at her, said something to the other two and pointed in her direction.

Iz's hands started tingling.

Don't come over. Don't come over.

But the three of them were walking toward her now.

"Hey, look who it is!" Vito boomed, clapping a hand on Teo's back. "My handyman."

"Anytime!" Teo said brightly. He turned to Iz. "Beaufort. This is Chloe and her boyfriend Dre. They drove three hours to be here tonight."

"Hey," Iz said tightly.

"Amazing performance!" Chloe's voice in person was as resonant as Teo's.

"Thanks."

Teo looked deliberately at Chloe like he was waiting.

"Iz," she said, "I have to apologize. I went at you a little hard on the phone."

Iz looked everywhere but at Chloe. "That's okay," she muttered.

"But," Teo said to Chloe with a dazzling smile, "we learned a valuable lesson, right? I'm actually capable of handling my own relationships."

"You are *totally* capable of handling your own relationships." Chloe turned to Iz and added impishly, "And on that note, I know something you don't know!"

"Shut up, Farrington," Teo said immediately.

Dre added, "Come on, let's leave them alone. Iz, nice to meet you." He practically dragged Chloe off into the crowd.

Iz was left standing there mutely with Teo, Vito, and Gisele.

Totally capable of handling your own relationships.

I know something you don't know.

The words jangled meaninglessly in her head.

"Uh," she said. "I'm just . . . I have to . . ."

She didn't even know what she was trying to say.

What did real people do at a moment like this?

When you'd ruled out meltdowns and running, but you still totally hated how you were feeling, what was your Fierce Voice supposed to say? What did bravery look like?

Iz stood there making faces apologetically at the three of them, smiling in what she knew was a weird, crooked way. She shook her head wordlessly, then nodded to nobody in particular.

"You okay?" Vito said, frowning.

"I'm sort of, like . . ." She crossed her arms tightly.

"Beaufort. Do you want to sit down?" Teo looked alarmed.

"Uh. I don't know."

"Come on, let's go over here." Vito put a hand on Iz's back and propelled her to a chair nearby.

"Do you want some water?" Teo was asking.

"I want . . ." Iz said.

She looked at him.

"I want . . ."

They waited.

She glanced at Vito then, remembering when she had gathered her courage to have it out with him so they could resolve their problems. She clung to that memory, got strength from it.

"I want . . . to talk to you for a minute," Iz said to Teo in a low voice.

Vito looked very suspiciously at Teo, like he was sure the boy had done something horrible. Teo flinched, genuinely cowed.

"Come on," Gisele said to Vito. "Come with me. Leave them alone for a minute."

Vito made a rumbling noise but followed her.

Teo squatted down so his eyes were level with Iz's. "What's wrong?"

Iz let out the longest breath ever.

Forced the words to come out slowly.

Tried to make sure that they represented what she was feeling without turning into something wild she couldn't control.

"I'm—I'm kind of upset," she said at last. "I don't know how to say it. I'm ... I think I'm kind of upset about *you,* actually."

Teo's eyes darted back and forth across her face. "Tell me what I've done," he said, voice thick with worry.

Iz stared at him in disbelief.

She wanted to shout, *you know exactly what you've done!*

But she forced the fury to slow down, swallowed hard, gritted her teeth till she was calm. "One thing happened a while ago. And something else happened ... today."

He waited, looking pained and bewildered.

"The phone." Iz put each word down like a paving stone building a pathway to somewhere she didn't know. "Outside Eastbourne. I ... heard you talking to Chloe on the phone and telling her how you call me Onion Girl. And I felt, I felt hurt by that. I felt like you were making fun of me."

His eyes flew wide. "Oh, Beaufort, no, wait—"

Iz went bravely on. "And ... earlier tonight. Shemar lost his necklace. I was looking for it. And I ... I saw you. By the stairs. With her."

He was frowning now with confusion.

Iz measured each word, analyzed it for honesty and fairness to ensure that it was occupying a middle place between extremes of emotion. "I ... heard you say she was perfect, and you spun her around, and then I think you kissed her. I don't know for sure though, I couldn't see that part—"

"I didn't kiss Chloe Farrington!" Teo's voice was high and tight.

"Okay. You didn't kiss her."

She forced her words to stay calm. Willed herself not to lose it.

"I ... I just wanted to say I saw it," she whispered. "I'm sorry I did. I wasn't planning to. I wasn't, like, sneaking around trying to catch you with her or anything. I was just looking for the necklace."

She paused.

"And I ... I just wanted to tell you how I was feeling when I saw it. That's all. I was ... I was really kind of sad."

Tears started trickling down her face. She wiped them away but kept staring at him.

Teo shook his head, eyes full of some intense thing she couldn't quite identify. Was he trying to figure out how to explain away what she'd seen? Or was he about to tell her he was relieved she knew everything at last—to point out that Chloe was low maintenance while Iz was a little too much for him to deal with, a little too filled with angst and drama?

Whatever it was, Iz steeled herself.

She could handle hearing whatever he was going to say.

Not only that, but she was going to feel it, acknowledge it, volley a reasonable response back without losing herself. Because it was better to know than not. She wasn't new to people leaving or making her go. She would face this loss with dignity.

"Beaufort." His voice sounded like it was full of tears. "I'm so sorry. I've been trying to keep this . . . thing a secret."

Iz took in that pain and felt it in her heart, in her stomach.

She breathed with it, forced herself to get to know its horribleness.

When she could trust herself to speak, she said, "I-I wish you'd just told me. But I get that maybe you thought I'd go ballistic or something. With good reason. I'm sort of working on trying to figure out what I'm thinking and feeling before I act. And I want to be better at considering, like, the effect of what I say. So . . . I won't stand in the way or be weird or anything."

He stared at her. "What are you talking about?"

"You and Chloe," Iz said evenly. "I'm sorry you had to keep it a secret. But you don't have to worry about me."

Teo shook his head vehemently. He pulled out his phone, started scrolling and tapping like he was trying to attack it.

"If you come with me right now," he said, "I-I can show you something and it will clear all of this up. It's still open but we have to hurry."

She paused, sifted through her thoughts. "I am really feeling kind of like emotional, and I don't actually want to go anywhere right now."

"No, you don't understand. I-I have been *planning* a thing, a-a *secret*, and I just totally wrecked it. Like, *wrecked it.*"

Despite the awfulness of the moment, he looked utterly compelling crouched in front of her, his eyes agitated and face taut.

She took a deep breath.

What would a normal person, a reasonable person, say in this moment?

At last, she said, "You were planning a thing?"

He nodded. "I . . . I . . . It's hard to explain. I'd have to show you. You'd have to come with me."

Iz paused. "Where is it?"

"Not that far. A couple of blocks."

Iz looked over at Vito and Gisele, who were standing by the opposite wall, pretending not to be paying attention. She thought back to that day when she had sat on her bedroom floor talking with Gisele about Teo.

You have big feelings. You're human. And believe me, so is Teo.

After a pause, she said, "I'd have to let them know where I'm going."

Teo stood up. "Of course. Of course. Let's tell them."

Chapter Forty-Seven

"Teo and I are going for a walk. Is that okay?"

Vito regarded Iz with narrowed eyes. He glared at Teo like he was still sure the boy had done something wrong. "You coming back here or dropping her off at home?"

"At home," Teo said.

"Have fun," Gisele said, with worried eyes.

"Okay. We will." Iz hoped it would be true.

Gisele ran a hand along Iz's cheek. "I'll be up when you get back."

Iz nodded unsteadily.

But a warm feeling spread through her, despite her worries. There would always be Gisele now. There would always be Vito and Dr. Perlinger and Métier and Eastbourne. They were powerful things she could carry in her heart. They were fuel for her Fierce Voice. She just needed to keep remembering that.

"You . . . ready?" Teo said to Iz at last.

"Uh . . . yeah, okay." Although she was nowhere near ready.

"Have a good night," Teo said to Vito and Gisele.

Iz followed him through the thinning crowd, out the doors, and into the whirling December snow.

Teo turned right along the sidewalk. They walked silently together for several minutes. At last, he stopped in front of a building, opened the door, and held it while Iz walked through.

Directly ahead was a counter behind which an elderly man was sweeping the floor. Teo half ran up to him. "Two tickets, please."

"We've just closed, son. Sorry. Come back tomorrow."

"Ahh." Teo took a deep breath. He leaned on the counter. "I'll pay you, like, whatever you want, if you could just let us in for a bit. I have to *show* her something . . ." He gestured at Iz. "It has to be tonight. It *has to.*"

"What's so important?" the man asked.

Teo lowered his voice and spoke urgently while Iz stood there cross-armed. The man looked over at her, then back at Teo.

"So," Teo said at last, "that's why I would be so grateful if you could let us in, even for a few minutes."

The man was quiet for a bit.

He straightened the volunteer badge on his shirt.

"I'm not supposed to," he said. "I'm shutting the place down."

Teo grimaced, his hands clenched.

"But as it happens," the man continued, "I don't have anywhere particular to be tonight. Nowhere out of the ordinary, anyway. *I'm* not a young man on a mission." He smiled. "Go in."

"Ahh!" Teo leaped into the air. "Thank you! Thank you!" He pulled out his wallet. "What do I owe you?"

The man waved his hand. "It's after hours. No charge. I'll settle in with my book and see you when you come out."

"We'll be fast," Teo said.

The man waved his hand. "Take your time. No sense rushing things." He gestured to his right. "Go through the door over there. Just make sure it's completely closed before you open the second one."

"Thanks! Thanks so much! We will." He turned to Iz. "Come on."

Teo opened the glass door the man had indicated and waved at Iz to go through. Puzzled, she stepped into a whitewashed area with a second door on the opposite wall. Teo followed, closed the first door firmly behind him and pushed the second one inward.

An unexpected swirl of tropical heat exhaled all over Iz. She smelled something fragrant. What was it? Flowers, maybe something citrusy too.

"Go in," Teo said, holding the door open for her.

So Iz walked through.

An object danced in the periphery of her vision. She shot around to see a brilliant blue butterfly zigzagging above enormous ferns. It came to rest on a little round platform that held orange slices.

Then Iz became aware of other movements. Creatures fluttered everywhere. Bright flowers waved. Somewhere nearby, a stream was bubbling.

"What *is* this place?" she said out loud.

"It's a butterfly sanctuary. You can come here and hang out with butterflies, tropical flowers, warm breezes . . ." Teo paused. "Just like you talked about that day. Remember? At Métier, when we stopped fighting."

Iz stared at him, frowning.

He added, "And I said we should go to Hawaii . . ."

Slowly, the conversation came back to her.

"Ohh," she said.

She had been so happy to be friends with Teo again. She hadn't wanted to sully the moment by sharing anything dark from her past.

One day I'll tell you about it.

Like, in some tropical place with butterflies and warm breezes and flowers.

At that moment, an orange and black butterfly landed on the top of his head. Totally unplanned, she barked out a guffaw. Teo looked completely ridiculous.

He misinterpreted her laughter. "I get it. You're, like, thinking this doesn't explain me on the phone with Chloe that day, or being with her tonight . . ."

"Uh, no," Iz said. "You have a butterfly on your head."

"I do?" He put up a hand to feel his hair.

"Be careful! You're going to hurt it!"

He dropped his arm immediately. "Well, you've got one on your wrist."

Iz looked down to see a brown butterfly slowly opening and closing its wings. She stared, fascinated. She raised her hand to see it better. A second butterfly, this one pale blue, fluttered around her fingers, then landed there.

"Oh," Iz breathed. The whole world was distilled down to these two delicate creatures gently fanning their wings. She could feel her heart slowing down and her lungs relaxing in the humid air.

Teo said, "Come on. There's this one place I want to show you."

He took off along a little stone path, and Iz followed. The path curved over little hills, and came at last to a small bridge overtop a stream. Teo strode to the highest point on the bridge. After a hesitation, Iz joined him. She leaned on the railing.

"You can see everything from here," Teo said. "It's like ... the whole world."

They were quiet for a while, watching the butterflies fluttering around and landing on the tropical flowers.

Then Teo said, "So ..."

Iz's stomach tensed right up. But she told herself that was okay. She could handle whatever was going to come out of his mouth.

Teo glanced sideways at her. "Chloe has these amazing earrings. They're ... custom made. One's Violetta and one's Alfredo."

Iz blinked. She wasn't sure what she had been expecting, but it wasn't that. "Oh. Right. So romantic. I heard you two FaceTiming about it."

"Violetta died a horrible death, so I don't know how romantic that is ultimately." He paused. "But anyway, the main thing is, those are earrings that were made for Chloe *specifically*."

"Well, obviously. I doubt you can go into any jewellery place and just be like, *Give me some* Traviata *earrings, my good man*."

"No." He leaned on the railing, looking down at the little stream. This went on so long that Iz started to think the conversation was over.

But he spoke again. "Her dad's a jeweller, though, so he makes her stuff like that."

"Oh," Iz said helpfully. "So ..."

"So." His eyebrows shadowed his eyes. "You probably don't care, and you maybe don't even want it now, but I ... I asked him to make me something for your birthday. And he did, although it wasn't ready in time for the party or even for the actual day."

A weird little feeling rippled through Iz.

"And anyway," he continued, "tonight Chloe brought it to the concert. And I stayed behind when everyone went upstairs to the Berenger-May Room so I could get it from her and pay for it. And when I said she was, like, amazing, it was because she'd brought it three hours in the snow from where she's going to school. And because I was totally happy with how it had turned out."

Iz blinked.

"And yes," Teo said. "I can be a gregarious guy. Maybe I didn't need to spin her around. But let's remember her boyfriend was right there at the time."

"He … was?"

"Yeah, Dre was standing beside her."

"Oh."

There had been a lot of people nearby.

"So, anyway … here it is." Teo fumbled something out of his jacket pocket. "If, I mean, you want it. If you don't, whatever."

He held out a long velvet box. Iz stared at it for a minute. Then she took it in her hands.

"This is for *me*?"

"Yeah, it's for you."

Iz was suddenly almost afraid to breathe. "Should … should I open it?"

He shrugged and nodded. "If you hate it, I'll take it back and you won't have to see it again. Or, like, *me,* if you don't want."

With trembling fingers, she opened the box.

"Oh," she said.

A thin gold chain nestled against blue velvet, shiny like a dragon's scales. But that was not the main thing. Attached to the chain was a pendant covered in tiny glittering white stones.

It was a small, perfect onion.

"Those are real diamonds," Teo said anxiously. "I mean, I know that they're small, almost just dust, but it's basically all I could afford."

"You got me an onion," Iz said, staring at it.

"I got you an onion." He started talking quickly. "Because, I mean, I thought about how you said you would one day tell me about your past when there were tropical flowers and butterflies and everything. But then ..."

Iz waited.

"You didn't get to do that at all." His voice grew angry. "You ended up telling everything to the police, and it was scary and hard, and you had to be brave even when you were probably terrified ... and it shouldn't have had to be like that."

Iz's eyes blurred.

"And so," he went on, "I was planning to bring you here this week, once the concert was over. I was going to tell you I couldn't fix that stuff, but I could at least give you the tropical things ... and then I was going to say ..."

He paused so long she looked up at him.

"Ahh," Teo said, rubbing a hand across his forehead, and causing the butterfly on his hair to take off in alarm. "I was going to say, you can be just as you are, like, complicated and prickly and ... and strong-willed and scared and brilliant and brave, and I will support you. And you don't ever have to tell me a thing, not ever, if you don't want to."

Iz was scarcely breathing.

"And I was going to say ..."

He looked totally anguished.

"I was going to say, like, would you ever want to reconsider this friendship thing? Because, Beaufort, eventually I'd really like to be your boyfriend, if that doesn't sound too cheesy. But obviously this whole thing got significantly messed up. And I get that you probably don't ..."

"Can you help me put it on?" Iz said softly.

"Oh! Sure!"

He lifted the necklace out, stood behind her, and looped it around her neck. She could feel his fingers fumbling as they fastened the clasp.

"There," he said. "It . . . looks great."

Iz ran her hand over the little jewelled onion. She looked up at his distressed expression.

"I love it," she whispered. And then, "I-I . . ."

He waited.

She took a deep breath. "I totally misunderstood. I'm sorry."

"Don't apologize. You had every reason to think something was going on. I'm sorry for, like, sneaking around . . . I should have realized you've experienced enough secrets to last a lifetime." He was standing really close now.

"Though this is such a good secret," she whispered.

Looking up at him, she tried to think about what she was feeling. Everything was so layered and complicated.

But then, as she kept staring up at those beautiful eyes that showed every larger-than-life emotion, all the noise in her head fell away.

Everything got weirdly simple.

He was *Teo.*

She was *Iz.*

A boy, a girl, and an onion.

Iz took the hugest breath of her life. "I-I kind of maybe don't *mind* if . . . it's like . . . official or something . . . Being your girlfriend or whatever."

A smile broke across his face like blazing sunshine. "*Yeah?*"

"Ha!" Iz gulped. "Yeah."

"Beaufort," Teo said, tipping up her chin.

Suddenly all of her nerves were firing.

"Iz . . . can I—"

His phone rang.

Chapter Forty-Eight

"Ignore it," Iz said.

But when Teo glanced down, he said, "It's Juliana."

Their eyes met.

"Get it, then, I guess."

Teo said, "Hey! Juliana!" Then he listened for a long time. "Yeah, she's right here. Let me put her on."

With shaking hands, Iz held the phone to her ear. "Uh ... hello?"

"Iz!" Juliana said. "I called Vito just now. He mentioned you were with Teo, so I took a chance and called Teo's phone." She paused. "I've ... got some news."

Something in Juliana's voice made Iz tense right up.

Her brain started racing through possibilities.

The police had closed the investigation.

The peace bond was being disbanded.

The People were free now to do whatever they wanted.

Nowhere was safe.

Then she forced herself to calm down. She'd been buffeted enough by fears about That Place. She was Fierce Voice. She was going to be in control of how she reacted, even if she was scared.

She summoned as much bravery as she could. "They're ... not going any further with the investigation, right?"

Teo stepped forward, face full of concern. "Beaufort ... Iz ..."

But Juliana's voice rose. "No, no, it's good news! The police charged them just now."

Iz's mouth fell open. She couldn't utter a single sound.

"Wha . . ." she managed at last.

"They finished their last interview this morning. And there was clearly enough evidence to lay charges."

Iz thought of Skye sitting with the police and *telling*. About the bravery of that.

"*But,*" Juliana said.

Iz sank down on the little bench behind her. Teo immediately sat down too, leaning in like he was part of the conversation.

"B-but?" Iz said.

"I'm told they're going to plead not guilty." Juliana's voice became careful. "That means . . . a trial."

Iz swallowed hard, nodded. Then she realized Juliana couldn't see her. "Uh . . . okay."

"We can talk more about this soon. Basically, you'll probably get called to be a witness. But that's going to be a while from now, and I'll help you through every step. Iz, you won't be on your own."

Iz was shaking. She put an arm protectively in front of her stomach, hunched over, and shrugged her shoulders up to her ears. "Okay."

"Hey. I'm really good at what I do." Juliana's voice was cajoling. "Don't worry, please, Iz. We'll take them down. And remember, none of this would be happening if you hadn't been brave enough to speak out."

"Right."

After that, they somehow finished the conversation, and she found herself hanging up.

Teo said quietly, "Everything . . . okay?" His eyes were on her like guard dogs or something. She felt the full force of his loyalty and strength.

She put her head on Teo's shoulder. "They're charging them," she whispered. "But I might have to testify or something."

"Ah, Iz." He put his arm awkwardly around her. "I'll be there."

They sat side by side on the bench for what felt like a couple of days, with the hot, wet air and the fluttering life all around. She felt protected and cared for in this beautiful space with this radiant boy. She pushed Those People away in her mind and drew Teo in instead.

"Remember ... that one thing you told me?" she whispered.

"You know I tell you a lot of things, right?" He smiled. "I'm like the king of oversharing."

"No ..." Iz took a huge, trembling breath. "That ... that *one* thing. At Métier, the day I came to find you and apologize, and we walked all around. The thing you told Chloe about me. And then you said, forget it."

Totally in love with you.

He looked perplexed a minute longer, then awareness dawned. "Oh! *That* thing."

"That thing ..."

He waited a long time then said, "Yeah?"

"Well." Iz swallowed. "I guess ..."

She squinted sideways at him.

"I guess like ..."

His yellow-brown eyes were scanning her face.

"... I mean, there's a chance ..."

His lips were starting to curve upward in amusement. "Take your time."

She drew in a breath saturated with humidity and flowers, exhaled her fears. "I'm ... possibly kind of in love with you too."

She winced. Saying it out loud violated all of her rules.

But then she reminded herself there were no rules. There was just being brave and trying to figure out what you honestly wanted to do.

And, she realized with growing joy—

She had wanted to say it! She had meant it completely!

Teo regarded her, a slow smile creeping across his face.

"Of course you are," he said.

Iz hit him.

Then she wrapped her arms around his neck and drew him close and stared at his tawny eyes. Everything got sort of fuzzy.

She kissed him. Or maybe he kissed her. With his hands stroking her face and hers buried in his loose, soft curls, she couldn't tell where she ended and he began. And after all of her worry and self-protectiveness, it felt like the most natural, beautiful, wonderful thing in the world.

With no Vito there to cut them off, they stayed like that for a while.

Afterward, they stirred and kind of laughed shyly.

"Hey, I'm Teo," he said, eyes crinkling.

"I'm Iz. I'm an onion."

"I can tell from your necklace."

Her hand went up to it, felt the perfection of its shape.

"Wanna go for a walk?" he said.

She nodded.

He stood up and half bowed, held out a hand like he was in an opera or something. "Madam?"

Iz took it and stood up too. "Thank you, sir."

They strolled along the path past the camellias, hand in hand, while fluttering creatures surrounded them. Iz half closed her eyes and imagined the butterflies looked like baby dragons dancing and cavorting in the air, ushering her toward something new and wonderful. Then she opened them again, and of course the dragons were butterflies and Teo was Teo and she was Iz. And that was exactly perfect.

As they walked along, they talked. About the future. About The Man and The Woman and the trial. About Eastbourne and the outreach program. About how Dr. Warren thought they should submit their opera to the international conference. About Meredith and therapy. About Teo's own therapy after his mother and sisters' deaths. About fighting to find Fierce Voices to advocate for others and even for yourself.

And about how maybe it really *was* Iz's turn to plan the next outing.

Except that now it wasn't an outing.

It was a date.

Acknowledgements

Thank you so much to Common Deer Press for taking a chance on my first book *Iz the Apocalypse*, and now the sequel, *Fierce Voice*! It has been a joy to be able to keep telling Iz Beaufort's story in this book.

Many people have played a part in bringing *Fierce Voice* to fruition. My editor Emily Stewart provided a meticulous eye and always insightful perspective on Iz's story. David Moratto did another wonderful job on the typesetting. Deb Greenberg did a fantastic job proofreading the manuscript. Bex Glendining created a cover illustration that not only brought Iz and Skye to vivid life but also contained tricky Easter eggs for keen-eyed readers. My husband John, always my first and most trusted reader, discussed Iz's journey with me often and provided many key ideas. My daughter Rachel read the manuscript and gave her perspective as a young adult. My dear friend Heather Cooke—Métier's most devoted fan, who has been there since the very beginning and continues to be a staunch supporter of Iz—read an early version of the book and provided valuable input. She and I have also shared many a conversation about the Métier crew.

I would also like to thank Alison Colavecchia for her brilliant insight and tremendous support. The idea of having a fierce voice came out of one of our conversations together. I will always consider her to have utterly transformed my life. A more talented therapist would be hard to imagine.

I must also thank the many young people I've met who shared their passion for Iz and her journey. A special shoutout goes to a girl who bought a guitar and taught herself to play after reading *Iz the Apocalypse*. Another goes to a talented composer who set all of Iz's lyrics to music. I am grateful for every conversation with you all and treasure the emotion and honesty you have shared with me. To those of you who feel a kinship with my complicated girl, I would like to say that you are seen and your voices matter.

And … to the audience at the OLA White Pine Awards, who screamed when I said that a sequel *Iz the Apocalypse* was coming, here it is at last! I hope you enjoy it!

About the Author

Susan Currie is an elementary teacher in Brampton, Ontario. Before she entered the public school system, she earned a living as an accompanist, pit musician, music director, choir director, organist, dinner musician, leader of various music programs for children, and piano teacher. In addition to *Iz the Apocalypse* and *Fierce Voice*, she has written four other books—*Basket of Beethoven* (Fitzhenry and Whiteside, 2001), *The Mask That Sang* (Second Story Press, 2016), and *Haudenosaunee: the People and Nations* and *Amazing Women in Canada: Autumn Peltier* (Beech Street Books, 2024). Susan is an adoptee who was in the foster care system briefly as a baby, and only learned of her Haudenosaunee heritage (Cayuga Nation, Turtle Clan) as an adult. She is happily married to John and has a wonderful daughter named Rachel.